T0354717

ONCE AGAIN

A Madrone Valley Bachelors Novel

BOOK 1

Char Lee Dressen

WESTBOW
PRESS®
A DIVISION OF THOMAS NELSON
& ZONDERVAN

WestBow Press books may be ordered through booksellers or by contacting:

WestBow Press
A Division of Thomas Nelson & Zondervan
1663 Liberty Drive
Bloomington, IN 47403
www.westbowpress.com
844-714-3454

Scripture marked (KJV) taken from the King James Version of the Bible.

ISBN: 978-1-6642-7395-5 (sc)
ISBN: 978-1-6642-7414-3 (hc)
ISBN: 978-1-6642-7394-8 (e)

Library of Congress Control Number: 2022913982

Print information available on the last page.

WestBow Press rev. date: 12/08/2022

PART I

"My foot hath held his steps, his way have I kept, and not declined. Neither have I gone back from the commandment of his lips; I have esteemed the words of his mouth more than my necessary food. But he is in one mind, and who can turn him? And what his soul desireth, even that he doeth. For he performeth the thing that is appointed for me: and many such things are with him." Job 23:11-14

CHAPTER 1

JULY 2002

Sitting at his oak office desk, Stan Perry, at 52 years of age, was a striking figure. He had mildly greying brown hair at the temples. He was of medium build, one would say robust and healthy, with the most blue eyes, one would often say electric, for they were sharp and wizened. Having just a moment of quiet in his busy schedule, he often took the time to think and pray for his family.

He sat thinking about Robert his son-in-law and the type of clientele he was reaching and attracting to their offices. He was often asked for by name which was no surprise, he was gifted. Robert was young in the construction trade and had a bright future ahead of him. He had a keen mind and willingness to keep up with modern ideas, yet keeping the integrity of a structure and its character intact of the older homes he came into contact with.

There seemed to be a renovation revolution that was beginning to take hold in their community. Their business was certainly enjoying an uptick in business and the subsequent revitalization of their town, as was everyone who enjoyed doing business with each other.

Stan loved Robert like a true son not only because he was married to his only daughter, but because he was a dedicated employee. One day he would hand the business over to them both if God willed. Reflecting on the goodness God had bestowed on them all, he began to pray for his daughter, Marie, for Robert and their three rambunctious children: Robbie Jr., Seth and Lizzy. Yet he couldn't forget the upcoming fourth, Sam, who was yet to enter this world. Counting his blessings, he looked at a framed picture of his family that sat upon his desk.

"Dear God, Keep my family safe from harm, bless them today, help them to accomplish all that you have for them. Bless them with love and guidance as they raise their children in the 'nurture and admonition of the Lord'. Help them to walk in truth and in your Word, Oh' God. Teach them your statutes, and help them to walk in your ways. You are an ever faithful and loving God. Thy Will be done, Amen."

Elizabeth Perry worked, kneeling in her garden, and at 46 years of age she was still very much a picture of youth and beauty. She never knew that she made many ladies in her church jealous of her youthfulness. Being generally a lighthearted person, she would never admit she was beautiful, perhaps 'pretty,' but never beautiful. Her hands and arms worked in the soil, finding and pulling weeds from her ever growing flower garden. It was her haven. Eve, the first created woman, was born in a garden, Elizabeth always mused on that thought as she worked at pulling out the weeds that had sprung up. Elizabeth's long brown hair was pulled back into a ponytail, and it brushed her bare arms as she worked.

A bird began to twitter in the trees so she stopped a moment to listen to his sweet song then enjoying the ensuing quiet and solitude. Her face was turned towards the sun, slowly breathing in the scents of summer and things to come. A few wisps of her dark hair dancing about her face in the breeze, her figure was still comely even after three children. She always wanted to look and be her best for her family and children, so she rarely overindulged with good food, except when it came to chocolate, now that was something she could hardly say no to. She chuckled to herself as she enjoyed the breeze and the quiet that soothed the soul.

Sitting in the silent backyard enjoying it's peacefulness, Eliza was enjoying the fact that she had gotten everything on her "to-do" list done today. It had been a while since that happened, and she was quite pleased to be able to enjoy her special place. The time and silence was broken at the sound of footfalls on the grass, making a swishy sound. John Antony, her youngest son, broke into her thoughts...

"Mom, hey, Mom...! Oh, there you are," she could hear the smile in his voice, "here's some lemonade."

"Thank you, J," she smiled up at her ever growing 15 year old son. He was a smidgen under 6 feet with no remedy to stop his growth.

"Dad just called, he wants to know if it's okay with you to have Sis over for dinner today, or maybe tomorrow?"

"What time is it?" Asking as she held out her hand for him to help her up. Taking her hand, he pulled, and she came up easily.

Looking at his watch he said, "It's 3:32. Do you want me to call and invite her over?"

"No, I need you to head over to Devon's and ask his mom for a cup of sugar. I forgot to pick some up when I was at the store, but I need it for the cookies I want to make."

"Ooh, what kind, mom? Are you making my favorite? Can I help?" John bombarded her with questions as they walked back into the kitchen. Eliza laughed.

"No and yes," She shooed him away, "now go get the sugar."

"Aw, Mom, come on. Tell me, whose favorite cookies are you making?"

"Dad's, of course. Who else?"

"Ugh, Mom, you know those are my favorite too! You're so mean to tease.'" He winked at her, gave her a squeeze, then left running out the front door to get the sugar at their nearest neighbors. Eliza liked to tease him, and he didn't mind as he took it well, unlike her daughter Marie. She sighed. That girl needed to lighten up, but all she could do was pray for her. The girl didn't even like surprises. Eliza did not understand for she loved a surprise from her husband, he knew her so well. She smiled at the thought of her handsome husband, as she dialed to call Marie.

"Robert Jr.!... Lizzy!... Seth!... what on earth are you doing? Look at the mess you've made in this kitchen! What am I going to do with you all!" Marie groaned in frustration.

The children all turned wide-eyed, looking at their mother and then each other, shock and surprise evident in their faces. Little Lizzy's lip began to tremble at her mothers' outburst.

Five year old Robbie piped up, "We only trying to help, Momma!" He put his little hand on his hip, like she was doing herself now. "We was going to clean it up. Honest."

Seth shook his head up and down like a bobble head toy.

"He'p Mommy."

Marie instantly deflated. She felt small and sorry for her outburst. She detested these emotional outbursts, 'It has to be the hormones', she guessed, that had her on this emotional roller coaster. She knew this, though it wasn't an excuse. Somehow, they should be controlled. She thought, "Couldn't they?" She sighed, blowing a raspberry. "I'm sorry kids, Mommy's just not feeling good today."

"Yeah, we knows. That's why we want to help make somethin' good" Robbie looked around, "Sorta. I'm sorry we made a mess, Mommy." He said this as he mixed something in a bowl.

Picking up one year old Lizzy, kissing her cheek as she did so, "It's okay," she sighed again. "What are you trying to make?" She put Lizzy down on the floor again beginning to wipe up the counter.

"Cookies, of course!" Seth yelled. Looking at the ingredients, Marie had to wonder, "What kind?" there was real bacon bits, raisins, flour, butter, salt, sugar, and mustard sitting all on the counter.

"Mm—," was all she said. The phone rang, walking over and picked up the phone from the kitchen wall. "Hello?"

"Marie, I have a question?"

"Oh hi, mom, what's your question?" She then whispered to the boys, "You boys put everything away."

"But, Mommy...?" they protested.

Putting her hand over the receiver, "No, Sirs!" she gave them "The Look." "Now," she said firmly. At "The Look," they knew not to talk back to their mother.

"Come on Sethy," Robbie handed his brother the mustard to put away.

"Marie? Are you listening?"

"Huh, sorry, Mom, just a sec." Marie walked out onto the patio and closed the sliding door behind her. "What were you saying?"

"What's going on over there?"

"Oh, just the boys 'trying' to make cookies," she giggled, "with mustard as an ingredient." She turned, watching the boys through the kitchen window, where they couldn't hear her conversation.

Eliza laughed, "Oh my," she giggled herself. "As I was saying, do you have plans for dinner?"

"If I do, they'll be late. I might just order a pizza or Chinese take-out. The boys made such a mess in the kitchen, and Lizzy will definitely need a bath, again," she sighed. "She's covered in flour, as are the boys. Mom, were you ever this tired in your second trimester?"

"Yes, of course. You shouldn't be so hard on yourself, dear. It's the way it's supposed to be. Try and rest frequently, let the house go a little. It's okay to not have your house completely spotless you know."

"But your house is so clean, Mom."

"Don't compare yourself amongst yourselves; it is not wise you know. Anyhow, my house was not spotless when you all were little. I have time now, and I do have help. I also don't have little hands making messes all the time."

"I thought I'd be feeling better by now. But I'm so tired these days. I'm not really motivated to do much."

"Well, I have some good news, at least for today. Dad would like to have you come over for dinner, so no worries for you on that account. I guess the Lord knew what your day would look like, so He made a way of escape," she laughed.

"Thanks, Mom."

"No, worries. Thank your Dad, he's the one who asked me to call you. And anyhow, why don't you tell the boys they can help me make cookies? That will make them happy."

"Thanks, Mom, I'm sure it will. So, what time should we come over?"

"Oh, you know your dad, he likes to eat early," she laughed at the truth of her statement. "No later than 5:30 okay?"

"Okay, that gives me about an hour to get everybody ready. I hope we'll make it on time."

"Nonsense, that's plenty of time, put the boys in the downstairs bath with the door open so you can hear them, and put Lizzy in her high chair so you can clean up the kitchen while they play. It shouldn't take you that long."

Marie heard a crash from the kitchen. "I've got to go, Mom. The kids broke something in the kitchen and Lizzy's on the floor. Bye," she hung up on her mother, rushing in as a cloud of flour rose from the floor, covering the boys and Lizzy, literally from head to toe, along with a broken jar of maple syrup.

The boys opened their eyes their faces white. All you could see were their eyes as they blinked them open and shut. Marie couldn't help it as the sight of them made her burst out with laughter. When the boys began to spit and sputter at the flour on their faces, Lizzy began to cry at the noise the broken glass had caused.

That started Marie to action, as she picked up the girl and brushed at her face with a towel, wiping up the excess dust. She set her into her highchair and gave her a toy to play with. "Boys stay where you are," she commanded over her shoulder, as they didn't have shoes on. They stood mute as soldiers, they were so surprised.

Next, she went for Seth, who had been the closest, and brushed off his face, sputtering herself at the amount of flour accumulated on his face, nearly unable to contain her mirth. She lifted him up and took him straight to the downstairs bathroom. "Now, get undressed, Seth. You're going to have a bath."

Turing on the water full blast, Seth yelled, "Yippee!"

"Now, settle down and get in when you're done undressing. I've got to get to Robbie and your sister."

"Yes, Momma, I'll be good."

"That's my good boy, thank you." He was struggling to get his socks off as she exited the bathroom.

Robbie sat on the floor, mixing the syrup and the flour together in patterns of his own design. "Robbie, please stop that, you're making more of a mess than I need right now."

"Sorry, Momma, but this is fun!" He proceeded to give her a coy look, with big eyes all wide and innocent. She had to laugh in spite of this little munchkin.

"Come stand up so that I can take you to the bath. You're worse of a mess than your brother. You weigh a ton you know that?" she chuckled.

"Do not!" Daddy says, 'I weigh a brick.' "What does that mean?"

"It just means you're getting very big and growing a lot. How did you get so big anyway?"

"God made me growed! Don't you know that, Momma?"

"Yes, I guess I do." They laughed together as she deposited him in the bathroom. "Now, finish getting undressed and in you go. I need to get your sister. I want you boys to get very pruny okay? Wash real well because we're going to grandma's later for dinner. She said something about making cookies at her house," she winked at them.

"Yeah!" they shouted. "Now, get to business. I have so much to clean up." Taking their dirty clothes on her way out, she passed Lizzy on the way to the laundry and undressed her in her highchair, so that she could wash her clothes too. She would worry about herself later. *Sigh* then, going to the washroom, she deposited the laundry in and set it to wash with an extra rinse cycle.

Next, taking down her cleaning supplies, along with mop and bucket and broom, she got to work cleaning the kitchen again. "Well," *sigh* "it shouldn't take too long since I already cleaned it earlier today. I'm sure glad Mom and Dad invited us over for dinner. I'll sure be ready to eat when we get there."

CHAPTER 2

Robert pulled into the open garage and parked his little Honda Civic. He thought to himself, "I should talk to Marie about upgrading my car, it really is starting to show its age." The drivers seat was torn and lumpy, more so than when he first bought it used, back in high school. The duct tape was wearing and becoming sticky. Today, it left a sticky patch on his shirt. "Yeah, high school, wow. That sure seemed like so long ago; only seven years, but so much has happened since then." He was now married to his childhood sweetheart, and she was about to have their fourth child. "Boy, I sure feel old right now." He laughed at himself.

Opening the car door, he decided to inspect his wife's mini-van. He wanted to make sure it was tidy for the trip to Mom and Pop's house. He opened the van door and out spilled a ball and a container of cereal. "O' boy," he thought. Pulling off his tie and his Oxford, he set to work taking out all the Sunday school papers

10

that had been discarded by the children, once treasured then forgotten altogether. "There was a sermon in there somewhere," he chuckled. He disliked the messy van, but there was not much that could be done about that until the children grew to be more responsible. They were young and still in the 'teaching' phase of life. Not that you were too old to learn a lesson, but now is when children were molded into the young adults they would certainly one day become. For now, the least he could help out his wife was to clean out the van most evenings.

Taking out the shop vac and he began to suck up all the stale cereal and whatever else he found. Marie rarely knew the kids had brought something into the van until it was too late sometimes. On many an occasion, she was so frustrated and fumed about it, but he sure loved that part because she was quite beautiful when upset. Her cheeks would hold a warm glow and her eyes would light with fire. That's when he would hold her tight until she would calm down and he would tell her he loved her. She would calm in his embrace and turn to him giving him a kiss when she was ready and a whack on the arm when she wasn't. He laughed at the reminiscence. He had a spitfire on his hands for sure and for certain. Robert couldn't imagine a life without her by his side. Realizing he was standing there daydreaming about his wife, he went inside to see her as he was all finished here. Shutting the van door, he put away the vacuum and took up his shirt and tie and walked into the house through the garage door.

Upon entering the kitchen, he heard little Lizzy squealing with delight and babbling something to her momma from the highchair. He could hear his rowdy boys splashing about in the tub. Marie had her back to him, mopping the kitchen floor. It looked spotless when he had gone to work this morning. "I wonder why she's doing it again?" He didn't mind watching her fluid movements, almost as if she was dancing. "She can be so inviting." He embraced her around the belly from behind. She let out a squeal and a shout and jumped back a pace, banging her head into his mouth. She had her hand to her heart when she turned around.

He held his lip, "I'm sorry, honey. I didn't mean to startle you." Lizzy began to cry, and just then the boys ran in, full of suds.

"Daddy, you' home. Is Mommy okay?" they asked.

"Yes, Mommy's okay, I accidentally scared her. Why don't you boys go get back in the tub, and I'll be right in to help you finish up, all right, fellas?"

"Shore t'ing, Daddy," Robbie said as he and Seth ran back, dripping suds as they went. Little Lizzy stopped her fussing since everything seemed to be all right.

Pulling Marie close, he nuzzled her neck, "I'm sorry, honey." She allowed herself to be held with the mop in her hand.

"I never heard you come in. Oh, my stomach."

Robert leaned down and began to speak with the babe. "Hello, Sam, it's Daddy. I didn't mean to scare your Mommy." He rubbed her stomach to soothe it. "Wow it's really hard!"

"Well, you did scare me pretty good, you know."

Rob kissed her stomach, "I'm sorry." He straightened and kissed her on the nose. "I guess it's time to see about those two boys. I'll take Lizzy while you finish up here."

"Thank you honey. You're the best."

"No, I got the better end." He winked at her and walked out with his little Lizzy, tickling her on the tummy as he went.

Marie tried to hold that picture in her mind. This was a nice memory of little moments to treasure for later as she watched her handsome husband walk away. Resuming her task, she knew he'd put on a little weight after they'd gotten married. His muscles he'd earned playing football in high school began to not be as taut, but he was still strong. He still ran a few miles about three times a week, but his upper body workouts were now done away with as they'd taken too much time away from his growing family. It had been something she had been praying about, and thankfully, she didn't have to argue with him about it.

A visiting Pastor at their church had talked about the importance of family. Hobbies or things that were not important in the sight of God should be "...put away and not get in the way of the family..." as in First Corinthians 13:11b- "...when I became a man, I put away childish things." That was all it took, as she recalled.

Rob had come to her that evening, after having spent the remainder of the day in quiet contemplation. He'd asked her forgiveness for being selfish and putting himself ahead of their family. She had been so happy that night. They talked things over and had come to a compromise. She didn't want him to completely give up what he liked to do, so he ran three times a week with her blessing. They had decided, if something really important came up, he would forego for another time or day. Otherwise, they had a nice routine that was comfortable for both of them and stable. He was the sunshine in their lives. He was the jokester: the fun parent. She didn't mind because he always knew how to get her out of any bad or unhappy attitude. The thought occurred to her that she was the moon, the dead planet that only reflected the light from a brilliant sun. She could only glimpse his brilliancy. Rob was her love for always, none other could take his place, his gentleness, his quiet nature, his steadfastness, but most of all, his love for the Lord and his love for her.

Shaking herself from her melancholy reverie, she got about to finishing cleaning up the kitchen. Rob walked out of the bathroom with all the kids hanging off of him, and she laughed at the sight of them. Seth was hanging off his back, while Robbie was hanging onto his leg, and Rob held Lizzy in his arms. He was the people version of a jungle gym!

"We're off to get dressed, Mommy!" Robbie yelled.

"I can see that," she chuckled at their antics. "I'll be up in a minute to help out. I'm almost done here."

"Don't worry about it, honey. You go ahead and hop in the shower. I'll take care of these monkeys." The kids all giggled, "Then, I'll join you." He turned back and winked in her direction. Smiling at him, Marie shook her head and went to put away her cleaning supplies back in the laundry room. Then, waddling her way up the stairs, she made it to the master bedroom at the end of the hall and into a very much needed shower.

CHAPTER 3

5:07PM

After loading the kids into the mini-van, Robert asked, "Okay, is everybody 'bunkled' in?" Robert chuckled.

"Yes, Daddy!" they chorused.

"How did we ever come up with that silly word again?" Rob looked to Marie as he began to back the minivan out of the drive.

"Don't you remember? Robbie was just learning how to say big words and he just couldn't say 'buckled.' It came out 'bunkled' and it stuck." She said shrugging. "How it made us laugh," she chuckled.

Rob pushed the button for the garage door before he pulled away from the driveway completely. They were now on their way to Grandma and Grandpa's, Marie's parents' home.

Seth asked from the back seat, "Are we almost there, Daddy?"

"Seth, we just got started, buddy. It'll be twenty minutes yet, "Why?"

"Grandma said we could help her make cookies. I love grandma's cookies cuz they're so yummy for my tummy," he giggled. Rob and Marie smiled at each other.

Robbie asked, "Is Uncle Johnny gonna be there?"

Marie looked back at him, "I don't see why not, honey."

"Good, but is his girlfriend going to be there?"

"I don't know, but I don't think so. Why?"

"I don't like her. She's mean to me."

"When was this?" She asked, her feathers getting ruffled.

Robbie gave a thoughtful expression, "I think it was the last time we went to Grandma's. She asked Uncle Johnny to go to the store, and I wanted to go too, but she pushed me back and said, 'I don't want trouble following us.' But I'm no trouble, Mommy, honest." He crossed his heart.

"Of course you're not trouble. You're my big helper all the time." Robbie smiled at his Mommy, pleased she agreed with his assessment. "I think I'll have a talk with 'that girl.'" Marie crossed her arms. Rob chuckled at her posture as he stopped at a stop light. He could tell her 'mom feathers' were ruffled and she was scraping for a fight. Nobody came between a mom and her chicks.

"Now, dear, don't go too hard on 'that girl.' Don't you remember how we were?" He bent over and gave her a kiss on the cheek. He glanced up to see the light turn green and proceeded forward.

Marie turned to make a retort, but before she could say anything, her eyes widened in horror, "Robert! Look Out!" The impact and sound of crunching metal and shattering glass amidst the screams of fright was the last thing Marie heard before her head hit something and all went black.

CHAPTER 4

5:47 PM

The sound of some kind of alarm woke Marie. "Is that the house alarm, hon?" Hearing the sound of someone stepping on crunching glass, "An intruder! Oh, God, keep us safe." She prayed, her eyes fluttered open as she began to wake so that she could tell Rob what she heard. Her ears began to ring something awful and a muffled voice from far away said, "She's waking up."

"Are they that close? Keep us safe, dear Lord." A hand touched her face and opened her eye, flashing a light in it. She screamed, "Help!" as loudly as she could, but it sounded soft, even in her own ears. The light flashed again in her other eye. "Stop that!" She had to get out of this compromising situation. She tried to roll over onto her side, she had to get away.

"No, no, no, ma'am, don't do that," the voice commanded.

Her ears began ringing, more insistent this time. No, not ringing... Was that a siren? Then, all came flooding back: an accident.

"Ma'am?" The voice questioned, "Ma'am? Can you hear me? What's your name?"

"What's going on? Where are my children? My husband?" Her eyes opened fully, "Are they okay?"

"They're being taken care of. What's your name?" the voice kept asking.

"It's Marie, Marie LaSalle," she tried to move, but couldn't. "Why can't I move my arms?" she looked around confused.

"Marie, you're on a stretcher. We've got to get you to the hospital. Your right arm is broken. Do you remember the car accident? Do you remember that?"

"Yes, someone hit us. We had a green light. My husband? Is he okay? How's my husband, can you tell me that at least? 'Oh, God of my father,' she prayed for her children to be safe. "The children, are they okay? Can I see my babies?"

The EMT looked at a police officer that had been standing by with a notepad in his hand taking notes. The officer replied "They're on their way to the hospital, ma'am. Don't worry, they are in good hands."

"Oh dear Heavenly Father, please help me." She cried out. "Officer, please, can you call my parents? They live close by. Someone needs to be with my babies. They'll be so scared to be by themselves. Please, please call my mom and dad." Marie pleaded with him.

"Do you know the number, where they can be reached?" He stood with pen at the ready. "What are their names?"

"Stan and Elizabeth Perry. I can't remember their number. 'Oh God, please help me to remember,' she prayed to herself. "What's their number? I know it I do!" she began to become frantic.

"Marie, it's okay. We'll find it, just have to call dispatch. It's not a problem since we can find out."

"But I know the number! I just have to remember," becoming hysterical with worry for her little ones.

"Marie, you're going to have to calm down or I'll have to sedate you. Please, don't make me do that." The EMT said, patting her arm awkwardly.

"But I can remember. I know I can, so please let me go. I need to get to my babies; they need me."

"I'm sorry, ma'am, but you give me no choice," the EMT put a sedative through in her saline drip.

"Is that even safe, Manning? She's pregnant!"

"I'm fully aware that she's pregnant, Rogers! This is better than if she codes or something because we haven't been able to see anything else that's going on with her because she's pregnant. At least this way, she's stable to transport to the hospital. They can deal with any emergencies with the baby there. We have to get her there as safely as possible. If she's worrying about her kids, you can see she was getting hysterical and possibly combative. You don't mess with a mama bear and her cubs!"

"All right, all right, you know better. Don't bite my head off."

"You asked for it! Go make that phone call, and get her family to be with those kids."

"I'm on it...Dispatch this is Rogers..."

CHAPTER 5

6:21PM

Douglas's date Jessica or 'Grayson' as she liked to be called by her model name caused him to ask, "Walter, what seems to be the hold up?"

"Looks to be a nasty accident up ahead. I see several ambulances up there, and here comes another tow-truck coming up behind us on the shoulder." Walter maneuvered the Maybach out of the way so the tow-truck could pass in the emergency lane. "Looks like they're finally getting traffic going here, sir. We'll be out of this mess soon."

Douglas sat back in his seat as they began to move a bit faster than a foot at a time it seemed from their previous position. They'd been stuck on the road for about half an hour with no way to get around, having been in the center lane with no way of escape. They were passing through this small town on their way to the city for the theatre; he'd had tickets to see a popular play that had been touring in their area. As they were passing the scene of the accident, he saw two cars, one a minivan, the other a jeep of some sort, both were badly mangled. The driver's and rear passenger's side was caved in on the minivan, and glass littered the entire roadway.

A firetruck had maneuvered itself to try and block as much of the scene as possible when he noticed an ambulance after the blockade and a woman on a gurney. The EMT was speaking with her before she wailed, "ROBERT! Cried out his name. Calling out in distress, "HELP ME, Lord, Save us!" asking for divine help, right before she passed out.

"Dearest Lord, Help the poor woman, give her peace." He prayed aloud.

"Douglas close that window, will you please? How awful! I don't want to see this or hear it while we're on our way to a happy place. I surely hope we won't be late for the opening act," said the petulant voice of his date. She looked at herself in a pocket mirror, patting her hair and then, he noticed her pouty lips as she applied her lipstick. In the light of the situation, it seemed to grotesque an action. He rolled up the window, though it had only been down about three inches. It firmly closed out the loud sound of the sirens pulling away fast down the highway and on to the hospital, hopefully to ward off the hand of death. Suddenly, he asked his date Grayson, "Do you fear death?"

"What? Do I... do I fear death? What kind of a question is that! What's gotten into you?" She sneered at him, then realized her own questioning attitude didn't go over well, with his imperceptibly shocked expression, and eyes that narrowed. She saw his jaw working in agitation and decided to acquiesce. After all, she was the benefactress in this situation with a wealthy suitor. "I would rather not talk about death, but since you brought it up, of course I'm afraid. Isn't everybody? I mean, who'd want to die? Especially like that, in a horrible car accident?" she shivered as if a cool breeze touched her.

"I suppose no one would really like to die in that way, but I don't fear death. It is 'precious in the sight of the LORD,'" he quoted from Psalm 116:15, then looked out the window.

Trying to play off this strange turn in conversation laying her hand on his knee giving him a coy look."You are incorrigible, you know that?"

Douglas turned back to look at her, then taking her hand, laid it back in her own lap, giving her a rueful smile.

Trying again she asked, "What are you really trying to say, that you don't care if you died, even today? Are you suicidal or something and nobody told me? Is that why we're on this date, to turn your thoughts away from other things?" manipulating the conversation away from herself and putting it on him.

"What?! No!" he wasn't sure if he wanted to continue this talk with her, but it needed explanation, he supposed. "I guess she really isn't a believer," he thought as he'd been led to believe. "I guess, to put it into terms you would understand, is that I'm religious if you will: a Christian. I believe in God, and I believe I will go to heaven when I die based on my faith and trust in Jesus Christ. Do you understand?"

"Do you really believe in all that heaven and hell stuff?"

"Yes, you don't? I was led to believe that you were a believer, and if you're not, then what do you believe in? Where do we go when we die?" Douglas asked.

"Nowhere." Shrugging her bare shoulders We don't 'go' anywhere," she said in quotations. "We just die like flowers or grass or animals. There is no heaven or hell or anything like that. That's what I believe. My daddy used to say, 'In all you're getting in life, get what you can, can what you get, then sit on the can!' Life should be a party, not about worrying about dying" she laughed trying to lighten this strange conversation she was having.

"Interesting," was all he remarked, then turned and looked back out the window at the passing scenery as they were finally on their way to the theatre.

Grayson didn't know where to go from here in their strange conversation, so she decided to say nothing after that. Perhaps later, she could get the conversation going in a different direction. "It wasn't likely," she thought, "that he would hold her own opinions against her. Everyone is entitled to their own opinion after all, aren't they?" She sat there next to him uncertain of her position with this very handsome businessman. He was a little strange, but she'd been with worse. At least this guy treated her kindly and with respect. "I guess being a millionaire allowed you certain eccentricities of thought, didn't it?"

CHAPTER 6

7 : 1 4 A M

At breakfast the following morning, Douglas sat at the farm table in his massive kitchen, perusing the paper, but also thinking about the previous evenings events. He awoke, irritated that the evening hadn't gone at all as he'd planned after having passed the accident. Taking a sip of his coffee, he paged through an article to find himself and Grayson on the front cover of the "C. A. T." or Celebrities About Town section of their local paper. 'Ugh' he thought, then shivered involuntarily. Turning past that section a few pages, he came upon a photo from the scene of the accident they'd seen the night before. He read the article all the way through, though there wasn't much information about the family or what condition the family members were in at the time of printing.

Walter, who was Douglas' personal assistant, stood at the counter taking a sip of his own coffee while his wife MaryAnne, made breakfast.

"Walt, did you read this article about the accident that happened last night?"

Walter turned around from speaking with his wife, "Yes, sir, I've read it through. I just couldn't believe it. I also read the update online."

"What update? What's happened Walter?"

Walter hung his head before saying, "It looks like the husband died and one of the children was severely injured in the accident he may not live. The other kids, two others, weren't as injured because their car seats protected them, they were seated in the center seats of the van. The wife or mom of the children is also pregnant. She is unconscious, and the doctors don't know if she'll come to."

"Oh, Dear Heavenly Father!" He exclaimed, shocked. "Walter?" he said thoughtfully, "I should do something to help in some way, I feel compelled."

"What do you have in mind, sir?"

"I'm not sure what I'd like to do, but I'll think of something soon. Maybe as we get more information or updates, I'll know better how to proceed. I think I'll give my friend Nathaniel Thurman a call. He's generally full of good ideas and solutions to problems."

Walter's wife, MaryAnne, set a plate of food in front of Douglas, but he wasn't sure he could eat a bite after this terrible news.

Interrupting his musings, Walter said, "Well, when you figure out what you would like to do for this family, just let me know. I'll take care of all the details." MaryAnn set a plate of food in front of him as well.

"Thank you, Walter. I appreciate your help."

"Just doing my duty, sir."

"As I always like to say, Good Man!" they laughed, sharing a joke between themselves. MaryAnn shook her head. She never figured out why they found that so funny.

CHAPTER 7

JULY 11, 2002 - 3:42PM

Sitting close to Marie's bedside, his own eye's red with many spent tears for it had been a long three days since the accident had happened. The doctors were concerned with Marie's condition. In the past three days anytime that they'd try to wake her she would become overwhelmingly hysterical with grief that they had to sedate her again for the sake of the babe in her womb. The doctor was afraid she'd go into early labor and it was too soon to deliver it. So they'd have to keep her sedated until such time as she could be calm in mind and body. 'That may be the hardest task of all,' Stan thought. Sitting with her and feeling completely helpless, but not without hope.

For he remembered there was another difficult time in their lives and God alone brought them through it. The Lord could and would do it again. But right now he would not go back to those too hard memories to bear to be thought of at this time. "Lord, give me…, give us the strength to move forward. Give my daughter the strength to press on during this difficult time. Lord, please help my grandchildren with their feelings, especially not to feel abandoned, because you, Oh God, do not, nor will you not abandon your children in their hour of need. And dear God how we need you now. We NEED your presence in our lives. Help us to overcome."

Doctor Morgan walked in on his prayer, adding a soft "Amen," when she thought he was finished. Stan looked up, "Please don't let me disturb your praying, inward or outward, voice your concerns, He hears you."

"I just want her to wake up slowly, maybe Doc, if you could slowly reduce the sedation, so that she can hear me while I'm praying, maybe that will help to ease the transition, if possible, that is, and maybe she won't be so frantic. You know what she's been through before, now."

"Yes, I do," she frowned, "that's why I'm concerned about her and her babe".

"Perhaps somewhere in her subconscious she'll be able to reconcile what has happened and my praying will allow her to have some sort of peace."

"Okay, we can give it a try." She pushed a button to reduce the rate of sedation Marie received through a drip line.

"Thank You doc, that's all I ask." Stan continued praying softly near Marie's ear while Dr. Morgan slowly reduced the sedation, praying herself for this to work, then walked out to give him some privacy with his daughter. He prayed and thanked God for sparing her life a second time. And for finding them all faithful to go through this hard trial, 'His will be done in their lives'. He pleaded "Please Lord, help me to find a way to break the news to her gently of all that's happened." He stopped a moment doing his best not to sob and lose control of his emotions. He opened his eyes and saw Marie looking at him, calmly. "Sweetheart, you're awake!" He attempted a smile, for he was thankful she wasn't beyond consolation.

"Yes," tears filled her eyes, "don't worry Dad, I know about Robert and Robbie."

"No dear just Robert. Robbie is in ICU." He patted her hand gently.

"No Dad you don't understand, I dreamt that Robert came with Jesus and they took Robbie with them to heaven. Just as I heard you praying."

John Antony came in just then panting from running. "Dad" he sobbed, "Marie you're awake!" With tear filled eyes he said, "Oh Dad, Robbie...," John couldn't go on and fell into his father's arms sobbing.

"It's all right son, God's got this, it hurts but they're both with the Father above. No more pain, no more suffering on this earth."

"But why Dad? Why them?" He sobbed questioning.

"Why?" He consoled his son patting his back, he expounded, "We don't know the mind of God or God's plan for any of our lives, but he does say in his word in Jeremiah 29:11 it says,

"For I know the thoughts that I think toward you, saith the LORD, thoughts of peace, and not of evil, to give you an expected end," he also says, "for 'my thoughts' are not 'your thoughts', neither are your ways my ways, saith the LORD. For as the heavens are higher than the earth, so are my ways higher than your ways, and my thoughts than your thoughts." (Isaiah 55:8-9),"O LORD, how great are thy works! And thy thoughts are very deep" (Psalm 92:5), "Many, O LORD my God, are thy wonderful works which thou hast done, and thy thoughts which are to us-ward: they cannot be reckoned up in order unto thee: if I would declare and speak of them, they are more than can be numbered." (Psalm 40:5), "How precious also are thy thoughts unto me, O God! How great is the sum of them!" (Psalm 139:17).

"So you see son, we must not despair, they are in the Lords' hands." John Antony calmed down, accepting his own fathers acceptance of the situation finding peace through the scripture his father quoted to them. Marie pressed the button for a nurse to come attend her.

A good friend of hers, Linda who was a nurse, came in with tears still in her eyes, doing her best to be brave for Marie's sake. "What can I do for you Marie?"

"Would it be possible to go see my boy, or could he be brought to me here? I want to say goodbye."

Linda let out a sob, then caught herself and stopped it before it came out more. She swallowed with difficulty and then said, 'I'll see what I can do about that.' She quietly left the room, as tears rolled down her friends face. Out in the hall it was a very solemn feeling. Not one nurse or doctor liked to have a death in their hospital. Not that it was any fault of their own what had transpired, but still, it was felt by those who may have known the family. A young life was received by his loving Lord along with his father into the Almighty's loving embrace.

Elizabeth, Marie's mother, saw Linda outside of her daughter's room, just staring off into space for a moment. 'Linda, are you okay dear?'

"Yes...No. Sorry." She tried to walk away but Elizabeth stopped her in her tracks.

'It's okay really, you can tell me what you're feeling. What's going on?' She asked sincerely, wanting to help if she could.

"It's just I've not known people that I've been really close to before that have died. I mean my parents are still living. My grandparents passed away when I was too young to miss them. So I guess it begs the question...', she left off asking.

Elizabeth prodded, '... and what question is that dear?'

"You know heaven or hell, have I done enough good to earn my way there? You know?" Linda shrugged, leaning against the wall.

Within herself, Elizabeth was sober a moment and prayed, 'O' Lord, I pray you help me lead this lamb home to you.' Pausing a moment, she then asked, "May I be honest with you?"

"Yeah, sure." Linda shrugged again uncertain where this was going.

Eliza began "The Bible states in Romans 3:10, 'As it is written, There is none righteous, no, not one: ... and Isaiah 64:60 says, "But we are all as an unclean thing, and all our righteousnesses are as filthy rags; and we all do fade as a leaf; and our iniquities, like the wind, have taken us away."

"So how are we supposed to get to heaven if we're not righteous? Is there some sort of formula or set of prayers, like hail Mary's or something?"

"Well, yes and no. Let me explain it better. Yes, it's true we are not righteous enough for heaven and we can't get there by doing only good works, though that doesn't mean you should stop doing right. But the way to get to heaven is by accepting Jesus Christ as your personal savior. In Psalm 51:7 it says, 'Purge me with hyssop, and I shall be clean: wash me, and I shall be whiter than snow.'

Linda interrupted her, "So where do I get this, hyssop? Can I buy it online?"

'Oh dear, Elizabeth thought, 'I'm not explaining this right. Lord help me get through to her better.' Eliza started again, "Okay, um, no dear, it's more of an analogy, but what I should have said was in 1 John 1:7 the Bible says, "...and the blood of Jesus Christ cleanseth us from all sin."

"You see Jesus came into this world as a baby, that's why you see nativity sets at Christmas because it is the celebration of his birth through a virgin girl. Jesus lived a life for about 30 years without sin, because he is both man and God. 'He was wounded for our transgressions, and bruised for our iniquities' (Isaiah 53:5), he was unlawfully tried then sentenced to be crucified. Jesus was buried the same day and then resurrected, he rose up from the grave three days later that's why we celebrate Easter, to commemorate his resurrection." She took a breath.

"In Matthew 26:28 Jesus says, 'For this is my blood of the New Testament, which is shed for many for the remission of sins." You see, he died on the cross and shed his blood as an innocent man, so that we could have life eternal our sins were put upon him. John 3:15-17 says, "That whosoever believeth in him should not perish, but have eternal life. For God so loved the world, that he gave his only begotten Son, that whosoever believeth in him should not perish, but have everlasting life. For God sent not his Son into the world to condemn the world but that the world through him might be saved. He that believeth on him is not condemned: but he that believeth not is condemned already, because he hath not believed in the name of the only begotten Son of God."

Eliza concluded, "So you see, "But as many as received him, to them gave he power to become the sons of God, even to them that believe on his name: (John 1:12)-if you believe on the name of Jesus and confess your sins "...if thou shalt confess with thy mouth the Lord Jesus, and shalt believe in thine heart that God hath raised him from the dead, thou shalt be saved. (Romans 10:9)" 1John 1:9 states, "if We confess our sins, he is faithful and just to forgive us our sins, and to cleanse us from all unrighteousness", He also goes on to say, "Whosoever shall confess that Jesus is the Son of God, God dwelleth in him, and he in God.(1 John 4:15)" One of the best things about accepting Jesus as your savior is that John 10:27-29 says, "My sheep hear my voice, and I know them, and they follow me: and I give unto them eternal life; and they shall never perish, neither shall any man pluck them out of my hand. My Father, which gave them me, is greater than all; and no man is able to pluck them out of my Father's hand."

"What Jesus meant is that once you've accepted Jesus as your own savior from sin, that you are kept by God safe in his hands. Not necessarily from problems, but he'll help you through them giving you peace. "Therefore being justified by faith, we have peace with God through our Lord Jesus Christ: (Romans 5:1)" Galatians 2:20 says it this way "I am crucified with Christ: nevertheless I live; yet not I, but Christ liveth in me: and the life which I now live in the flesh I live by the faith of the son of God, who loved me, and gave himself for me."

Linda asked, "Do I have to pay for this salvation, I have a friend who says we have to pay for penance or something like that."

Elizabeth smiled, 'This is the beauty of salvation, it is absolutely free! "For the wages of sin is death; but the gift of God is eternal life through Jesus Christ our Lord." (Romans 6:23) So you see no amount of money can save you, God's gift to man is Jesus and he gave of himself freely to us, isn't it wonderful?"

"So what you're saying is that all I have to do is accept his free gift by asking Jesus into my heart and life? Is it really that simple?"

"Yes, on both accounts. It really is that simple. The reason it's free is that God wants to reconcile himself with man. He wants to resume fellowship with us but we have to want to accept his invitation of our own accord, even a child can accept."

"I've never heard about this, but I want it for me. I want to accept it, is that all I do?"

"Yes, you pray to God, tell him you are a sinner and you agree with him that you are. Next ask him to wash away and forgive you of your sin through the blood of Jesus Christ having faith and believing he will do it. And you accept his pardon, that Jesus took your place on the cross therefore making you clean and thank him for taking you to heaven when you die. Thats it."

"Can I pray right now or do I have to wait for like Sunday?"

Elizabeth smiled with joy, "Absolutely you can pray now. Go ahead I'll wait here with you." She bowed her head, and Linda did the same.

Linda cleared her throat, 'Dear God, um, it's me Linda ... Linda McCallister. I certainly know that you know that I'm a sinner," tears streamed down her face, "I drink too much sometimes I do want to stop that. I know I cuss too much and I want to stop that too. God I'm sorry for being a bad person, a sinner. I didn't know it was wrong until now, but that's not a really good excuse I want my kids to be good, but how can they when I'm not? Please forgive me for sinning against the Bible, against you and people I know, even my husband and kids. Please clean me inside and out, you know from all of it. I want to be clean and new like. I ask Jesus to come into my heart, make my heart as white as snow. If you could do that I would be so grateful. Oh yeah, and take me to heaven when I die, cause now I'm in your hand and nobody can take me away from you. Amen."

"Amen." Elizabeth echoed. "So how do you feel?"

"Like a heavy weight has been taken off my shoulders." She giggled. "Wow, I feel so good," tears of joy streamed down her face, "I don't know why I'm crying." Elizabeth had tears in her eyes as well.

"They're called tears of joy, my dear, and it's all right to feel so good!" She chuckled as well. "You know what else is good?"

"No, What?"

"Melina is going too. I just had a talk with her before I came over here.'"

"Really?" She said shocked, her mouth agape.

"Yes isn't it exciting? You'll have someone that you can share your faith with and you are very welcome to attend our church. We'll save you a seat if you like" Eliza handed her an invitation from their church.

"Yes, I'd like that very much". Linda looked at it closely, "Oh, I get these all the time" taking the invitation from Elizabeth, she stowed it in her pocket.

"Well, now you have no excuses, you know me and Melina said she'd like to come as well. Maybe you two can come together?"

"Maybe I can get my family to come too. Thank You Mrs. Perry. I guess I'd better get back to work."

"Yes, you go on ahead, I'm sorry if I kept you from your duties.'

"I'm Not." Linda smiled, then sobered for the task at hand.

CHAPTER 8

AUGUST 2002

For Marie it was the longest month of her life by far. Bless her
parents, they were such a tower of strength for her and the kids.
They cried many times together when they were alone with one
another. Thankfully no harm had come to her or the baby because
of the sedations that she'd been given, she just felt so weak and
drained of any kind of life whatsoever. Her emotions were so
fragile, the littlest thing would set her to crying buckets of tears.
All of her joy seemed to vanish with Robert and Robbie Jr. She
loathed to go to the funeral service because that would mean that
her beloved's death and that of her son were truly final. Her father
and mother in fact had made all the arrangements for her as she
just couldn't cope with any of it. She was broken more so than she
could ever imagine in her life, worse than before. Why had her
loving savior done this to her? Hadn't she suffered enough? Didn't
she deserve good after all the bad she'd been through before?

"Where were you God?" She'd railed at God speaking back verses from scripture to him... "Behold, I go forward, but you are not there; and backward, but I cannot perceive you! On the left hand, where you work, but I can't see how you are at work in my life? You hide yourself on the right hand from me, I cannot see you,"... whispering the verses Job had asked the Lord in chapter 23 verses 8-19, "God where were you?"

Her heart whispered back, "My grace is sufficient for thee: for my strength is made perfect in weakness."(2 Corinthians 12:9) Job said in verse ten, "But he knoweth the way that I take: when he hath tried me, I shall come forth as Gold".

It soothed her soul somehow she would gather her courage and strength from The Lord. She would make it through, she just had too, for the sake of her children, for herself, for His sake and purpose. She would let "his will to be done here on earth, as [it is] in heaven" (Matthew 6:10). She would submit to his plan although it was hard and it hurt.

The funeral service was simple and beautiful. She could not believe how many people had attended. Not only their church family but all of Roberts' associates from work and their families and people whom he'd done work for on their homes. Robbie's entire student class had come. The Pastor had delivered a beautiful message of salvation and trust in Jesus Christ. Many parents and children alike had come to Christ for the first time that day.

For the first few weeks after she came home. Marie's parents had stayed at her house to help with the children and to help her get settled back into a more normal routine, it was difficult having had a broken arm, being nearly six months pregnant and feeling so weak, her body was battered and her heart was bruised. It was hard getting up most mornings, she just wanted to not get up.

One sunny morning Elizabeth forced her to get up and dressed that morning and eat some breakfast. "It will help your over all attitude and recovery. You can't forget about little Sam growing inside you." She said rubbing Marie's belly.

"How can I forget, I feel as big as a house and I'm not even full term yet. Thanks for taking care of me mom. I love you, you know, I appreciate your help."

"I know you do, I love you too, dear. It's that love that compels me to help,

But I have to tell you that your Dad and I talked last night... and well" *sigh* "It's time for your Dad and I to head home, we'll come often. But it's been over a month now and we both feels it's time for you to move forward by yourself."

"But Mom! I can't! Not yet! Please don't" she whispered, begging.

"I hurt for you dear, I really do, but your cast comes off today and your body has healed physically. So now you need to think about the future. Your dad and I are always close by, you know that, but we too have lives and your brother, Bless him, has been somewhat neglected and he needs us too. We didn't even celebrate his birthday because of you. He's hurting too, you know?"

At that statement Marie deflated, she had been quite needy and she knew her mother was right. "Okay mom, just stay one more night though, please, help me tell the kids."

"We already have and they're fine with it. Children are sometimes more resilient than us adults. God softens the blows for them sometimes. His grace is sufficient, and they believe it."

"Yeah. Sometimes I wish I had a faith like my children do." *sigh*

"Tell me about it" she chuckled, "kids say the funniest and the most wise things sometimes, out of the mouths of babes you know."

"Yeah..., so how is John Antony these days? I guess I've been so self-absorbed with my own pain that I've forgotten about everyone else."

"He'll be all right eventually. With Valentino not being able to return from overseas because his tour isn't over, well, Robert was his next big brother. You know they talked about many things, now he'll have to bounce his girl troubles off your Dad" they shared a small chuckle. "What your brother doesn't realize is that your Dad is a hopeless romantic. We live a good life together."

"Yeah me too" her voice shaky, "we did" she amended, "we lived a good life together didn't we, Mom?"

"Yes, I believe you did have a full marriage, short though it was. I knew you two were happy and I never worried about you when you two married, not even when you went away to college. The Lord gave me the strength to let you go."

Marie remembered the day too. "You know I almost backed out, but Robert said something to me that forced me to take that step forward."

"What was that? I don't think you've ever told me this."

"Baby steps." He also quoted Job 23:11 and 14 to me. I memorized them after that to help remind me."

"What does it say?"

"My foot hath held his steps, his way have I kept, and not declined...," she scrunched her face in remembrance, "...for he performeth the thing that is appointed for me: and many such things are with him."

"He was a wise young man."

"Yeah that and I think he wanted me there with him at college. Even though our schedules would be varying, with our different interests. But God helped us work it out. Somehow I knew I would marry him eventually."

"Turned out sooner rather than later, huh." Elizabeth nudged her arm.

Marie smiled at the memory of her wedding day, "Yeah", she sighed, "I've known him practically my whole life, how will I move on without him?"

"Baby steps". They both broke into tears holding onto one another, allowing the healing tears to flow. After a spell, they released one another, Elizabeth saying. "Enough of this, you've got your doctor appointment to get ready for."

Marie nodded and her mother left her alone to get ready. As she dressed memories of the past wove their way through her head. Remembering the first time she'd met Robert...

CHAPTER 9

JUNE 1985

Elizabeth called out to her ten year old son. "Valentino, come get this box, will you?" He dutifully came taking the indicated box and taking it into the house for her without complaint. After all it was moving day and they were all excited, they were now at their new home in the neighborhood on the outskirts of downtown Madrone Valley. Located in the renowned Silicon Valley, just north of the garlic capital of the world, in California. Close to San Jose where her Dad had many of his jobs or even all the way to Saratoga. He drove to where the jobs took him, but decided to relocate them here in this smaller peaceful community. "A good place to raise a family away from the city with a bit of land."

There were a few homes on their tree lined street. She did remember that there were nice sized front yards, she hadn't realized at the time they owned an acre of land. Next to the garage most of the homes had nice landscaping out front except theirs. The mid-century modern house had been a rental property previously and was not very well cared for. Her father saw the potential in this ramshackle home. He'd bought it at a slight discount enough for the necessary repairs to the roof and patching that needed to be done in certain parts of the ceiling in her room and the living room which fronted the home. Dad had that all done before they moved in this week, he even let her pick a color for her room. She chose a pale pink to go with her white furniture and her miniature rose quilt that her grandmother had made for her when she was younger.

Her room was smaller than her brother's, but she didn't mind. Mother handed her a box for her room she went down the ramp then up the driveway through the front door and turned left down the hall to her bedroom while Val's room was next door to hers, they would share a bathroom between them. Her parents room was at the other end of the house with their own bathroom with the living room dining room and kitchen in the middle of the house. They called it a split home.

She liked the backyard with it's ancient willow tree in one corner a patio large enough to hold a small party and the grass, that needed a lot of help, the roses that lined the back of the property didn't look to good, but Mom would soon take care of that she was great with flowers.

Setting down the box Marie looked through her window, she saw a boy across the street, wearing a baseball hat over blondish brown hair, he was in the shade of the tree, so she couldn't see his eyes. He was lanky, sitting on the swing in his front yard, wearing a sling on one arm and throwing a baseball up into the air and catching it with the other. She loved baseball and hoped this town had a team. Mother called again, she knew she was dawdling, this was the hundredth trip, probably. She held in a sigh and headed out again for more boxes. As she headed out Val passed her, she asked "Did you see the boy across the street?"

"Yeah, his names' Robbie."

"How old is he?"

"He's a year and a half older than me. He seems nice though. He said he'll introduce me to the other fellas on the block. It looks like we'll be going to the same school, he'll be a sixth grader."

"Does he know if there's any girls around here?"

"I don't know I didn't ask." Val shrugged and continued to walk past her to his room with the box he held.

Later that day once they had finally emptied the moving van, and the moving guys were gone, they sat on the living room floor having a 'picnic' and eating pizza for dinner. The table had not been put back together yet and the sofa Dad had ordered as a surprise for mom, wouldn't be there until later in the week. So they sat on the floor having a laugh and enjoying their new home though they were all tired. Suddenly the doorbell rang. Mom rose up to answer, it was Robbie.

"Hi, my mom had to leave for work, but she asked me to bring these over."

"Oh, I'm sorry I missed her, please thank her for me, would you like to come in and meet the kids?"

"I already met your son Val, but not his sister. I should get back though, our dinner's almost ready. I just didn't want to forget."

"Well, thank you...I'm sorry I forgot your name..."

"Robert LaSalle, but everybody calls me Robbie."

44

"Nice to meet you Robert. Please come over anytime you like and bring your siblings if you like."

"Thank you ma'am but I don't have any siblings."

"Oh, well, you're welcome anytime."

"Thank you, Mrs. Perry. Maybe tomorrow I'll come by."

"I'm sure Val would like that." She waved goodbye as he walked away a wistful look on his face. 'Hmm,' she thought to herself, "Look what the neighbor made for us," she opened the package. "Cookies, yum, they smell good." She smacked her lips and took a cookie out biting into it. 'Mmm'.

Everyone else took a cookie and had a bite savoring the chocolatey goodness. Stan said, "That was a nice ending to our day."

"Yes, that was quite thoughtful of Robbie's mother, but apparently she works this evening."

"That's too bad, you didn't get to meet her, honey."

"Sure makes me ever so grateful that you allow me to stay home with the kids, love." Mom smiled at Dad with affection. He had pulled her to himself and gave her a kiss that made her blush.

Val gagged, "Ew, Dad gross."

"Don't knock it till you've tried it son, after you're married that is," he chuckled when Val looked at him doubtfully. Marie giggled and looked at them just seeing her father dote on her mother, it made her happy to see her parents all gooey, making goo goo eyes at each other.

The following day Val went to see if Robbie could play, he was an outgoing boy and wanted to make friends before school started, he didn't think it would be good to start school before he'd made some friends in the neighborhood. The school was only a few blocks away so most days they could walk to school.

Robbie came out and Marie soon joined them, but Val didn't want her there, Robbie was 'his' new friend. "Why can't I be friends too?", Marie asked.

"Because you're a girl, obviously!" Val rolled his eyes.

"That's dumb, Val and you know it. Girl's can be friends with boys."

"Nu-uh!"

"Uh-huh, they can too!"

Val got in her face, "Nu-uh, why don't you go play with your dolls or something. We're going to play baseball."

"I can play, I'm the best-est on my team."

"Yeah, a girls' team." Val snickered. Marie ran away back home with tear-filled eyes; with her feelings hurt. She watched the boys play, until some other boys came along riding bicycles, Robbie introduced them, they talked for a while, then Val came in, she heard him talking with Mom, then he left again.

Robbie watched as they all rode away, he walked over to his swing and sat down looking forlorn. Mom came in then, 'Val went to play with his new friends, but I see Robbie didn't go with them. I wonder why? Why don't you go and see why he didn't go with them? I'm sure he could use a friend to talk to."

"Val said I couldn't be friends with boys."

Mom pursed her lips, "That's nonsense. I'll have a talk with Val, why don't you go over there and see if you can cheer him up.'

"Okay Momma."

The rest as they say is history. That day they had fun, they swung on his tree swing, she'd persuaded him to play hopscotch and he'd persuaded her to play 'Jacks'. They played tag then she'd asked him why he didn't ride bikes with her brother and his friends."

"My bike has a flat and my mom can't fix it."

"What about your Dad? Can't he fix it, my Dad fixes mine."

"I don't have a Dad. He died last year."

At this Marie began to cry, she had a tender heart. Robbie didn't know what to do, so he put his arm around her and began to comfort her. "It's okay, don't cry."

"I'm sorry about your Dad." She wiped her eyes, sniffling. "Do you miss him?"

"Everyday," he said with emotion, trying not to cry.

Marie got an idea "My Dad is home, I'll go ask him to fix your bike" she took off before he could protest.

Marie had told Dad about Robbie and about his Dad and his bike. So Stan walked over with his tire patch kit and pump. He proceeded to fix Robbie's bike without question. As Robbie watched, Stan explained the process as he worked, talking as if he spoke with Marie. Knowing the boy could use a little guidance without making him feel useless, he would ask for a specific tool and Marie would point to it as they worked together to help her father fix the bike.

When they were done Stan said, "If you need any other help, don't hesitate to ask, or if there's something your Mom needs, just ask my wife and we'll help if we can, Okay?" Stan held out his hand to shake hands 'Man to Man'.

Robbie gave a crooked grin, "Yes, sir, Thank You."

"Can he come over and have lunch with us Dad?" Marie jumped up and down, having had this great idea.

"Sure, pun'kin' if it's okay with his Mom."

"She won't mind, she's at work right now, she had to pull a double shift today."

"Yeah!" Marie shouted with glee.

They had lunch then settled in for a game of Scrabble after their meal. They'd had fun laughing and giggling at the words her Dad tried to put on the board. He would tease them with silly mixed up words before he would put down his actual words. They had a great time laughing and being silly.

Then Robbie heard his Mom calling for him. "I'd better go, Mom will be worried. Thanks for everything Mr. and Mrs. Perry."

"You're quite welcome, come back anytime."

Marie walked with him to the door, "Can you play tomorrow?"

"I don't know, maybe?" He shrugged.

"Oh, okay," she said eyes downcast. Robert then bent down and kissed her on the cheek before taking off for home as fast as lightning.

"That rascal," Marie heard her mother say behind her. As she waved to his mother across the street.

Mom never stopped him from coming over all that summer, except for Sundays which were church and family days. That is, until he got saved at VBS that summer and started coming to church with them regularly, then his mom came when she could.

They were pretty inseparable from that point on. Even throughout junior high, and in high school they began to officially date. When she was 16, he was 18, taking classes at the local college, besides working a job at the local restaurant. When they went on dates, they always had her little brother, John Antony, in tow as chaperone.

John Antony was eight at the time, so they often went to go bowling or skating in the summer. In the winter, they went ice skating or to the local football games. A few times, they were allowed to go up to the observatory at night and watch the stars and take night pictures. With her Mom or Dad in tow, sometimes Val would accompany them as well. Marie was a hobby photographer, and so, of course John Antony wanted to be a photographer as well. He did have a knack for it. Marie could tell, as he showed great promise with some of the pictures she let him take on her camera.

So many of these wonderful memories came to her mind during those dark days. She loved Robert so much and would miss him more than she cared to admit. She didn't think she could ever marry again. He had been her whole life. She would not have any memories of them together seeing their children being raised getting married, nothing special anymore, no memories of growing old together. She would be alone. She was a widow at twenty-eight.

Of course, father would help to stand in the gap where Robert's influence would be missing with the boys. Life would be so different now.

CHAPTER 10

SEPTEMBER 2002

After that first month, her stress level began to increase. She would have to make phone calls to all the billing companies, she dreaded it. She hated talking to people she didn't know, and they weren't very friendly most of the time. Somehow she would have to manage the household budget, which meant she had to call the mortgage company.

Once she called the mortgage company, she found out she needed a copy of Robert's death certificate so that the loan could be changed, but that also had to be recorded with the county recorders office. Did she work? Could she make payments? Did she have insurance on her husband to make a payoff?

"I don't know!" She exclaimed before bursting out crying and slamming the phone down. "Ugh, these dumb people," she said out loud.

"Yeah," Seth shouted, "dumb peep's."

"Seth! Don't say that again. Mommy was just upset. I'm sorry, I won't say it again, so you don't say it either okay? It's a no, no word."

"Okay, sorry, Mommy, no-no" he looked genuine, putting his finger to his lips in the shushing motion.

"Me too, Sethy, me too." Marie hugged her boy and the baby kicked him.

"Hey," he said, "who did that?"

"The baby in Mommy's tummy. His name is Sam. He's just saying hello."

"Hiyah, Sam! Why don't you come out and play?"

"Oh, now, he can't come out for a while, but when he is ready, he will."

"Okay," and he traipsed away happily.

If only she could recover so well. Stan saw the look on her face and said, "You will, sweet-pea."

"Dad, when did you get here? I never heard you com in."

"I'm sneaky that way, you know." He winked and gave her a kiss on the cheek. "I know you don't want to hear me say this, but you will heal. It's hard right now, I know. You just have to trust God, and trust in His plan. "Don't be angry with Him, honey. He knows what you can and cannot handle. Don't you remember another time when you didn't think you could handle it? But, you know, with His help and grace, you did. Look at what a blessed life you have."

"You call what's happened to me, to us, a blessing?"

"Yes". He paused looking at her seriously, "I know it doesn't 'feel' that way now, but think of all the lives that have been saved because of what's happened, fifteen souls, by my last count, but, even if only one had been saved, Robert and Robbie are saying, 'It's worth it.' To die so one might be saved, but so many more than one, they are up in heaven rejoicing over those salvations. How many more will be impacted by the end, we don't know. 'For the LORD [is] good; his mercy [is] everlasting; and his truth [endureth] to all generations.' (Psalm 100:5)

"Dad..." she sighed.

"Yes, sweet-pea?" He came over to hug her.

"I need help with this," she held up all the bills and notes she tried to talk with each of the companies she tried to contact. "I'm lost with all this. Robert always took care of the bills, and I just can't talk to these people. They have no compassion or decent courtesy when I try to explain what happened. I'm just so frustrated I could scream," she sat down, heart racing, feeling light-headed.

"Oh, my dear," shaking his head, "he did you a disservice by not keeping you informed. Your mother knows all our financial information should anything befall me."

"Dad!" Marie protested.

"Don't get me wrong. I loved the boy, but answer me this: do you know any of the passcodes to access the accounts or where they may be located?"

"I suppose, in his office, or maybe the safe deposit box at the bank? I know we have one of those."

"Okay, we'll do this together. I'll help you with this and teach you some basic accounting skills, but I think it would be wise for you to brush up on the household management aspect. Maybe you should take an online course through the college, or maybe

Pastor Fogley has some recommendations from the congregation, someone who could teach you."

"Yes, a plan of action. This feels much, much better now." Marie thought to herself. "Okay, let's get started."

"No, we'll start tomorrow."

"But, why?"

"Because you'll feel better and be rested when we begin. Also, I'm afraid it will take all day, maybe even a few. We need your mom or brother here to help mind the kids while we work on this. Some things are going to change drastically for you. Do you even know how much money you have in the bank?"

"No, not really. I just have what he gave me: cash to spend on groceries and gas and that was it. When it was gone, it was gone. I had to ask if I could have a little more, but I tried not to."

"Well, that's at least a good start. Anyhow, it's almost dinnertime and most places of business are closed or closing, and they rarely pick up the phone. Bad customer service, I say."

"Dad?"

"Yeah, sweet-pea?"

"I love you." Marie hugged his neck and sighed with relief.

"I love you, too."

CHAPTER 11

Her father had been right of course, about it taking days, it was closer to a month. All the regular bills, like the utility and phone company, had been easy. The life insurance and mortgage companies had been a much more difficult and complicated matter entirely!

The life insurance company wanted so many things before a payout would happen, documentation about everything: death certificate, police reports on the accident, the whole shebang! It was worse than going to the dentist, and the mortgage company was no different. Robert's life insurance did not cover the entire mortgage on all their property or any kind of stipend for Marie and their kids. So, she had to have her mother and father co-sign for the remainder of the loan.

She would have to go back to work. She didn't know what she'd do. She had worked since she was 16, cleaning houses for friends and neighbors, after they married and she got pregnant, Robert didn't want her to work anymore, even though they'd been finishing college at the time. He'd wanted the focus to be on family, not money or her education, because the Lord would provide what they needed and help them, so she quit college to focus on their coming child.

The Lord always did provide for them, ever faithfully. Now, all of that would change, not his faithfulness or provision, but now she was the head of her family, life would be more of a challenge. "Dad, what should I do now? I don't exactly have any "real" life skills, and I'm six months pregnant. Who would hire me?"

"Well, for one thing, I have been praying about that for several weeks now, and you will come to work for me, Sweet Pea."

"But, what would I do? Clean the office? It's about the only thing I know how to do. Clean up other people's messes." Defeat in her voice.

"That isn't true and you know it! When you were in school, you were always a top student in math, science, and English, remember?"

"Yes, well, that was a long time ago."

"Not so long ago. Perhaps you're a little rusty, but soon enough, you'll need those skills for work. I would like you to work as my assistant until the baby is born. We have just enough time for the insurance to kick in, and cover you at delivery time. You'll get three months off, and then I'd like for you to go back to school. You should take either online college courses or go to the local and take some economics and finance. Perhaps you could be our payroll officer and do things like budgeting and math to keep me on task."

"Dad, why are you helping me so much?" She asked with tears in her eyes.

"Simply, it is because I am you father. But it's not entirely unselfish you see. My payroll officer will be retiring in a year and a half. She already has warned me to get her a replacement and you will be trained by the best, and go to school and learn all the current technology for your job. But Marie…, am I supposed to just stand by and watch you suffer and struggle alone? Do you think in the Bible, if Jacob could have helped Joseph he would have!"

"I guess so, but then things would have been a lot different for Egypt, for them too."

"Not necessarily! The Lord would have done things differently perhaps, but the results would have been the same."

"Perhaps."

He sighed, "What am I going to do with you?" He asked rhetorically with a smile quirking up his lips. Marie smiled back. It was a question he always asked and she never answered. He pulled her close and hugged his daughter. Stan thought to himself, "That's her first smile in weeks. I'm glad."

"So, when do we start, boss?"

"How about next Monday? That should give you a couple of days to find the help that you need, and if not, you could work from home for a while with simple stuff, until you can find someone on a permanent basis."

"How should I dress?"

"At this point, whatever's comfortable, but afterwards, I'd like you to dress 'business casual.' Obviously I'd prefer skirts, but Friday is denim day, just to keep things fun."

"Dad, it doesn't matter what you wear; you're always fun."

He gave a mock punch to her jaw and said, "That's my girl." He then pulled her to himself, 'You're going to make it, honey girl, with His help. You will make it. Remember this: 'Jesus said unto him, if thou canst believe, all things [are] possible to him that believeth." (Mark 9:23) "So... believe."

Marie sighed as he held her safe in his arms as unwanted tears escaped from her eyes. The seeds of belief were planted for the impossible. Now came the watering.

CHAPTER 12

Marie complained, "I'm so glad school is over and done with, at least for this week, I think I may burst, this baby is so big mother."

"It'll be good to have a big boy. I was so worried about you during the summer, but it looks like your little guy made you take care of him."

Tears filled Marie's eyes then, "Oh, Mom, will the ache I feel ever go away?"

"I honestly cannot say. When your Gran passed, I missed her so much. For about two years after, I would catch myself calling her and then remembering she wasn't there anymore. She would have loved seeing your babies grow up, but it's not for us to know the seasons of this life, or how long they will last. But to know that it all has a purpose in His economy is the best knowledge to have, although we may not understand it. Christ feels our pains,

He knows how we suffer, but if we do it by His grace, He will heal us in due time."

"And now? After ten years, mom, how is it? The pain?"

"Yes. Well, it's bittersweet really. It has lessened, so I cherish the good memories of her. I have your father to comfort me, and you kids can be a great balm. But, mostly, I'm thankful she's in Heaven and doesn't have to suffer from the cancer anymore. That is something I can be thankful for this Thanksgiving." She sighed, "Okay enough of a tea break. We have a feast to get on! Except for you Marie. Your legs look so swollen today, so you sit and I'll bring you something to do."

"Sounds good to me. My back has been achy all morning."

"Do you want a pillow to support your back?"

"That would be nice, yes."

"Here, why don't you sit on the sofa and put your feet up?"

"You're spoiling me, Mother!"

"Well, you are my only daughter, and the men outnumber us, so we have to stick together." Little Lizzy climbed onto the sofa then blankie in hand, and sat next to Mommy.

"Stick togeder, Momma," she said as she laid her head on Marie's bulging belly.

Elizabeth chuckled, "Yes, now, I'll go get that pillow."

"Hey, Mom, where's Dad and the boys? The house is so quiet."

"They're outside. Your father had the notion to deep fry the turkey this year. John Antony saw it on one of those cooking shows that he's always watching. He planted the seed about two weeks ago, so they are in the backyard tending to it. Don't worry about Seth, John is playing a game with him."

"He's going to be a good dad someday, isn't he, Mom?"

"I sure hope so. He's grown up a lot these past few months. I've never seen better grades, even though he has that part-time job working at the grocery store," she mused.

"Mom, can I have that pillow now?"

"Oh, yes. Sorry, I'll be right back."

Marie sat stroking Lizzy's hair and she felt her baby girl fall asleep. It had been a fun morning for her, and now it was nap time. She yawned, "A nap doesn't seem like such a bad idea."

Elizabeth came back with the pillow to find her daughter and granddaughter fast asleep. She snuck slowly to the mantle where her camera was and snapped a picture of the two of them. Marie never flinched. "Poor dear." Her mother thought as she inspected her daughter more closely. There were still dark circles under her eyes, and her hair wasn't neatly in check. She realized her daughter was still hurting, even with all the activity in her life, and her children to distract her. A tear escaped as she watched her daughter slumber.

About two hours later, Marie woke with a start, as a sharp pain encircled her belly. "No, it couldn't be. Did Lizzy accidentally hit me?" She looked down, but Lizzy was gone. "Don't panic, Marie, it was nothing. I should go to the bathroom." As she tried to get up, another pain shot through her and she winced aloud. Her mother heard her stirring, and from the kitchen she asked, "Did you have a nice nap, sweet-pea?"

"Yes, but, ooh—" Marie groaned, the contraction stronger this time. Eliza ran over to her with pie-floured hands.

"Is it the baby? Is he coming?"

"I think so, Mom," she looked at her, worried.

"I'll get your father and John," she flitted off, clapping her hands in happiness. Marie didn't feel very happy. She just felt scared. A dozen thoughts filled her mind, "How am I going to raise this baby alone? How am I going to get through the delivery without Robert there? My dear, dear Robert!" She began to cry as another contraction came, stronger than the last.

Stan came in, followed by John and Seth, who pushed his way to the front, asking, "Are you gonna have a baby, Momma?"

"Yes, Sethy"

"Yippee! A new brudder ta play wif!" He grabbed her tummy. "Hey, Sam, come on, hurry up."

Everyone chuckled, but just then another contraction took her. Marie gritted her teeth so she wouldn't scare Seth. When it passed she said, "Well, I think he's listening to his older brother." She looked up at her dad.

He smiled at her with tear-filled eyes. "It's gonna be okay, sweet-pea."

She held out her arms for a hand up, and a hug. His hugs were the best, aside from Robert's. "I miss him, Dad. What am I gonna do?"

"One step at a time. Baby steps. One day at a time, and by His grace and help. I heard a sermon once, long ago and it stuck with me through the years. God's not going to take something away if he isn't ready to replace it. He takes away hate, and gives back love. He takes away selfishness, and gives kindness. He takes away pride, and gives humility. Understand?"

"He takes away Robert and Robbie to give me Seth?"

He pulled her away, "NO!" He looked her firmly in the eye. "He didn't take them. He received them unto Himself. They are here," he pointed to his chest, in my heart and in the bosom of God. And they are here, pointing to her heart. He is going to give you something so wonderful we won't even know how to respond to His kindness. I'm sure of it." As another contraction seized her, she held tight to her Dad. Stan led Marie gently towards the car.

"Be safe and drive carefully, dear," Elizabeth called after them. "I love you both." She joined everyone else in waving until they were out of sight. She heard the timer go off in the kitchen, "Oh, my pies!" Elizabeth pushed through the crowd of her family to the kitchen.

As they drove towards they hospital, Marie thought at an interminably slow pace. She looked at her father, "Dad?" He concentrated on the road.

"Yeah, sweet-pea?"

"Thanks for being here with me, and helping me, especially since..." she couldn't continue as tears rolled down her face. Stan squeezed her hand in knowing where her thoughts were.

"I'm glad I'm here too, Pun'kin" he said. She sniffled, "Dad, I'm afraid." She confessed, as a terribly strong contraction took hold of her.

"Just hold on, Marie. Hold on to faith. Hold my hand however you must and just think that you're holding onto the hand of Jesus. For he's certainly holding onto you even now, he is with us in this situation." Pulling into the parking area designated for labor and delivery. There were attendants waiting for them. "Marie LaSalle?" one of them asked.

"Yes," she nodded and began to cry in earnest. "Your mother called ahead for you" she cooed, "Don't fret or worry, dear, it'll be all right." Stan grabbed her bag out of the trunk and followed close behind them.

He pulled the arm of the attendant to stop their progress as Marie went on with the other in a wheelchair. "My daughter recently lost her husband. Can I go with her into the delivery room?"

"Yes, you can, and we did know who she is. We've all been praying for her, everyday," the older attendant said.

"What's your name?"

"I'm Bethany, but I know Linda and Melina. We were saved shortly after Linda was, and we decided to start a prayer group before we start our shift and we always add Marie to our list. It's very hard losing a loved one, especially the first year. Lord knows I was a wreck when my husband passed on. But thanks to the Lord, the pain is lessened."

Stan clasped her hand. "Thank you for that."

They began to walk again. "She's in good hands, because she's in the Lord's hands." Stan began to tear up.

Once inside the Labor & Delivery Department, the nurses buzzed around Marie like busy bees, hooking her up to monitors and all kinds of equipment, and asking a thousand questions. At least, that's how it seemed to Marie. Her father, she noticed, was sitting in a corner of the room praying. How it reminded her of Robert, who would do the same until most of the "hubbub" died down. Then he would come over, rub her belly, and soothe her nerves. For, even though this was a joyous occasion, she hated being in hospitals. It brought back too many dark memories. Her pulse began to race as the memories flooded her mind. Her eyes closed unwillingly. Everyone, everything disappeared, save the memories...

"Robert watch out!"

"Ma'am you have a broken arm."

"My babies, where are they?"

"Robert! Help me! Somebody help me!"

"I'm sorry, honey. Robert's dead."

"Dad...Marie..., Robbie's gone."

Stan shook her gently, "Marie, you need to calm down. It's not good for you or the baby."

"I know, dad, but being here... Oh, I'm gonna be sick, Dad!"

"NURSE!" Stan hollered.

One came rushing in, "Yes?" She was too late as Marie expelled right then.

"Oh, dear. Let me call the doctor, and we'll get you cleaned up. Bethany, a little assistance?" She called out, as she began to pull the soiled sheets off of Marie.

Bethany, the older nurse came over to Marie's side and looked her straight in the eyes. "I know you've had a great loss," she began to stroke her head as only a grandmother could do. Marie began to cry in earnest again. "Oh, dearie," she pulled her close and let her cry as she spoke gently to her. "Your husband was a good man, who loved the Lord and you all very much. But I think he would say that what you need is God's grace right now. To fill you because you have a hard road ahead. I'm not going to lie, but if you trust him to help you through. He is the only one who can and will do it. He promised it in his word."

Once Marie began to calm down Bethany said, "Good, now, it's time we probably start pushing. Something is telling me this little fella wants to see his momma face to face and just love on her." Marie smiled at that. The doctor on duty walked in.

"Can I have an epidural?" Marie asked, but another contraction came and her water broke.

"I'm afraid not even a 'saddle-block' will help at this point. How long have you been having contractions?"

"Only about two hours, right, Dad?"

He looked at his watch. "More like two and a half."

"Well, this little one is eager to get out since your water broke. Let's take a look and if I don't miss my guess, you can start pushing."

Within another half hour Marie delivered a very robust and sleepy baby. The doctor was surprised at how calm he seemed to be. Marie cried as she held him, but this time, they were happy tears. "Hello, Samuel. I'm so glad to see you."

Grandpa was watching and looking on with a satisfied smile. God's grace would bring another aspect of healing to Marie. For Stan had prayed and asked in his prayers, for Him to bring his daughter a semblance of peace. He could see that little Sam would help her do just that. He knew she'd still struggle because humans are so prideful, and we tend not to let go and let God work. Through Samuel, he hoped Marie would have another part of healing work in her life. He would help her move forward with her life because she'd have to keep going on with life for his sake.

Marie held Samuel up for her father to take. He held him close and prayed aloud.

"Dearest Heavenly Father, You are the Father of us all. Please, bless this little one, Samuel David to be as his namesake: a child "asked of God" and "beloved" by all. May he be a healing balm to his mother, to all of us? You have designed our lives this way to feel pain and sadness, so that we can see and appreciate the love and joy You have to offer us, through your son, Jesus. We bless your name, Oh God. Amen."

CHAPTER 13

SATURDAY, NOVEMBER 30, 2002

Seth sat at the front room window, waiting for his mom to arrive. Grandma had told him Mommy, Papaw, and baby Sam would be here any minute, and he wanted to be the first to greet them. He played with his favorite car on the windowsill. Then he heard a car door slam. "Momma's here! Momma's here!" he shouted. Two and a half year old Lizzy almost ran to be let out of the house at the word, 'Momma'.

Elizabeth stopped her, wiping her face with a paper towel, and took her to the door to welcome home her daughter and baby Sam. She saw her husband struggling with the car seat, while Marie took the diaper bag and her luggage. "Ha ha!" She heard her husband shout, "Success!" He pulled baby Sam out with his baby seat. She smiled adoringly at her husband. "Baby equipment had changed a lot in fifteen years," she thought.

As they came towards the house, a flat bed tow truck began to back into her driveway. Everyone stopped to look, Marie thought he was just using it to turn around, but then the driver turned off the engine. He got out of the truck, put on a baseball cap and grabbed a clipboard as he started walking towards them. Another older man got out the passenger side of the truck and began to undo the chains hooked up to the brand new blue minivan with a giant bow on the top of it.

"Can we help you?" Her father asked.

"Ya shore can!" said the man with a southern accent. He had a scruffy beard and sun-glass covered eyes. "I'm lookin' fer a Marie La Sale? er... La Sally. Sorry if I got the name wrong. Not too good with names sometimes," he finished with a toothy grin.

"I'm... I'm Marie Lasalle," she corrected him, slowly, haltingly.

"Please, sign here then!" He held out the clipboard and tapped where she was to sign.

She hesitated and said, "I don't understand..."

"Why, this 'ere is a new car, and I'm 'ere to deliver it!" He grinned again. "But I didn't buy a new car... you must be confused on the address, or the name." She turned to head into the house.

"Well, let me see 'ere. You are Marie La Salle", he corrected himself smiling at her, with that toothy grin again, "of 1542 Jumping Juniper Drive, Madrone Valley, California, are you not?"

She turned back, "Yes, that's me."

"Then, this 'ere is yer new car, Ma'am."

"Dad," she cried, "you didn't!"

Stan looked befuddled, "No, I didn't!" shaking his head in the negative.

"Don't look at me!" Elizabeth said. "I do what your Dad tells me, and he certainly didn't! Although we had thought about it."

Marie stammered, "I... I can't... I can't accept it." She said to the driver, "I can't afford the payments." She looked sad as she turned away again.

The driver gently took her shoulder. "Ma'am, the car is already paid for. It's free," he grinned. "I'm so dumb, I forgot to say. It says right 'ere. Bought and paid for by Arimathea Foundation as second grand prize for entering their drawing. All taxes and fees have been paid by the company. Alls ya gotta do is sign 'ere and the car is yours, Ma'am," he grinned again.

"But, I didn't enter any drawing," she said confused.

"Well, maybe someone else did it fer ya." He scratched his chin and held out the clipboard again. She set down her bags and, with a shaking hand, took the clipboard and signed her name. She looked up and saw the other man lowering the flat bed.

"Thank ya kindly, Ma'am," he said, as he touched his baseball cap and went to help his partner. They backed up the minivan into her driveway, and parked it. He came back and placed the keys into Marie's hand. "You enjoy now. It looks like you needed it," as he looked at the children standing next to her.

"Thank you," she said hoarsely and burst out crying. Elizabeth reached out for her daughter in an embrace. Seth came up and said, "Hey, Mister, that car's for us?"

"Yes, sir, it is."

"For always?"

"Yes, fer always, and always," he smiled his toothy grin, the driver took his cue and began to walk away. Then Seth yelled.

"Yippee! Thank you Jesus. I prayed for a new car for Momma." He shouted and ran to inspect it.

Nearly chocking on his chewing gum, the driver had to hurry away before the tears came at the unexpected words of sweet faith in the Lord from the boy. Neither had realized the sweet savor they were leaving behind.

Walter said as he grinned as wide as a crocodile, "Well, that was exciting,"

"Shore was!" Douglas said in his fake southern accent. As he swiped at his eyes, then both men laughed as they drove back to the towing company's yard. "I'm so glad I called Nate. What a great idea he had! It was great your friend Bob could let us use the tow truck for the delivery," Douglas said.

"Yes, Bob is a good man, and he won't let our secret slip if any of them decide to ask." Walter stated.

"But it was our genius to set up a false company so no one would be the wiser and trace it back to me," Douglas said.

"Well, we gotta do what we gotta do to keep your secret safe. I guess I better close down that operation when we get back."

"No, I think I like this approach. I'm thinking she needs to 'win' free diapers for a year next," Douglas said.

"Do you have any idea how much that will cost? A small fortune I remember well," Walter said.

"Yes, exactly. Do you think she has that to spend? She's going to struggle no matter what. So why not help her in this way?"

"But why her? I mean, there have been other women in her situation, and you've not helped them."

"I don't know," Douglas shrugged, "somehow, it feels that I should help. This family was put into my path. Ever since I witnessed their particular suffering that awful day, I had the thought that someone ought to help. It's as if the Lord allowed me to witness it so I could be that help, and I have the means to do so, so why not me? I think she's worthy of help. She didn't even want to accept the car because she didn't 'enter a contest' and then she thought she'd have to pay for it, so she refused. When I told her that it was paid for, she started to cry."

"Okay, I'll go along, since you're the boss."

They both laughed and then began to make even more plans to help, but Douglas decided he would let MaryAnne handle the baby stuff for the contests she would know more of what was needful than himself. He began to make a plan of people he would talk to to help him set up the Arimathea Foundation for real.

PART II

2 YEARS LATER

CHAPTER 14

11:48 AM - APRIL 5, 2004

Marie sighed, as she sat at her desk in the offices of "Dean and Perry" an architectural firm. With so much to get done today, it looked to be a late night again. So, she put her head down and went to work, crunching numbers for end of month. "Everyone loves a paycheck." When she next looked up, her father stood in front of her desk an amused expression on his face. "What is that smile for?" Marie asked.

"I've been standing here for about three minutes. I was waiting to see how long it would take for you to notice."

"Really? I'm sorry to have kept you waiting. I was just so bent on getting this done, so I won't get home too late."

"Have you had lunch yet, Marie?"

"Lunch. Is it that time already?" She looked at her watch, confirming it was 11:51pm. "Wow, where does the time go?" She said rhetorically.

"So, you haven't had lunch, then?" He asked kindly.

"No, sir," she replied, and her stomach growled just then, she blushed. "Well, then, allow an old man to treat his favorite bookkeeper," he added winking, "before your blood sugar gets too low." He smiled gently, "And we can talk about Lizzy's birthday party."

"Well, if that's the case, where to?" She put her computer to sleep, grabbed her purse, rose to get up, but quickly sat back down.

"I knew it! Marie LaSalle!" He scolded, "You didn't eat breakfast this morning, did you?" He came around and helped her get up and steady herself.

"Yes, I did!" She said defiantly.

"What, a banana and a cup of coffee?" He said mockingly, she blushed deeply at his accurate guess, he continued, "That is no breakfast. It needs to include proteins and grains to keep you going. I can't have you passing out when I need you most, it's end of month after all," he said as he tweaked her nose. Then they walked out of her small office. She laughed as they reached the entry.

"I'm not going to pass out—," she was protesting, but stopped suddenly.

Just ahead, in the foyer, stood a very tall, distinguished-looking and incredibly handsome man looking vaguely familiar, like someone that tickled the back of her memory.

Mr. Perry stepped forward, "How may I help you, sir? We are currently closed for the lunch hour."

"I'm sorry," said the gentleman, "the door was unlocked, but I heard voices and decided to wait as I could hear you coming closer. I was wanting to make an appointment with Mr. LaSalle," he held a card out, "in particular, about some plans I'm making for a summer home in the area."

"Oh, well, I'm sorry to say he's no longer with us. I could meet with you though if that's amenable to you. Though it seems my secretary has gone to lunch already. Can you call, or come back in a hour or so? We were just heading out ourselves," he looked to Marie, who had stood where he'd left her, a quizzical expression on her face.

When he stretched out his arm for her to come, her expression changed and she was feeling strange but came towards him, then began to feel dizzy. She held out her arms to steady herself on the way to him, but missed the wall and instead was caught by Stan who ran to her on her way down. "Whoa, there." He sat her down in one of the leather chairs in the waiting area.

The tall gentleman came near, "How can I help? Shall I call 911?"

Mr. Perry said, "No, that is not necessary. If you go through that door, behind the desk is a mini-fridge. Please, get me a bottle of orange juice, quickly."

The gentleman walked quickly, doing as he was told. On returning, he handed Stan the drink already opened.

"Here, take a sip, Marie" he said to her, tenderly, softly. This continued for a few minutes. Marie did as instructed, then suddenly she looked fully aware.

"Thank you, Mr. Perry. I think I'm okay now." She sat up and straightened her outfit, clearly feeling embarrassed.

"Are you sure?" He asked nervously.

"Yes, sir," she looked him straight in the eye, willing him to stay quiet. "Okay, then," he stood up and his knee gave a popping sound. "You know, Marie, I am too old for you to be doing this to me. Next time, it will be my heart." He felt an arm continue to help steady him as he got up. He'd almost forgotten about their visitor. "Thank you, Mr...uh..."

"Fairbanks. Douglas Fairbanks," he held out his hand.

Stan took it. "I do apologize for all this drama," he half-smiled and shrugged.

"No, don't be. I was glad to be of help. But now that everything is fine, I'll see myself out and call at another time perhaps."

"No!" It was almost a shout from Marie. Both men looked at her, surprised. "I mean, for your help, why don't you join us for lunch? Unless you already have other plans."

"Well, I do have a reservation for two at Demitrio's. I hear they have spectacular food, but I can cancel."

"No, that won't be necessary. We will go there. Demitrio won't mind you joining us. I made reservations for two at our usual table, but there is room for you also. Would you like to follow in your car or come with us, Mr. Fairbanks? It is not a far drive from here. Really we could walk, but I don't think Marie will make it in her condition." She looked down at the floor as Douglas glanced at her.

"If it is that close, I will let my driver know to return for me in an hour?"

"Make it two. Demitrio or Nonna will not let us leave before then, and in the meantime, you can tell us of your plans."

"That is not necessary. I can make an appointment to discuss that at a later time," Douglas not wanting to take any undue advantage.

Stan, seeing his integrity, said, "Fine, if it will make you feel better about the situation, we can call it a lunch meeting and free consultation."

"But, sir..." he was not allowed to finish. Stan held his hand up, "Son, all my first consultations are free. You may as well take it, because I do believe I'm not free for another six months."

Douglas took the hint. "Okay, let me speak to my driver, and I'll be with you shortly." He turned and walked out.

Stan turned to Marie, who had been silent this whole time watching their exchange. "Come, let me help you up," he did so and waited.

"I'm fine, really, but I won't be if we keep standing around here. I'm starving." She walked toward the door saying, "Let's go."

"Are you sure? Do you know him? He seems to have known Robert."

"I'll be fine, and no, I don't know him, but he seems familiar somehow..." Stan smiled to himself as he walked out after her, and locked the glass doors behind him. He walked towards his car where Marie waited and Mr. Fairbanks came up behind her to open her door.

"What a gentleman," she thought. "Oh thank you, but you can sit up front." "No, I'll be fine in the back. I'm used to it."

"That's not what I meant. There's more leg room in front, than the back." "Oh, I see. Thank you," he opened the back door for her holding the top.

"Thank you," and she held the door to slide in, only she accidentally brushed his hand with hers. She looked at him momentarily, but he just smiled and shut her door. He got in the front and adjusted the seat further back.

"OW," Marie yelped.

"Oh my, are you okay? Let me scoot forward again."

Marie began to laugh, "I'm sorry, I'm just teasing. I couldn't help it. You have such long legs like my brother, I tease him when I can," she continued to giggle.

"Marie," Stan said sternly. "What in the world has gotten into you? Do you like your job?

"I..." she looked down sheepish. "Not really," she said drolly, "I'm, Sorry."

"Hmph! You pixie."

She brightened mischievously "You know I love my job. You know that, and you can't threaten to fire me. You can't live without me."

"True enough, now, no more teasing."

"Yes, sir, I'll behave, pinky promise."

"You mean pixie promises!" He half grinned.

"No, a solemn promise, to behave from this point on and not tease or exasperate anyone, especially you."

"Okay, that's better. Now, let's go have lunch."

The drive to Demitrio's, a few blocks away, was a silent one. Douglas was feeling discomfited by "Marie's" actions.

In turn, Marie knew she needed to apologize for her ridiculous behavior. She just couldn't seem to help herself. She teased her younger brother John Antony, who was almost 17, all the time about it. He was tall too, but not at all like Mr. Fairbanks.

"You must be, what, six foot four?" She inquired.

"Six foot six," was his only reply.

Mr. Perry parked. Douglas, being the gentleman that he was, opened the door for Marie. As she got out, she looked him in the eyes as he was looking down at her with a stiff expression.

"Please forgive me, Mr. Fairbanks. I took liberties that I ought not have. I gave in to my wicked heart and would ask that you not take what I did, and put it against Mr. Perry. He is truly an honorable man, with a very faulty auditor."

Douglas was struck with her sincerity and humor. "I can see that, and I forgive you," and he meant it, so he smiled which released the tension in his jaw.

Exhaling her pent up breath, Marie felt relieved. Everything would be okay, so she smiled back.

Stan called from the entrance, "Hey! You two want to eat?"

"Coming!" Marie called back. Douglas closed the car door.

"After you," She walked ahead of him, and Douglas watched after her. She looked lovely, her slim figure and nearly waist length dark hair was a pleasing picture. Then he noticed Mr. Perry watching him looking at her, and his look was not pleasant.

Douglas sheepishly grinned, swallowed hard, feeling a bit embarrassed for getting caught looking at the pixie. Doug pulled at his collar as he walked toward them then followed the two of them into the restaurant.

CHAPTER 15

LUNCH 12:12PM

Nonna greeted them, "Hello, Mr. Perry. Marie, child, how are you?" Taking her by the shoulders then hugging Marie.

"Very hungry, Nonna." Marie kissed both Nonna's cheeks the Italian way.

"Excellent!"

Douglas walked in just then. "I'll be with you in a moment, sir." Marie looked back at Mr. Fairbanks.

"Oh, Nonna, he's with us, a client, Mr. Fairbanks."

"Oh, excuse me. Then, your usual table, Mr. Perry?"

"Yes, thank you, Nonna," he replied.

"Right this way then." She led them to a lovely table that overlooked the lake with small boats going by.

"What a picture," Douglas said.

"Yes, it is lovely," Marie said dreamily. "One of my favorite places. I think

I'd like to live on the lake. I believe it'd be peaceful." She sighed, "But, it's very difficult to buy the land around it and improve it. The city wants a majority of it to remain a lakeside sort of tourist attraction. I can understand that, but it'd still be nice..." she let her mind drift to dreams that died with Robert.

Douglas could see her mind had gone somewhere he wasn't allowed to go. The solemn look on her face, the sparkle of a dream, a smile, and it was then extinguished suddenly by a frown. As she noticed he was looking at her, "You're beautiful."

Feeling like a heel that he had intruded on her thoughts with that comment, "I'm sorry," he looked down at his menu and blushed. "Why did I say that? You are so dumb? No, but it is true, she is beautiful." He hazarded a quick glance up. She was also buried in her menu, blushing. "So beautiful... Stop it!"

Stan, who was not oblivious to the exchange between them, said nothing, his beautiful and broken daughter and an "Apollo" of a man, sitting across from her. She was blushing of all things. Stan knew who he was the moment he'd said his name. Mr. Fairbanks was a giant in the business world. He could hire anyone with his big name. "Why was he here of all places?"

Nonna came by "So, is everyone ready to order?"

Marie sat biting her lower lip, which she only did when flustered and bashful.

Stan, noticing they were both blankly staring at their menus, began, "I think I'll have the gnocchi pomodoro and a salad with vinaigrette, with an iced tea."

"Excellent," Nonna said, turning to Douglas "And for you, sir?"

"Everything sounds amazing. What do you suggest?"

"Everything!" They all laughed, "But, my favorite is the spaghetti and meatballs. It is my grandmother's recipe, from the old country. Delicious!" She kissed her fingers, "Mangia".

"Okay, I'll have that, and a salad with balsamic dressing if you have it. Thank you."

"I make it just for you," she said with a wink. "And to drink?"

"Iced tea, thank you," handing Nonna back the menu.

"And for you, Bella Maria?"

"Soup and salad, Nonna, and water please."

"Is that all? You will wither away. How about some sausage on the side?"

"No thank you, Nonna," her eyes sparkled, "I'm saving room for dessert!"

"Ah- tré bien! Tiramisu or Cannoli?"

"Tiramisu, What else, Nonna?" She said laughing.

Laughing also, Nonna took their menus and twirled them under her arm, as she walked away, yelling in Italian to Demitrio as she reached the kitchen.

"This is quite the place," Douglas commented. "Busy too. Nearly every table is filled with the lunch crowd."

"Yes, Demitrio and Nonna have been here forever it seems like," Stan replied.

"They seem very friendly."

"They are family," Marie emphasized. "They come to our church. You won't find them open on Sundays."

"Really? But doesn't their business suffer from not being open?"

"To them, their business is in God's hands. They are only the stewards of it, and I'd say they are doing fine. I just finished remodeling their kitchen at their home, and they paid in full. They aren't foolish with their money and know how to save for the future. They are wise." Stan mused. Douglas looked toward the kitchen with new respect.

"So, Mr. Fairbanks, what brings you to 'Dean and Perry'?"

"Well, for one, Robert LaSalle did." Marie choked on her water.

"Are you okay?" Stan patted her back, looking concerned.

She took a deep breath, "Yes, sorry. Excuse me." She got up and almost ran to the bathroom.

"Is she going to be okay?" Douglas asked concerned.

"Yes, she will be." "Eventually," he thought. He smiled to put Douglas at ease, albeit half-heartedly. Nonna brought the salads and bread, the food momentarily, distracting them of Marie's hasty departure.

"Oh, that bread smells wonderful, Nonna!"

"Ah, so you know my name now. Yes, it is made fresh everyday for every meal."

Meanwhile, Marie was staring at herself in the mirror. She wanted to cry, but kept telling herself, "Get a grip. Get a grip, Marie! You can do this without crying. You can do this! Don't give in to the tears!" She felt hot, so she took off her blazer to cool off. She splashed cold water on her face, then realized her mistake. "My makeup, ah, Wow!" Oh well, there was nothing left to do now but wash her face. Thankfully, Nonna had face-wash below in the sink cabinet, only a few women knew about it. Washing off all the makeup thankfully felt very refreshed. She applied her mascara and lipstick that she always kept in the front pocket of her blazer.

She took a second look in the mirror. "Not bad. It's me," she told herself. "Yes, it's beautiful you," the memory replied, she smiled and walked out.

The men had not begun to eat. She realized they had waited for her, so she walked more briskly to the table. Douglas saw her coming and reached for her chair. She smiled at him and sat as he pushed in her chair, then he followed suit.

"Shall we pray, Mr. Perry? I'm starving." Marie said, as if nothing at all had happened.

"As well you should be, you pixie," he winked at her, took her hand, and bowed his head. Douglas was surprised when they held hands and Stan went directly into prayer. Stan began...

"Dear Lord, thank you for this bounteous feast. Bless this food and fellowship. If we can be of help to Mr. Fairbanks, may we do so with thy grace and by thine hand. May we do all and be all for Christ's name's sake. Amen."

Douglas was stunned, but gratified. "He also wondered if they were an item? It wasn't necessarily unlikely, many men in "the business" world had trophy wives. But..." he realized Stan was finishing the prayer as he was contemplating the situation, he lifted his head at the end of the prayer. These seemed to be honest people he could do business with, even if they were married, which he doubted, and not worry about anything else as much as other projects, he hoped.

"So, how do you know Robert?" Marie asked, trying to remain calm as she took a bite of bread.

"Oh, I don't know him personally, just by reputation. I have a house I bought a few years ago in 2000 near here, and at the time, I asked around with some of my contacts in the area. They said he's the one to go to if I need a restoration done. I'm afraid the house has been sorely neglected for a long time. I am just now getting to it. I've been busy and I actually forgot about it. I was told it had 'good bones'. A new roof, so I bought it sight unseen, it's the old craftsman on Shore Drive. I need someone with a caring eye and the ability to bring it back to life. I'm just sorry he's left your company."

"Me too," she smiled, but her eyes were full, and her voice husky. She took a bite of bread so she wouldn't have to speak further.

Stan patted her knee under the table.

Something strange was going on here, "Had the man been a boyfriend or something? Left on bad terms?" but Douglas didn't know how to ask.

Stan said, "I'm going to have to tell him."

Douglas looked back at her. Her eyes went wide, then she gave a slight nod in resignation, a sigh escaped, as her shoulders drooped. She began to put her spoon into her soup as if to eat, but knew she couldn't really, leaving it there.

"Come with me," Stan said to Douglas. They both stood up, and Stan led him outside to the patio that overlooked the lake.

"I know you may think us a bit strange," Douglas waited. "Let me just say it." He raked his hands through his hair. "Marie is Robert's wife. Robert is no longer with us because he died in a terrible car crash a few years ago. Marie has not fully recovered. She's known Robert since childhood, they married just after she graduated from high school. They had four children together, one of whom he never met because of the accident, she was pregnant at

87

the time. Her eldest also died a few days after from complications after the accident."

"Oh, my! The poor girl," Douglas looked back toward the table. He hadn't realized it was the same Marie of years ago. She looked different he certainly hadn't recognized her. 'Well, duh, she wasn't pregnant anymore. She was slim, really slim.'

"No, no," Stan protested. "She will not take your pity. We don't fully know or understand why this happened to her, but she is strong and stubborn, determined that no one pity her."

"But doesn't she deserve our compassion?"

"Yes, she does, but I must tell you, this is the first time it's happened to her. That someone has asked for Robert after all this time. We thought everyone forgot about him, or knew what happened to him."

"Well, it's hard to forget genius."

"Thank you for the compliment. I'll tell her later, but for now, when we go back, please don't talk about Robert. Let's just move forward on to what you'd like from us and we'll go on from there. Deal?" He held out his hand.

"It may prove difficult, but I'll try. Deal," Douglas shook the proffered hand. They came back inside and their meal began.

"So, what would you like us to do?" Stan began.

"Well, first of all, I'd like to have a walkthrough with the architect who will be on my project along with my general contractor to see which walls can come down. I would like to open up most of the downstairs. It's a little choppy right now for my taste. "I host a lot of parties for my business, and I'd like to have people walk all throughout the lower part of the house. The upstairs needs major updating. I'm thinking it will be a complete gut: plumbing, electrical, insulation, windows..."

"Oh, not the stained-glass windows!" Marie chimed in startled.

"No, not all of them," he chuckled. "I will save the ones I can, and the others will be..." he rubbed his chin, "...art, or gifts maybe. I have an affinity with stained-glass, and so does my mother."

Surprised her eyebrows rose, "Really?" She asked, taking a sip of water.

"Was that 'really' I like stained glass, or 'really' as in I have a mother?" Marie choked on her water again. Stan patted her back until she regained her composure.

"You, sir, have a bad habit of saying something baffling and making me choke on a mouthful of water."

"How is it baffling that I have a mother? Am I so horrible looking that I don't deserve a mother?" He teased, but she didn't notice his inflection change. She just saw his stern face, but not the hint of his laughing eyes.

Swallowing hard, "No, I mean, yes. I mean, you're very handsome." She blushed deeply. She was confused and didn't know why, so she looked down at her plate.

"Marie doesn't do well with teasing, Mr. Fairbanks. I learned that early on."

"My apologies, Miss LaSalle," and he touched her hand sympathetically. Marie retracted her hand quickly. It was as if a shock of electricity shot through her hand. "I'm sorry," he said. "I didn't mean to offend you."

"It's not you, sir. It's me. I'm sorry..., boss." She nodded towards Stan. "Excuse me, I'll see you back at the office." She grabbed her purse and started to get up to leave.

"But you haven't had your meal or your dessert yet?" Stan questioned.

"I'm not hungry anymore, Good day, gentlemen." Marie rose up and left without looking at either of them.

"What did I do wrong? Will she be okay?" Douglas asked for the second time that day.

"Like I said, she will be, eventually. I think, I'm sorry to say, that you frightened her."

"But how?" Douglas asked, bewildered.

"Simply put…, you showed her compassion and touched her hand. She doesn't allow people to touch her, especially now that her husband's passed."

"But you helped her into that seat when she almost passed out."

"That's different."

"How so, sir?"

"I've known her a long time, so she trusts me." Stan gave a sad sort of smile.

Nonna came up to the table. "Where is Bella Maria? I have her favorite dessert ready."

"I'm sorry, Nonna, but she had to go. I'll take it to her."

"Why'd she go? You should have made her stay. You are her boss, are you not?"

"It was my fault," Douglas said. "I did something I did not know she didn't like."

"Oh, so you teased her. Tsk tsk tsk. I think you should take her the dessert and say sorry."

"I've apologized twice already," he mused.

"With women, all apologies are not good without chocolate and flowers" she patted his cheek. "I'll go get the dessert," and with that Nonna flitted away. Stan could only smile after Nonna. "I hate to say it, but she makes a valid point, don't you think?"

"I don't know. I'm trying to think what my dad would have done. I don't think he apologized in that way. We lived in the country, so I don't think chocolate or flowers were readily available to him."

"Well," Stan said sardonically, "we are in the city."

Nonna came back with her dessert and a card. "I called ahead so you can go pick up flowers from my cousin Teresa. She is just down the road." Nonna handed him the card and dessert. "Come on, now you go. Go on," she commanded in a motherly tone, as if he was a boy in trouble and needed to make it right.

He stood up and kissed Nonna on the cheek. "Thank you, Nonna," he smiled.

"Cheeky!" She smiled back.

"I guess I'm off, sir. I'll give your secretary a call to finish with our appointment?"

"Yes, I will make room for you, though it may be a while yet."

"I understand. Thank you."

"Now, go, go," Nonna shooed him away again. Douglas saw Walter walk in just then, and they left together.

"He is handsome," Nonna commented to Stan.

"Yes, but I'm afraid Marie is still full of Robert and his death. She may have put him on a pedestal no man can reach. I'm afraid she's made an idol of him without knowing she's done so. I will have to pray that isn't the case."

"I will pray too. It's been a few years for her, no?"

"Yes, two long years. I've prayed for her to have the pain lessened, but I think it may have just been activity that has kept her going and not true healing. I saw a lot of hurt still in her face today."

"I think she may have a lot of fear too."

"Fear? Why?"

"Fear to begin again, to love again. To have to share her past all over again with someone who does not know her from childhood, like Robert did."

"You are wise, Nonna. I had not thought of that. Now I know how to better pray for her."

"The wisdom comes from reading my bible. Now, Demitrio and I too, will know how to pray for bella Maria."

"And so do we."

CHAPTER 16

1:32 PM

Marie walked briskly at first, trying to clear her mind for work, but it didn't seem to work. Her pace slowed as the thoughts darted through her mind, especially, "Why did I react that way? His touch was shocking, 'did he not feel it? Did it mean anything? But those eyes... they felt hurt by my reaction? Why? Maybe it is because he is handsome, though I am not beautiful, perhaps he has never faced rejection before. But he did say I am beautiful. He was just being polite. Why did he blush then? Why did I blush in return? When he said I was beautiful?

"You are beautiful, inside and out," her own mothers voice sounded in her mind. Always encouraging her because she had lost her self-esteem.

"My yoke is easy, and my burden is light...' Matthew 11:30, floated through her mind.

"God will not give you more than you can handle". That was her practical mothers' voice again.

"Then why is my burden so heavy?"

"Because you don't want to relinquish control." Roberts' voice again, he knew her so well. She wanted to protest.

"But... but..." Marie's heart and mind searched for an answer and knew there was none to reply except to accept the truth of that statement. Somewhere along the way, she had taken back control of her life, instead of leaving her life in God's capable hands.

Crossing over to the park across from the office she found a bench under a shaded tree. It was warm for April and humid, which meant rain was on its way. As she sat, she contemplated the thoughts going around her mind, and what they meant, as well as what she had been doing. Had she really taken back control of her life and not let the Lord have his will? She looked at her relationship with her parents and she realized she was heavily relying on them. Not that they had necessarily minded watching the kids from time to time. When was the last time they'd had a vacation by themselves? Or even just a weekender? She realized that it had not been since Robert died. They took her and the kids on vacations and paid for everything. She had allowed it.

Marie now realized she had been selfish. "And here I thought I was being selfless all this time and sacrificing, when in reality, it was may parents who were being selfless these past two years. Somehow, I need to change that." Marie took out her mini notebook and wrote in it…

#1 - Let parents vacation alone

Thinking of her relationship with her children, how Seth was four and a half in Kindergarten. Wow, Kindergarten was almost done with just a little over a month left for school. He was happy for the most part, but tended to be quite serious at times. Was she doing enough to ease his tension, to help him feel like just a boy and not "a boy without a father"?

Lizzy was just a happy-go-lucky little girl who was in K-4 and had many little friends. She had a little crush on the Pastor's teenage son who came to volunteer in her class before lunch time. She wanted a male to look up to.

Finally, little Sam, He didn't know what it was really like to have had and lost a father. He only knew Papaw and John Antony.

He didn't know Uncle Val because he'd joined the military right after 9/11 happened and the world became an uncertain place to live. He rarely came home on leave. She didn't think he felt he really had anything to come home to: no wife, no children, no prospects. She wondered if his heart was still hurt after Jessica? Surely there was a woman more worthy of such a man as he had become. Had she been a good sister to him? Did she really listen to him? Or did she just talk about herself and her own sad woes?

What about John Antony? He would be a senior in high school soon. Was she a good sister to him, or was she bossy still? He had shown himself to be responsible, saving up finances to put himself through nursing school. He was self-employed as a wedding photographer on weekends and putting his other artistic photographic abilities on the shelf for the time being.

"They will keep," he had said to Marie when she'd asked about it. He was a wise boy. Did she still treat him like one, even though he was becoming a man?

So many thoughts, and so many decisions to make. Her head was swimming, she closed her eyes and pinched the bridge of her nose. She didn't exactly know how to pray, or where to begin. She opened her eyes to look at her list which had grown while she sat contemplating her life.

#1 - Let parents vacation alone

#2 - Encourage Seth to have more fun

    A)Find a way to take him to a ball game

    B)Love my children more freely

#3 - Write to Val more often. Apologize

#4 Apologize to John Antony. Be more involved if he allows me into his life

#5 - Let God be God; allow him to work in my life.

#6 - Be a better friend/employee, etc. Be kind

#7 - Have a little more fun, Don't be so serious

"What about forgiving Robert for leaving?" Her heart asked.

Tears streamed down her face as she prayed for forgiveness and for not living a better or right life. Forgiveness for all the worry and doubt and fear she'd placed on herself and everyone else. Asking forgiveness for not trusting in His eternal promises for her life. "I want to change Lord, but I'm afraid. Please, give me the courage I need to live a life pleasing to you. Please help me, O' my savior, my God, I need thee, amen."

The age old hymn came into mind and she hummed what she remembered, "~Every hour I need thee, every hour of the day~"

CHAPTER 17

THE APOLOGY

Douglas had picked up the bouquet of flowers from Teresa, as
Nonna had commanded, and was now being driven by Walter back
to the firm where they'd started. Douglas spotted Marie under
the shade of a tree across the park. She looked deep in thought.
"Walter, pull the car over."

"Sir?"

"I see Miss LaSalle over at the park across the street," Doug
pointed in her direction, so Walt pulled over in a parking spot
that just opened up. "I'll walk over, it might not be so awkward
delivering this out there than in the office with all the other staff
witnessing my being a buffoon." Douglas thought he saw a smirk
on Walter's face, but his only response had been all too eager to
help.

"Yes, sir," as he opened the door, he let Douglas out the back
of the car.

Douglas walked over, he was determined to get this over with as soon as possible. As he approached, he could see she'd been crying. Had he offended her that badly that she had to hide away from prying eyes? Drawing nearer, slowly, he saw the notebook in her lap with her hands folded on top as if in prayer. Her eyes were closed and he realized he was about to interrupt her prayer or quiet time with God. "Oh dear," he thought to himself, "I can't interrupt her now, so what do I do?"

Marie had heard footfalls through the grass as she finished her prayer and hoped it wasn't anybody she knew passing by because the footfalls stopped nearby. She decided to take a quick look as she mentally said her amen, wanting to prolong the peace she felt after praying. *sigh*

Whom, and what she saw upon opening her eyes, she did not expect. Her eyes grew wide as she saw Mr. Fairbanks standing not five feet in front of her holding a bouquet of flowers, and a costly one at that, from Teresa's Flower Shop, no doubt. Teresa was the only florist she knew who used wide gold ribbon on all her orders. Even on Valentine's Day, she tied it together with red, it was her signature. This one, on the other hand, was her "apology" bouquet as it had a black and white ribbon. Black representing the trespass, and white representing the asking of forgiveness. Hopefully, after being forgiven, the red rose in the center was to be handed back to the giver which represented the accepted apology of the recipient of the bouquet. Douglas stood there, seeming at a loss for words and unsure in more ways than one.

Marie began, "Hello, Mr. Fairbanks, it seems we both are at a loss to see each other again so soon." She sniffed, snapped her notebook shut, in her haste the slip of loose paper fell out. Putting the notebook quickly in her purse, She then pulled out a tissue and dabbed at her eyes with somewhat jerky movements.

"Is she annoyed with me? But I didn't really do anything wrong?" He decided to begin and get this over with, 'How strange that he was the one apologizing, but here goes,' "My apologies again, Miss LaSalle, but Nonna made me..." he faltered for words, proper words.

She sat up a little straighter, cocking an eyebrow at him, shocked. "Wait!' She held up her hand, "Nonna 'made you' do this..." she gestured at the flowers, then crossed her arms, "You sound like a ten year old that has to go to the dentist."

He saw the smirk she was trying to hold in. 'Was she laughing at him?' Then, she burst out laughing at his severe and mortified look. She stopped long enough to say, "You should see your face, it's priceless!" Tears began to escape her eyes, but this time was from laughter. She had a loud, boisterous laugh as if she'd been caught off guard and hadn't intended to laugh, but it just burst forth. Attempting to calm herself. "I'm so sorry. Whew, I haven't laughed like that in so long," she immediately sobered.

"A merry heart doeth good [like] a medicine," he quoted Psalm 17:22a, then hazarded a few steps forward.

"So, why the apology bouquet?"

He took a few more steps forward. "Well, in all honesty, I wasn't sure at first, but, both Nonna and Mr. Perry were under the impression that I needed to 'properly' apologize, gesturing towards the bench, 'May I sit?"

Scooting over on the bench, making room for his large frame. "Sure."

He lay the bouquet between them, not ready to actually give it to her. "Oh, yes, here's your dessert. Nonna made me bring it." Douglas handed it to her.

Marie's eyes twinkled, and she said, "Nonna has made you do a lot of things you didn't want to do." She giggled.

He sighed, 'So, she has another type of laugh'. "I don't really know how she did it, other than to say she was compelling and I dare not refuse. Otherwise, she might hit me over the head with a rolling pin or something."

She burst forth in laughter again at the image that brought to fore.

'Another laugh different from before, more mirthful'. He thought.

"Yes, Nonna can be very 'persuasive.' Have you had Nonna's Tiramisu?"

"No, I've not eaten in this town before. I'm usually just passing through."

"Well, you're in for a treat." She opened the box and stuck the plastic spoon in it. Handing him the container, she urged, "Take a bite. You'll think you are in heaven." She smiled contentedly, as if she had already eaten some.

"Well, if you insist, I never say no to dessert." He winked at her.

"I do insist, but I want it back." She smirked. Douglas took it, and as their hands touched he felt a little shock, and she blushed quite prettily. He took a generous forkful. "Now, eat it slowly and savor it."

Looking at her out of the corner of his eyes, he took the bite and did as instructed. The rich espresso flavor and the cream, cake, and cocoa flavors were all mingling together, yet individual in taste and texture...closing his eyes for a moment. *sigh* 'Mmmm...', This is so good. It's just like home. Wow! That is so amazing!"

"I told you so. It's heavenly, isn't it?" She held out her hand for him to return it.

He hesitated, holding it away from her, "Can I have a second bite?"

She laughed out loud like the first time. "No, this is my dessert, remember?" She reached for it.

He held it away, "Just a teeny bite more? I promise."

Normally, she wouldn't give in. "I'm selfish," she realized. "Yes, that's fine," she sobered.

He took his bite quickly, then realized her mood had changed again. "Are you okay? Did I offend you again?"

"Huh, uh," she curled a wayward hair behind her ear. "No, no, it has nothing to do with you."

"Uh, oh. When a woman says that, it's almost always the man's fault. Good thing I already have an apology bouquet." He smiled at her, trying to lighten her mood.

She smiled, "Yes, you do." She took out the single red rose and handed it to him.

"All is forgiven then?" He took the proffered rose, smelling it.

"There was never anything to be forgiven for." She stood up, "I must get back to work now."

"May I see you again?" his expression changed, "Where did that come from?"

Stammering, she noted, "I'm not an architect. I do finance, so I doubt we'll see each other very often." Although she knew what he'd meant.

"No, you misunderstand, I meant socially. May I see you again?"

"You mean, like a date?" Looking puzzled, 'Why would he want a date with me?'

"No, well, yes." He also looked perturbed, "Why not? We're both adults."

"I'm sorry, Mr. Fairbanks, I don't date."

"Why not?" He blurted, "Why would she refuse me?"

"There are three reasons waiting at home for me."

"So, logistically, it's difficult? So you don't want to bother with it?" "Something like that. I'm sorry, I have to go." She turned to leave, uncomfortable with where the conversation was going.

He stopped her. "Why don't we all go then? Something fun the kids would like."

"I don't involve my children in 'dating schemes', I'm sorry, Mr. Fairbanks, What kind of mother do you think I am?" Contempt in her voice, she eyed him severely turning again she walked away, this time he let her go. He did spy her holding the bouquet closer to her face and inhaling the sweet scent. A slip of paper fell on his shoe, it looked like the notebook paper she had. He picked it up. Thinking he'd just throw it in the trash, he read the first line...

Things I Need to Change

"Oh, boy. This is personal. I need to return this, but she might be offended that I read it. Maybe I should just throw it away instead, 'she can just write another one when she doesn't find this one."

For some reason, Douglas couldn't make himself throw it away. He looked after her walking into the office, being met on the way in by Mr. Perry. They conversed as they walked inside. Douglas stood in the shade and looked at the list again. His eyes lit up, feeling compelled, he knew he could help with some of it. Smiling to himself, he didn't know why he felt he should help. But his steps became lighter as he thought of a plan to get Marie out on a date. It would do her good. He felt she was hiding herself away, letting life pass her by, hoping to remain an anonymous background figure in the play called 'Life'. Well, he was about to shake things up for her..., just a little bit.

CHAPTER 18

JUNE 11, 2004

"Stanley Miles Perry!" Elizabeth yelled through the house. "What have you gone and done?" Stan and John Antony, who just got home from a graduation celebration, came running down the hall.

"What is it? What's happened, my dear?"

She held out the UPS envelope to him. "Explain this!" She said sternly.

"Oh boy, what'd you do, Dad?"

"I haven't the slightest idea, son!" Stan took the papers and looked them over, glasses on the end of his nose. He smiled when he finished reading, then began to laugh out loud.

"What in the world, why are you laughing?" Elizabeth said.

"This, he held up the envelope, my dear, I did not do it seems we have been selected to take a cruise to Alaska on a new ship, all expenses paid! It leaves port on Tuesday and returns the following Friday for a total of ten days at sea."

"But that's only a few days away! How are we going to get there?" Stan held up two plane tickets with their names on it.

"And from the airport to the dock?" Again, he produced two tickets for a shuttle pass, round trip.

"This is a dream come true. It can't be real," Elizabeth said.

"Oh, but it is. It is a gift from God for you, my dearest. You've always wanted to go see Alaska. Now is the opportunity, and it's been gifted free and clear with all expenses paid."

"This is too wonderful to imagine," tears welled in her eyes.

"You softie" Stan said, "Come here love." She embraced him as John Antony looked on at his parents.

"I guess I'm fending for myself for a few days, huh?"

"No, I'm calling Marie right now." Elizabeth replied.

"Oh, great," John Antony rolled his eyes. "I get to be lectured instead of having leisure for the next ten days."

"Don't be so hard on Marie. She's changing, you'll see," his mother said.

"I'll believe it when I see it," he mumbled and began to walk off.

His mother heard and said, "Have faith, son. Give your sister a little consideration. Of whom else have you known of that has gone through the pain and suffering she has and come out unscathed? No one, no human, save Christ, can handle all the pain and suffering with true humility and dignity. "Even Christ said, 'If this cup can pass.' He had a human moment of despair, but said, 'not my will, but thine.' He was willing to lay down His life for us. God the Father, willed His son to die, so that we may be saved from or sins, but He also felt the pain of separation from His beloved one. Your sister is only human, not God or God-man. She has her failings, just like we all do. Do you know that she apologized to us?"

"What for?" He asked, interest piqued.

Elizabeth asked, "What exactly did she say, honey?"

Stan said, "She was sorry for being a selfish daughter and for taking undue advantage of our relationship. Said she'd asked the Lord to forgive her for trying to control her own life and her surroundings. She also said she wasn't living, just existing to survive the next day. "So, you see, son, she still has a long way to go, but she's trying, slowly but surely, to mend her heart. What she doesn't realize, is that that's the Lord's job: to mend the broken-hearted."

John Antony sobered a little, "I'm sorry, Dad, Mom, that I was so quick to judge her," he said, repentant.

"We're not the ones you should apologize too, dear," Elizabeth said. "When she comes, find a quiet moment with her, and have a brotherly-sister talk like grown ups should."

"I will. Thanks, Mom," he kissed her cheek and hugged his dad. "Now, don't you two have to pack?"

Elizabeth fluttered, "Oh, goodness, what am I going to wear!" and ran off. Both chuckled in her wake.

"I guess I'll call your sister, then rearrange my schedule." Stan said, but just then, his phone rang. "Hello?"

"Mr. Perry, Douglas Fairbanks here."

"How did you get my number?"

"My apologies, sir, I got it from your secretary as it's an emergency. I had to tell you in person as you weren't in your office."

"Is everything all right?"

"Well, it seems that there was a miscommunication on my part to the flooring company, and the job will have to be on hold for two weeks until the new flooring that I want installed arrives."

"So, that means all the finishing touches and cabinetry will have to be delayed as well."

"Yes, my apologies again. If need be, I can still pay your men for their missed time on the job. I don't want for someone to go without a paycheck for my mistake."

"No worries. There are other jobs I can switch my men over to that can begin right away. I'll just have to switch it up when I get back."

"Are you going somewhere?" Doug sounded interested.

"As a matter of fact, my wife and I won an all expenses paid trip to Alaska. It is a long overdue vacation. My wife needs it, although she'd never say so."

"Well, sounds like congratulations are in order, I hope you have a wonderful time."

"Thank you."

"I guess I'll see you when you return."

"Yes, call Denise to schedule an appointment."

"Thank you for understanding, bye."

Stan hung up with Douglas then decided to go to his office and do some re-arranging with Denise and call his foreman, Jack.

The phone rang three times before Marie answered. "Hello?" she answered breathlessly.

"Marie! You will never guess what's happened!" Elizabeth said in a happy voice.

"Wow, you seem excited, Mother."

"It's so wonderful. I don't remember entering any contests, but your dad and I have won an all expenses paid trip to Alaska on a cruise. Can you believe it! God is so good."

"Wow, that is exciting! Amazing!" She felt glad for her parents.

"So, besides that, I want you to look after John. We'll be away for two weeks, so just make sure he's eating."

"Would he like to stay with us? I can set up the spare room for him, that way I can really make sure he's taken care of. The kids would love Uncle John to have a sleepover as well."

"That sounds like a great idea, even better than what I thought! I'll get him to pack and send him on over."

"Great! It'll be fun to have him around. I'll see him soon, so I'd better get the room ready. Bye, Mom!"

"Bye, honey. We'll see you soon."

Marie call up the stairs, "KIDS?" The came running to the landing.

"Yes, Momma?" They echoed in unison.

"Guess who's coming to have a sleepover for a couple days?"

CHAPTER 19

SATURDAY

"Seth, can you come and set the table, please? Your Uncle John should be here from work soon."

"Coming, Momma!"

"Lizzy, can you get the juice and put it on the table?"

"Okay, Momma!"

Marie set the napkins on the table after putting Samuel in his high chair. "Thank you for being so helpful."

"You're welcome, Momma!" They chorused and giggled. Marie smiled as she stirred the pot of spaghetti sauce. The doorbell rang.

'Ah, that must be John.' Marie thought. 'Why would he ring the bell? I did give him a key.' "Seth, can you see who that is?" She continued to stir, "It's probably Uncle John. He may have forgotten his key."

Seth ran off, and she heard the door open. "Momma, Momma, come quick."

Alarmed, Marie ran over, spoon in hand, to the front door. She saw a man holding balloons and an envelope. "Yes, may I help you?"

"Are you Ms. LaSalle?" He asked reading the envelope.

"Yes, that's me?" Marie replied, confused.

"These are for you," he handed her the giant balloon, bouquet, and the card. "What do I do with these?"

The man looked confused and shrugged, "Enjoy?" The young man walked off just as John was coming in.

"Are those really for us, Momma?" Seth asked.

"I guess so," she looked at the card, but there were no markings. She opened it, pulled out the card, and out spilled five tickets. She picked up the tickets as the balloons bobbed around her engulfing them all. Lizzy trailed some balloons after her and was bopping them with Sam in his high chair.

"Can we play with them?" Lizzy asked.

"You already are, aren't you? Hmm, what do I do with them?" Marie asked no one in particular.

"Let them go?" John Antony responded.

"In the house?"

"Why not? Live a little, huh, sis? Let 'em go. What harm can a few balloons do?"

"This is not a 'few balloons,'" she emphasized. "There must be at least 50 here. I'm going to float away."

"Really, Momma?" Seth asked, holding onto her leg.

"No, silly, but it feels that way."

"Just think of it as a party," John said. "Let 'em go. We can make fun, squeaky voices with them later." She smiled at the prospect.

"Okay." She let them go in the house. They hit the ceiling gently and began to bob around up there. It made her smile. John picked up one of the tickets she'd dropped.

"So, what are these for? A ball game? Who are they from?"

"I've no idea."

"Well, come on and read the card," he said impatiently. She pulled out the card. It read...

"Congratulations

You are the select winner of this month's Friday Family Day at Springer Baseball Park.
Enclosed, you will find 2 adult's tickets, 4 children's tickets a parking pass is included.
Please enjoy with the compliments of the
Springer Baseball Committee and Madrone Valley City Council

"Look, John, do you think it's for real?"

"Sure does seem that way. Can we go, sis? I don't work on that Friday. It should be fun." He ginned at her. She looked dubious.

"I don't know."

"Oh, Mom, please? You know I want to go to a real live game once in my life," Seth said. "Puh-leeeze!" He looked at her with those puppy dog eyes and pretended to make his lip quiver. "Pretty please, Mom, with sugar on top?" Lizzy chimed in, and even John. "Come on, Mom, please, please," they chorused together. Marie could only laugh at their antics.

"All right, all right, you win you silly heads, we'll all go. But, John, you have to help keep watch and have bathroom duty with Seth."

"Yes, Ma'am," he saluted. "I gotta get my glove from Mom and Dad's."

"Why, Uncle John?" Seth asked.

"Because, we might be able to catch a fly ball or something. Then, if you do, the players get to sign it for you!"

"Awesome! Mom, can I get a baseball glove?"

"They're too expensive, honey," she regretted it as soon as it came out of her mouth. The excitement left his eyes. "But, we can try to find your dad's old one in the garage maybe?" He brightened up again.

"Thanks, Momma," and he hugged her fiercely. A tear escaped her eyes. John squeezed her arm in support, then distracted the kids. "Let's go to the garage ad look for it. It'll be a treasure hunt, argh! Right, me hearties?"

"Argh!" Seth and Lizzy echoed as they sprinted towards the garage, saying "pirate-y" things as they searched for the hidden treasure.

CHAPTER 20

JUNE 18, 2004 -
THE BASEBALL GAME

Friday had come before she knew it. With her father away, Marie had stayed late Monday through Thursday to keep on top of the bookwork so that she could leave early Friday afternoon. She found herself excited and apprehensive. She'd never taken the children to big events and a crowded stadium, small as it may be, by herself. She had John to help at least, so he gave her a measure of comfort.

The Springer Oaks were a minor league team, but it was a baseball game nonetheless. Seth had found his Dad's old glove and slept with it under his pillow every night since. She smiled, the hurt not hurting as much, but loneliness filled the space. Marie had never really liked being alone, she realized, even when she was young. She had always wanted someone to play with, and it didn't matter who the person was.

After "The Incident," as she'd come to refer to it, had happened to her in her teens and had reinforced the rule: two were better than one. After Robert died, she had to get over the loneliness and dread of being alone. Although most days she knew she was not alone because of the children being with her, and her office was full of people coming and going, day in and day out. But, so many times, she felt alone in a crowd. Feeling she had no one to really share her burdens with because she felt no one understood. At least no one from her set of friends.

Drifting apart from all her married friends, feeling like a third wheel. Hating the sympathetic looks, and it just made her feel worse. They'd tried to be kind, but one of her friends had tried to set her up on a date asking her over for dinner. It had only been a year after the accident, and it had ended in total disaster. Marie swore off dating and her friend after that. She still saw them at church, but she never spoke to her friend anymore, preferring to keep to herself.

In the last two years, she'd overheard many times that she'd become a recluse. She'd thought it'd be better than being a gossip and a busybody like they were being. They never realized how much it hurt to hear them gossip about her.

She was alone in taking care of her children, and only she could do it alone. No man wanted a widow with three children in tow. She was content, hard though it may be, to raise them by herself. She had her father and brothers that set good examples. True, they couldn't be there all the time, but she felt it was enough. She didn't discount her faith to see her through any storm. So far, the only major one had been hers to overcome.

Once at home, she packed some juice boxes in her backpack and a few handy snacks to keep them from the temptation of the hawkers selling hot dogs and other things she couldn't afford to buy at stadium prices. It would have to do.

Checking for last minute details on her list, she'd marked every box except for sunscreen. "Kids, come down and get sunscreen on, then we can leave for the ballpark." It always amazed her how they sounded like a herd of elephants that were stomping through the house. She smiled when Seth was the first to arrive, having had Robert's longer stride.

"Do we hafta wear sunscreen, Momma? It's gonna be dark soon."

"Yes, because I don't know exactly where we'll be sitting. If we're in a sunny spot, you'll get a sunburn, and that's worse than putting on sunscreen."

"Okay, Momma," he said, resigned. Marie had everyone slathered and off to the game in no time.

Upon arriving at the parking gate, Marie showed her pass to the attendant. "Oh, VIP I see," he said. He gave her a placard with the team's logo on it, told her to put it on the dash board, and that all the parking attendants would guide her to the correct parking area. "You're lucky since it's right up close. If you'd like, you can stand by the players gate and get their autographs. Their bus should be here soon."

"Really? Marie asked surprised, and the children squealed in delight, including John.

"Yes, Ma'am," the elderly attendant replied, "You all have a fine time tonight."

"We will," she said, with the biggest grin he'd ever seen on anyone.

After parking, getting player autographs, the players giving the kids special attention and gifts, she couldn't believe it! Eventually finding the way to their seats, Marie couldn't believe her eyes. Their seats were directly behind Home Plate! How could that be? She checked their seat numbers and row again to be certain, but her eyes did not deceive her.

"How awesome is this!" John Antony said. "I wonder how the council pulled this off? These seats are amazing the tickets must have been expensive!"

The seats were great the whole game. They cheered; they laughed; they ate. A vendor had stopped by and gave them all hot dogs. Marie hadn't wanted to buy them, but he'd said someone up top had already paid for them and that they were free. She was so grateful as the kids had started getting a little hangry.

"I wonder who paid for this?" She'd looked around to see if she recognized someone, but there wasn't anyone she recognized to be seen. "Hmm! Oh well, just be thankful to God, Marie. Yes, Thank you, Lord, for your wonderful gifts. Thank you for this time to spend with my family and having fun," she paused and glanced at her smiling children. They were eating the hot dogs and getting ketchup and mustard on themselves, but she didn't care. They were having so much fun, so she continued, "Thank you, Lord, for this day. Thank you for always being the provider for my family. Thank you for my family and..."

"Mom, I gotta go potty," Lizzy whispered loudly.

Marie heard a few snickers, but everyone around her was friendly and lively, true sports fans, unlike herself, but she enjoyed the time with her family and they were having fun. That's all that mattered. She looked to John, who nodded his head to watch the two other boys.

Douglas was watching Marie and her family through binoculars on a different level. When he wasn't watching the game, he took advantage of the team changes to see if it looked like they may need something. He'd glanced over and saw her and her daughter head up the stairs. "They must be headed to the restroom" he thought. When Marie and her daughter hadn't returned for 15 minutes, he began to worry. Walter was with him when he saw Douglas's countenance.

He asked, "Is everything all right, sir?"

"Well, yes. I think Marie took her daughter to the restroom, but they haven't returned. It's been 15 minutes already so I hope nothing happened. Can you just check it out? Buy something at the concession nearby."

"Sure thing, boss. Be back before you know it."

CHAPTER 21

THE BATHROOM

Douglas was almost beside himself when Walter returned 30 minutes later with a self-satisfied grin on his face. "What happened? Why've you been gone so long?" Douglas demanded. Walter chuckled, "Boss, you're gonna love my story."

"Spill it".

Walter chuckled knowing something Douglas didn't realize, but decided it was best just to "Spill it" as asked. "I sprinted over to those restrooms, and there was a long line out the door. Poor girl had a terrified look on her face. She was dancing around and telling her mom she had to go now!

I heard Marie say, 'We have to wait. Everyone else has to go too.' Then, the unthinkable happened. I was first in line for a soda when she began to bawl her eyes out because the girl couldn't wait any longer and had wet herself, the poor dear. So, I did the manly thing. I pretended to trip as I passed by and threw my soda all over her."

"You did what?"

"I know that sounds cruel, but wait, hear me out before you fire me."

"Okay, explain away, go on."

"Since she was already wet, I figured I'd cover her embarrassment with the soda. Then, I profusely apologized for getting her daughter all wet. After her shocked expression, I said, "Oh, she looks like my niece (which she did when she was little), let me buy her some dry clothes, please." I begged her, "I feel, so terrible, I'm so sorry."

"She reluctantly allowed me too, so we went to the shop. She found a sweat suit in her size, then she saw the price tag and was arguing with me about paying half. I told her 'No,' firmly. "Let an old man enjoy buying something for his 'look-alike' niece. Plus, I get points on my credit card." She half-heartedly agreed when her daughter's teeth began chattering.

"Oh, you'll need a towel to dry her off too."

"Her daughter hopped around then. "Yeah, Momma. I want to get dry." She chattered through her teeth, "Seth is gonna be worried. We've been gone a long time, Momma."

I asked, "Is Seth your brother?"

"Yeah, he and Sam and Uncle John are waiting for us."

"Oh, boy" I said, "Won't they be sad if you get something and they don't?"

"Yeah, maybe." She looked over wistfully at the ball caps, so I grabbed two and a t-shirt for the uncle and put it all on the counter.

Marie protested, but I insisted! I told her, "Think of it as God's blessings on a life well-lived. I can tell you're a good mom."

She blushed, cried her thanks and gave me a big bear hug. "I sure liked going undercover. They should be back to their seats by now." Douglas looked through the binoculars just as Marie was handing out their gifts. He could see the two young boys waving their hats about, whooping in ecstasy. "It was worth it," he smiled and enjoyed himself more than he'd remembered before in a long time.

When the game was over, Douglas decided to sit and let the crowds file out and die down a bit before he would head out since the traffic afterwards was always bad. Looking through his binoculars one last time he saw Marie was pushing a stroller with a sleeping Sam and had her arms full of bags with John following behind who held a sleeping Lizzy. He was also trying to herd an uncooperative and tired Seth up the stairs. Douglas put down the binoculars and for a moment didn't know what to do. He looked to Walter.

"Let's go help. We'll just 'accidentally' bump into her again." He had a wide grin.

Douglas laughed, "All right, let's go." It took them a few minutes to locate Marie in the crowds of people heading towards the gate, he spotted her long hair up in the wispy bun he was fond of. Once they did, she actually bumped into them. She didn't even look up since she'd been apologizing all along her route because of the stroller, and all the bags she had been carrying were bumping into people.

She stopped when he didn't budge from in front of her, and she looked up finally held Douglas's gaze, surprised.

"Hello, Ms. LaSalle. It looks like you could use some help."

Marie felt flustered, she hadn't thought about getting out earlier with the kids, and she'd been struggling to just get out of the stadium. And now there stood, "Mr. Fairbanks!" he was blocking her path Marie squeaked out his name, then saying, "No, really, I'm fine."

John Antony piped up, "Maybe you don't need the help, but I do. Lizzy weighs a brick. Here you go." John hefted Lizzy into Douglas's arms, grabbed a bag from Marie and took Seth by the hand leading the way. She sighed with audible relief, exhaling her pent up breath.

"Come on!" John Antony said. "We still have to make it to the car. Get the keys ready, and remember 4C." He started walking away from her.

Walter said, "I'll help with your bags, miss."

She looked at Walter and blinked, "You know him?" Pointing at Douglas, with a nod of her head.

Douglas answered as he looked at Walter, "Yes, he's my..." he paused, "friend. We came to enjoy the game since his wife's out of town on a special birthday surprise he arranged for her, so we fella's are home alone." Douglas thought, 'That's not the only reason, but it's not a lie either'.

"Oh, okay. Thank you again for the clothing, as you can see, she's very warm and happy." She looked at Lizzy asleep in Douglas's arms. Lizzy never stirred except to wrap her arms around his neck. Marie's heart ached at the sight. Her eyes began to well up with unbidden tears.

Douglas cleared his throat, "Shall we get going?"

Marie nodded and led the way. She slowly followed the crowd out and down to her minivan. She searched for the correct row and saw John waiting for her leaning against the van along with Seth. She unlocked the car as they came into view.

John opened the door and helped Seth buckle in. He took Sam from the stroller as Marie folded it up, and buckled him in as well. After doing so, he took the pack he had and other bags from Walter, and put them into the trunk.

"Where does she go?" Douglas asked.

"On the other side, in her booster seat," Marie replied, as she put the stroller in the back as well.

As Doug placed Lizzy gently, she held on tight and said dreamily, "I love you, Daddy," and kissed his cheek and fell back into blissful sleep. Douglas had a hard time buckling her in after that. He looked at the little girl sleeping beautifully, a picture of her mother with gentle eyes and soft brown hair.

Walter cleared his throat, "Douglas?"

He snapped to attention quickly and banged his head on the roof of he car. "Ow," he hissed and rubbed the sore spot. "Yeah, Walter?"

"The wife just called. She's on her way home early."

"Early? Was she successful?"

"Yes, sir," and he winked at him.

"Great. Time to say goodbye to our friends here. John is it?"

"Yes, so, you work at the office?" John gave a quizzical look to Marie.

"No, actually. They work for me. I'm a client." He shook John's hand and John shook back, almost in a test of wills, then he laughed and let go of Douglas's hand.

"So, has my sister been 'gophering' for you?"

"Gopher? Whatever for?"

"Oh, you know, the paint isn't the right color, so she has to call around and get the right one or whatever to make the client happy."

"No, I wouldn't' demean her so. She does the books as far as I know, and keeps the budget for my project on track that's all."

"Oh, I thought she was doing the interior decorating too."

Marie spoke up then, "No, John, not everyone requires my services, and besides it's only for extra..." she stopped short of what she was about to say.

Douglas guessed, but didn't say anything except, "Well, Ms. LaSalle, it was wonderful seeing you. Give Mr. Perry my regards. I'll see him soon if all goes well," and he began to walk off with Walter.

"Wait!" Both men turned around. She ran up to Walter and kissed him on the cheek and said, "Thank you," she shook Douglas's hand and said, "You have a good taste in friends," and impulsively kissed him on the cheek as well. After realizing what she'd done, she blushed and ran back to her minivan.

John Antony gave him a thumbs up, winked at him then got in the minivan. "So, you like him?"

"Be Quiet, John!"

He laughed because he was happy for her if she did like him. "It's about time for you to be loved again, dear sis," and he meant what he said.

Douglas stood and stared after her for a long moment, touching his cheek after she'd driven off into traffic. Walter waited, then cleared his throat. It was getting chilly out, and he wanted to see his dear Maryanne. The fog began to clear Douglas's mind after he put down his hand, stuck it in his pocket, and continued walking with Walter. "You know, Doug?" Walter said after a time. "Yeah?"

"We're gonna be here for a while."

He looked up then, "Why do you say that?"

"Because the car is in the other direction," he said as he hooked his thumb and pointed behind them.

"Well, why didn't you say so?"

He laughed, "You wouldn't have heard me anyway."

"I would too..." Walt gave him a look that said, 'No, you wouldn't have.'

Douglas began to grin. "You're right, I wouldn't have. Marie just caught me off guard, and then that little Lizzy. She must have been dreaming. She called me 'Daddy,'" and he gulped back an emotion he didn't know what to call.

"Well, if you want, it could be that way."

"Me, a dad? I'm nearly 37 years old. That time has long since passed."

"Maybe, maybe not," Walter shrugged as Doug looked back to the area they'd just left as if seeing Marie and her family there. Walter left him to his thoughts as they wended their way back towards their vehicle, yes it was going to be a long night.

PART III

ONE YEAR LATER

CHAPTER 22

JUNE 24, 2005

On this cloudless evening drive where the stars shone as diamonds clear and bright through the sunroof of the limousine, Douglas sat. Relaxed in his seat, something he rarely did, looking pleadingly at Marie his eyes afire. She felt the heat of his gaze burn into her soul as he spoke again, she wondered if it was a dream? He repeated himself, imploringly, he realized she had not understood his meaning the first time, so he sat up.

"Please consider the offer to marry me, Marie. It's all I ask. I can tell that you respect me, but are unsure of yourself, I think, or perhaps of my intentions? I must confess that I'm hoping in time, you will come to love me," he said, slowly but assuredly.

Marie had been watching him as he spoke, and he'd looked directly into her eyes, they'd sparkled when he said he loved her. Sitting back resting her tilted head on her fingertips, her elbow propped up on the armrest. She looked out the window, her heart feeling heavy within, then said with a sigh, "You are and have been a good friend to me," there was an ache when she spoke, "but marriage...?".

Closing her eyes she thought of Robert, "I don't know what to do..., I don't know if I can." Looking disconsolately at him then back out the window.

Douglas sat up straighter, took her delicate hand in his, and waited until she turned and looked at him. He seemed to turn the flame down in his eyes as he said, "Please consider it at least, I will wait for your answer," his voice contained something that made her heart ache and feel funny. He kissed the top of her hand and placed it gently in her lap, all the while, looking at her with those blue eyes, glistening in the full moon-light.

She sighed again, "I will consider it." Turning to look out the window again, Douglas let her be with her thoughts. She thought of Robert, what did he say... she was trying to locate a memory that wouldn't quite materialize. She had closed her eyes to stop the erratic pounding of her heart as she controlled her breathing, *sigh* breathing deeply trying to still her rapidly beating heart.

Eventually she dozed off as they were driven along the back country roads. They would reach their destination within the hour, but not before she dreamt of Robert.

*She was dressed in the dress he had liked best, the white summery one with the ruffled eyelet and tastefully done lace. He was wearing her favorite suit, the gray pinstripe. She ran to him, and he held her close, then just as suddenly he said, "I have to go, and where I go, you cannot come."

In great despair she cried out, "I want to come with you!"

He called back, "You cannot come. It's not your time, my darling. I love you, but it's not your time."

She heard the children call to her, "Mommy?"

"It must be this way, your life it is not done."

She sobbed, "No, it can't be... it can't be..."

Marie found herself in someone's arms, stroking her hair and speaking to her in soothing tones. "It's all right, darling. I'm here... I'm here."

Hearing at first, Robert's voice then coming to the realization that it was Douglas, broke the dam of her grief stricken soul. She cried like she'd never done before, ever since her son and husband's death.

Douglas just held her as the storm blew inside her soul. He was touched by her sorrow that came from deep within. Her heart rending sobs tore at him.

Walter was nearing their destination, but pulled off into a lighted area to give them both a sense of privacy while he had a stretch of his legs at the rest area. He knew when to be discreet and this was one of those times. It hurt his own heart to hear Ms. LaSalle cry out in her sleep in such anguish, it had startled him as it had Mr. Fairbanks even more so. Being grateful for his long coat, Walter walked up and down the area praying to the Lord to bring her some form of comfort, having seen Douglas hold and console her, he'd known it wasn't right to continue to travel any further. They needed time to themselves to work things out or come to an understanding of some sort over the situation.

Douglas kissed the top of Marie's head as he felt the storm beginning to subside within her. He took out his handkerchief from his coat pocket and placed it into Marie's hand. She was quite warm from her crying as she moved away from his bosom he felt cold at her absence.

Wiping her tearstained face and blowing her nose, she turned away feeling shy and not a little embarrassed by her outburst. 'I must look such a fright.'

Pulling her back against himself he stroked the head that lay on his shoulder, "You are more beautiful to me than ever before." Fresh tears came into her eyes as he lifted her face towards his and kissed each salty teary eye. 'Beautiful,' he whispered, 'so beautiful.' At this gesture of affection hot tears spilled out faster than ever. For the first time in years for Marie it was as if the cold harsh winter wind that had blown and battered her grief filled and weary soul began to loose its mighty grip from her soul. Attempting to regain her composure, she began to exercise her breathing in even breaths. The exhaustion from her emotional tears caused her to yawn.

Douglas commented, "You're feeling a bit better, I take it?" As he tried to pull her from himself so he could look at her lovely face.

Instead she held him fast stating, "No, I don't want you to look at me. I must be a mess with a red nose and puffy eyes."

'Oh, Marie I don't mind how you look right now, I just want you to look me in the eyes. I have something I'd like to say, I promise I won't look at your swollen eyes or your red nose.' He teased, a smile from her, he could tell. 'Besides. I'm not averse to tears nor are they foreign to me as I do have a mother and a sister who cry at puppy commercials', he chuckled. 'Now please, look me in the eyes.'

Pulling herself from his shoulder, but keeping her head down and in shadow. Douglas slowly lifted her chin with his finger, 'Please look at me darling,' he pleaded softly.

Slowly she lifted her eyes, first seeing his chest then, creeping slowly up to his neck, his chin, his lips, his nose, then to his eyes, they were moist with tears as well. That surprised her, He waited until she locked gazes with him, then he said in an unsteady voice, 'I hope you will always feel as safe as you do now with me, I hope for you to always find peace in my presence.'

As he spoke hot tears streamed down her face, she wanted to turn her face and hide, but he held her chin fast, gently saying, 'No, please don't turn from me. These tears are mine, I want to see them washing away the pain that I've seen in your eyes more often than I care to count. Let them fall darling, allow them to cleanse your soul.' Douglas wiped away each one with his thumbs gently.

Her features were much more controlled this time, it did feel as if her soul was being washed with a gentle rain, she even had a tremulous smile at God's goodness toward her, by sending this strong yet gentle man. Breathing in and out deeply getting her emotions under control. She heard him begin to pull tissues from a box, releasing his hold on her, he handed her the tissues to finish wiping her face. Dabbing at her eyes she gave him a weak smile averting her eyes, "Thank you, Douglas. I...", she didn't finish the thought, instead she said, 'I think I'll go freshen up," she visibly swallowed. "Uh, how long until we reach our destination?"

"About twenty minutes, give or take". Marie squeezed his hand meaningfully, then exited the sedan and nearly ran towards the restrooms.

Walter was at the further end of the area on his return paces back, he saw Marie dart past him in the lamplight, while he'd been in the shadow, seeing her expression, she wore a smile that he'd not seen before, it was simply radiant.

Douglas had walked up to him, "Thank you my friend for understanding the delicacy of the situation, for giving us the privacy we needed." He held his shoulder in friendship.

"From the look on her face as she ran past, I'd say it was really my pleasure, I assure you, she'll be all right now."

"You think so?"

Walter grinned, "If that Cheshire of a smile she wore is any indication, well....," he shrugged, "I believe she's on the mend for certain, but it doesn't mean it's over."

The thought gave Douglas pause, for what lay ahead. He put the thoughts away for now. Giving his friend a hard squeeze of the shoulder in gratitude, he walked around also needing a stretch from the hours of being seated for so long.

CHAPTER 23

IN RETROSPECT

On arriving at the hotel, Marie looked even more radiant than she had at the beginning of this trip. As Walter opened the door, he held out his hand to give her a hand out. Upon taking it she smiled at him saying, 'Thank you kindly Walter, I don't know what I'd have done without your help earlier.' Holding his hand meaningfully.

He squeezed back, giving her a wink and said, 'It was truly my pleasure Miss.' Before he knew it she reached out and gave him a quick hug and a kiss on the cheek, then she ran looking free as a pixie, her dress floating about her, to Douglas' side taking his arm, shyly looking up at him as he stood by the entrance waiting for her.

Smiling down on her the valet opened the glass doors for them as they entered the hotel lobby. Douglas whispered in her ear, "I'm so proud of you My Darling." She blushed as she tried to hide her smile at his compliment, he loved that blush, it made his heart swell.

Douglas could not hide his wide grin. As they walked forward they were greeted by a young cheery voice behind the Front Desk. "Good evening, Welcome to the Fairbanks Hotel and Suites. I'm Mandy, she pointed at her badge, "How may I be of assistance."

"Hello Mandy, Reservation for Douglas."

She clacked away at her keyboard looking up the reservation, "Okay here we are, I see you've already paid and are in the penthouse three bedroom suite. May I have an ID and credit card for any incidentals?"

Douglas handed her his ID and credit card, she looked at it, her eyes lit up going wide giving him a second glance. She remained composed. "Props to her for maintaining her composure." He smiled. Mandy handed him back his information.

"And here are two room keys…" she began handing them the key cards. Marie stood about a pace behind Douglas.

Douglas interrupted her "I need another key for my personal assistant".

"Oops, sorry, this will be a just a sec…" she scanned another card, just as Douglas gave his key to Walter.

"Please check the room out please." Walter took the key card gave a slight head bow and headed towards the elevators.

Mandy mouthed, 'Wow!' To herself. Marie saw it and smiled to herself at the young girls obvious glee and trying not to gush. 'Who wouldn't gush,' she thought. Douglas was a very good looking man and quite imposing if anyone had an inkling of who he was. Anyone would be intimidated by his presence alone which was magnetic, he was respectable, powerful, and wealthy. Such a winning combination that any girl would swoon. Only thing was she wasn't a girl any-more, she was a single widowed woman with children that she needed to protect against the world, a daunting task. But so far one she'd been doing fine with, she hoped.

"The valet will bring your luggage up when you're ready to receive your luggage." Mandy handed Douglas the other key card.

Nodding his head, "Please have it all brought up in about ten minutes, he looked to Marie in question, she nodded affirmatively, 'if you don't mind".

"Absolutely sir. We can do that. No problem".

Directing Marie towards the elevators, he whispered in her ear, causing her heart to flutter his breath grazing her ear. "Go on ahead, I'll be there in a minute" she turned to look at him, he winked at her causing her to blush, just as the elevator doors opened. Entering Marie pushed the button and turned around only to see him watching her board the elevator, then he winked at her again as the doors closed. She smiled putting her head down shyly.

Turning around, Douglas, smiling broadly at causing Marie to blush shyly, he found he liked doing it. He walked back to Mandy, "I would really appreciate some privacy, it hadn't escaped my notice that you know who I am."

"You can be assured of my integrity sir, I can change the name of who is in the suite, shall I leave it as Mr. Douglas? That is someones last name too." She winked and then blushed at her audacity.

It made Douglas chuckle at her discomfiture, "Thank you Mandy. I appreciate your discretion." He pulled out a fifty dollar bill to ensure her silence.

"Oh sir, please don't that's too much. Plus as an employee of this company I would be discreet with whomever our guests were should they wish to remain anonymous." She handed back the bill.

Astonished he took out more bills, and told her "Consider this a bonus, from the management." He winked at her, conspiratorially, "Make sure the papers don't get wind that I've arrived if at all possible."

"In that case sir you may wish to avoid the pool and patio area tomorrow evening also the fourth floor is currently having a reception that is still going on until curfew tonight."

"Thank you, for the heads up I appreciate that Mandy."

"Sir, if I may, I'd like to say Thank you, patting her pocket where she'd put the 'bonus', my Dad will appreciate the extra help. He was a big fan of your high school football days."

"Really?" He was amused, he leaned on the counter willing to listen to her story of her father. "I didn't think anyone would care anymore."

"Yes, he used to tell me about your games whenever he would see your picture in the paper. He would bring up some tidbit not many people knew."

"Really? Not many people remember those days, me included" he gave a self-deprecating chuckle.

"Don't be so hard on yourself sir. Dad was a few years behind you in school. The memories stay with some people."

"Is that so...? What's his name? Maybe I remember him?'

"John Davis."

"Little John Davis? Red hair right?"

Mandy nodded yes, happy such a man remembered her father. It made her glad she worked for his company.

"Wow, small world...well, we are back in my hometown, tell him, I do remember giving him a ride home from school once, he had a flat tire on his bicycle if I remember correctly. Please tell him I said, "Hello" maybe we can have a coffee sometime before I leave town again.

"I'm sure he'd like that, he'd be so delighted." She smiled broadly.

As he waited for the elevator on its return descent, he suspected Marie had sent it back down to collect him. "Sweet Marie," he thought. She wasn't anything like the other girls, the actresses, the super-models, he had dated in previous years.

He had assumed dating those types of women because of his status was expected. Reflecting, 'but "who's" expectations was he giving into by dating those types of women," not that they couldn't be nice, but he found some to just be so... so... 'grasping? Haughty? For things that he couldn't give of himself to them for. Sadly in retrospect many of them weren't believers, naturally letting the relationship die, when they didn't want to join him to go to church. No doubt were they beautiful than most, but something in their character was lacking in many of them.

Now he saw what it was they lacked ... like a lightbulb going on in his head... that thing he'd been searching for in a woman. Humility, sweetness, and above all modesty. The bell to the elevator dinged confirming the solidarity of the thought.

Walter stood there waiting in the elevator, "I was just about to get the bags sir, also Ms. Marie asked me to fetch you."

"She did, did she?" He quirked a smile as he entered the elevator.

"Yes, Sir." Walter smiled back about to exit. Douglas halted him

"I already asked for the valet to do the work. Your work is done, Walt, for the day anyway." The doors closed and Walt pushed the button.

'As you wish. May I see you to the rooms sir?"

"May as well, because you're sharing the other room in the suite with me." Doug chuckled, "Can I ask you a question?" Douglas switched topic.

"Sure, Sir." Giving a slight shrug.

"Anything?"

"I suppose, if it's anything I can do or help with, sure."

"What was it that first attracted you to your wife, MaryAnne?"

Walter guffawed, "Now that is not what I was expecting. Are you sure you want to hear? It's a long story."

"I'm good, I'm up for some conversation tonight I think, if you are, that is?"

Walt chuckled, "Sure, if you wish. I don't mind talking about how I met my Mrs."

The bell dinged, the doors opened and there stood Marie blushing ever so prettily. She was looking down feeling shy and embarrassed as Walter walked past them both. "Excuse me, I'll see to things" he winked at Douglas, as he entered their shared apartment.

Standing in front of her, Doug waited for her to begin. She pulled a strand of hair behind her ear. Attempting to speak what was on her mind her voice cracked, she cleared her throat. Quickly giving him a glance before averting her eyes once again. As she blushed, she said, "I feel like such a school girl" his heart tripped, continuing "My room... you did all that," fidgeting with her bracelets, "for me? Why?"

"I don't know what you mean?", he asked trying to get her to look at him, it worked. Her head shot up, eyes narrowing. He attempted not to smile but it played at the edges of his mouth. Taking him by the hand, he felt electricity shoot straight to his heart, as she hauled him to her suite and showed him the room. Again she reiterated "You did this, didn't you...?" her arm swept the room everywhere there was an empty surface, were now filled with intervals of lit vanilla scented candles and yellow roses in vases, her favorite flower.

He gave her a cheeky grin, "Do you like it?"

"Do I like it?" she paused, looking around the entire room. It was sumptuous with comfy cushions and pillows. The room overlooked the pool and the gazebo. Beyond in the distance one could see the mountains cast in shadow by the moonlight tonight, it was a nearly unobstructed view of God's handiwork. "I love it, though it is a bit excessive" she pointed to the minibar set with a chilled bottle of sparkling apple cider then over to the package sitting on the bed.

"I over did it, did I. 'Huh?' I didn't think I did, I..." he stopped himself before he mentioned 'the other girls he'd dated" Smart man. "Thank you God for stopping my mouth and ruining the moment." Whoa, he was thanking God? That felt different, but good.

"Just a wee bit. What's in the package Douglas?"

"Why don't you open it? Are you afraid?" Walking over to the package she picked it up, but her hands trembled as she held it, she couldn't get herself to unwrap it. Douglas hated seeing her in distress so walked over and said, "Here, let me. Taking the package out of her hands, "It's not what I think, you think it might be," plucking it out of her hand he then sat on the edge of the bed as she stood before him, watching him, watching her quivering. "Let's open it together shall we?" Nodding her head he untied the ribbon deliberately, slowly, her eyes gave a twinkle of pleasure and a tiny corner of her mouth quirk up. Opening the little bag slowly pulling out a little envelope, he gasped, inhaling 'Ah!' With eyes wide in delight, "Ooh, what's this?"

Marie's trembling began to ease as he opened the envelope, "Just a note from your gentleman caller," he teased. At this, she gasped in horror at his words and snatched the envelope from his hands and retreated to the overstuffed wingback chair that sat by the window over looking the patio below tucking her feet beneath her, the full skirt of her dress draping over the chair.

Douglas propped himself up on the end of the bed resting his chin on his hand watching her every move. She fascinated him, her hair piled up on her head in some intricate way, that showed off her neck and dangling earrings. She pulled a molasses colored strand that escaped behind her ear exposing her left ear with the smallest freckle that sat there winking at him, as her head turned to and fro as she read the note, making him want to kiss it. "Whoa!" His thought brought him up, he sat up thinking he ought to leave before his thoughts completely ran away from him. She noticed he was heading towards the door.

"Wait please" pausing at the door, she finished the letter then made her way towards him and his pulse kicked up a notch, her eyes all aglitter as she looked at him, inviting him? 'Danger, Will

Robinson!' He swallowed hard, "Thank you, for this" she took his hand and kissed it then brought it to her cheek. "What a woman!"

"I believe Mademoiselle, that is my job," he then kissed the top of her hand. She reached up on tip toe and kissed his cheek. Letting her hands slide down his arms. He stood speechless for a moment, he gulped, leaving the room before he pulled her into his arms and kissing her senseless. He turned back as he entered his room to see her watching him as the door closed shut. Douglas stood in the doorway with this thought in mind. "Did I finally meet 'The One?' The one I've been searching so long for?"

"Yes," came an audible reply. Douglas jumped out of his skin. He looked up and there stood Walter in the living room staring at him. "What? You asked?"

"You scared the life out of me!"

"Sorry sir, I didn't mean to scare you. I thought you were asking me."

"So, I asked that Out Loud?'

"Yes".

"Do you really think so?" asking as he walked into the kitchen, "I need something to drink, I'm parched."

"Probably to do with the long drive. Tea?"

"Yes, I think a cup of tea would be great, so my nerves will calm down." He wasn't about to let him know how much she was affecting him, he probably already guessed. Taking a glass from the cupboard he got himself a drink of water. While you're doing the tea I'll be in my room let me know when its ready."

"Take your time sir"

Walter turned and smiled to himself "She got to him" it wasn't always a bad thing when a woman got under your skin, especially one as sweet and kind as Miss Marie.

Once in his room Douglas looked in the mirror, seeing his reflection assessing himself as if for the first time. There were so many emotions playing on his face that it was confusing. In that moment he began to truly search his soul for things that truly mattered.

"What were those things that really, truly mattered"? He knew he'd asked Marie to marry him earlier, but 'what was his motive behind those reasons...?' He was always striving forward in his business, he knew if he married Marie others in the business world would respect him perhaps a little more, he knew she would be the perfect hostess at dinner parties for she is beautiful, genteel and would show off well on his arm, without a doubt they would fall in love with Marie, she was intelligent and would be able to hold her own against the other wives or trophy wives in some cases, but 'to what end' was he trying to achieve in all of this "getting and doing"?

Dating girls before her, had been without end it seemed like, but 'why had he done that? What was the point of dating anyone? He hadn't found it to be very stimulating, 'until now'. Here lay the crux, there was just something about Marie that called to him, that motivated him to be a better version of himself. She challenged him, just by being who she was. And who could deny her kindness? 'What was his true reason for marrying her really?' He thought perhaps to get an 'in' with her boss and maybe buy in a partnership, but that was a rather callous way of going about it, he could simply become a silent partner without marriage. And 'what of the children?' He would then become their step-father.

"Could he be a father to them? Be what they needed him to be? Would they accept him as," gulp, "dad?" Suddenly he wasn't so sure about what he was asking of Marie or of himself. He would have to change... everything. 'Could he do it?' Looking again into the mirror of his soul he took a long hard look at himself in that mirror as he changed into his casual clothes. He thought himself to be a very good looking specimen for being only thirty-seven. A successful entrepreneur, still athletic in build and fit. Also about to be that much richer if the merger he was planning went well. *sigh* Tired of thinking about himself and his selfish motivations, he exited his room.

Walter was just pouring the tea and adding cream and sugar to each cup as he walked into the kitchen. "Walter?"

"Sir?"

"Have I ever said, 'Thank You,' for being such a good assistant and my friend?"

"Not in so many words, sir."

"Hmm," Well that must be remedied at once, my apologies for not saying it often and sooner. You've been a valuable assistant and friend. You've been in my employ now what, ten maybe fifteen years now?"

"I believe it's been about twelve years. I've worked for you since you were twenty-five. I was thirty-five back then."

"Really, that long?" Walter nodded in the affirmative, "Wow time sure does go quickly doesn't it?"

"Yes, sir, that it does."

"So back to our earlier conversation, how did you meet Miss MaryAnne, your wife? I don't think I've ever heard the story." Walter smiled, his thoughts afar off...

CHAPTER 24

JUNE 18, 1983 - WALTERS' STORY

It was a beautiful day in San Diego. I was on shore leave from the Navy back then. I'd already had in about eight years and I wasn't sure if I should reenlist and become a lifer and retire from the navy or get out? I had three months left.'

My buddy Maurizio Bellafore had invited me over to his house for the weekend. We were pretty much best friends and I wasn't able to get home to Colorado in such a short time. So I had accepted his invitation. Walter chuckled at the remembrance.

"You know I never made it home until Christmas that year and that's when they'd meet my wife for the first time".

Douglas choked on a sip of tea, sputtering, "What?"

Taking a sip of his own tea, Walter said, "Let me get on with my story."' He began again.

Maurizio's father, Ernesto, came to pick us up in a great cherry colored '57 Chevy pick-up. It was sweet.' He smiled at the remembrance. 'Maury, as the fellas on the ship liked to call him, cause most of them farm boys had never met a proper Italian, who also happened to be a first generation American. They could never say his name correctly so he became, "Maury".

Well, Maury sat in the center because he was quite a bit smaller 5'6" to my 6" feet of bulk. I can remember his Dad's look of affection, he'd missed his son, you know. He actually had tears in his eyes, he hadn't seen him for about three years having been in different ports around the world. That was the Navy for you.

Once we left Coronado, we headed to a town called Lemon Grove, we drove off the highway and into the outskirts of town and turned onto a dirt road with only a mailbox for a marker. The avenue was filled with Lemon and orange trees on one side of the lane and a rose garden on the other. Behind the house was an apple orchard that was coming off its bloom time.

There was a lone cherry tree in the front of the house next to the veranda.

Douglas interrupted, "Wait, wait a minute! You mean to tell me that your friend is "The Maurizio" of the 'Lone Cherry Tree' farm? And your wife is his sister?"

"Yes the very same."

"Why have I not known this before now? I love their products!"

"I know that's why I guess it never came up, you were already buying their products, it went without saying." Walt shrugged, "Would it have made any difference, about us working together?"

"You're probably right. It wouldn't have made a difference. But wow, small world." Doug sat for a minute before saying, "All right Walt continue with your story."

As we were driving up to the house through the grove, I thought I had glimpsed a boy with bare feet and wearing overalls, a newsboy hat running parallel to the truck. When his father pulled to a stop in front of the house, his mother came out of the house an apron about her waist wiping her hands, a smudge of flour on her face, looking very much like a 1950s photo. The scene was picturesque you know. Walt painted a pretty picture and Doug could see it. I exited the truck with Maury right behind me, we were walking towards the veranda when out of nowhere he was jumped on from behind, presumably by the boy I'd seen running through the grove. Maury was so caught off guard that he almost fell over. Catching himself, I'll never forget what he did next. He grabbed the arms of the boy and then began to spin round and round with them on his back. "Then I heard it, a sound I'll never forget."

"Heard what?" Doug asked on the edge of his seat, his tea chilled.

"The shriek of laughter that I will never forget as long as I live. You see as Maury turned around faster and faster, the hat flew off and an extremely long flowing mane of hair unrolled out of the hat, revealing not a boy but, ...

"MaryAnne"..., both men said together.

"Exactly, so".

Maury stopped before he fell down, she let go.

"Oh, I've missed you so brother!" With such feeling, I was blown away. You see my family is very reserved, they don't show their feelings all that much. But they were full of affection for one another, it is a blessing to witness."

She continued saying, "There's nobody here to pick on me or take me out anymore"

"Oh, what am I?" Ernesto asked, "Chopped liver? Did I not take you out last Friday?"

"Yes, of course Papa, but you cannot skate or ride bicycles like 'Zio." She petted her father and hugged him as if patting down his ruffled feathers. Oh she was coquettish with her father and brother. When she let go of her father and realized I was looking at her specifically, the whole family really, how they freely interacted with one another, well she seemed to shrink in honest embarrassment her enthusiasm curbed. Then all eyes turned to me, and Maury saved the moment and introduced me to the family.

"Mama, MaryAnne this is my good friend Walter Peters."

"Hello Mr. Peters, Welcome to our home. Please let us all go inside, supper is almost ready." Then an aside to MaryAnne "Child where are the apples I sent you to get?"

"Oh Mama" she explained as she twisted her hair to put it back into her cap, "I dropped them when I saw Papa's truck I was so excited to see Zio. I will go fetch then now." She took off like a sprite, she was quite a runner. Maury led me inside where Mama B had lemonade waiting for us.

It is a lovely farmhouse, with a wide veranda with wisteria growing up the trellis on both sides of the porch. It was two stories tall with five bedrooms two and half baths. You know Ernesto built the house himself, he is an amazing carpenter with a keen eye to detail, along with being an excellent orchardist. You would love that house Douglas with your own keen eye for architecture, you would say he was a forward thinking man for his time. His love, besides his wife though are his orchards and gardens. They really are a lovely.

Mama turns to us then and says "Why don't you two go and freshen up before dinner is served. "Zio, why don't you show Mr. Peters to the guest room and get him some fresh towels while you're up there."

She was paring apples for dessert. I can still remember the smell of the lasagna cooking in the oven and the smells of pie dough and cinnamon and sugar for the pie she was baking. I was in for a fine Italian meal especially after all that chow that just kept a body alive while onboard ship. It smelled heavenly. Mmm-mm!

"I bet it did" Doug commented and they both laughed.

When I came back down the stairs with Maury, we went into the kitchen and sat at the old farm table where Mrs. B set down two glasses of lemonade for us. MaryAnne had come in then with her arms and pockets full of apples. Her long hair was hanging down her back in a twist, her cap off. Her cheeks were rosy from her exertion and her lips a natural pink.

"Of course you noticed those features." Douglas ribbed him.

"Of course, who wouldn't? To me she is the most beautiful woman alive. She still has a youthful vibrancy to her, she was, is so lively. In the military you learn to be hard and tough. And here I'm confronted with this sweet innocent young lady who loves and lives for the love of her family. She adored them and they adored her in return she was the picture of innocence, personified.

As I looked on at MaryAnn, Mrs. B stood just behind her within my field of vision and I could tell she was questioning whether I was looking at her or her daughter, so as not to cause a social faux pa, I asked if I could help her as she was still paring apples. I'll never forget the look on her face, she about passed out. She was quite alarmed, 'No guest of ours will do work, what are you saying?' She asked Zio, "What is he saying...?' and she went off in Italian like nothing I'd ever seen or heard before.

I asked him, "What did I say? What did she say?" I could see Ernesto was trying to calm her down as she stabbed the air with her paring knife. She looked awfully dangerous to me, I didn't want to mess with this mama bear" Walt snickered. Maurizio tried to explain to her that I was a cook on the ship and that I was just trying to be helpful, that I was not trying to insult her. At that she seemed to calm down then and handed me a knife and some of the apples.

Challenging me, "We shall see, how good you are." There was a hidden meaning in there somewhere, I was sure. MaryAnne just stared at me the whole time out of the corner of her eye, as she rinsed & dried the apples in the kitchen sink. When Mama noticed her wandering eyes, she sent her out of the kitchen.

"Go change into something respectable MaryAnne, we have guests." She was about to protest but Mama had given her such a severe look that only a mother can give her child, that she left straightaway toward the stairs. Before she went up she caught my eye, not looking very pleased. Wearing a look that said she wanted to stick her tongue out at me. I gave her a quick smirk, she then tossed her head of hair like a proud filly tossing her mane and took off up the stairs in a huff, I smiled to myself. I certainly didn't want to draw any attention to myself or her, so I set to work quickly paring the apples. I was done paring the apples when Mama was just finished laying out her pie crust in the pie pan.

She was amazed and satisfied with my work having inspected each apple carefully. "Good," was her only comment, then sent us out of the kitchen with Ernesto. I had offered to help, but she would have none of it.

I asked Maury about why she wouldn't let me help. He said she was "old school" that way, only women in the kitchen being a good hostess and all that. I told him that my mom always let me help with dessert once saying "Any heart can be won with the execution of a good dessert" apparently that's how she won over my father, he sure loved his sweets. He reminisced a smile on his face.

They showed me around the place Ernesto leading the way pointing out trees and herbs and things that they'd planted in the vegetable garden for the summer and fall harvests. We ended up near the rose garden by the house. I hadn't realized how large it was, he had two hedges bordering it. He had turned it into a maze of roses and they were blooming, the fragrance was heady. Store bought flowers have nothing on those blossoms.

Ernesto gave us a lesson "One must be careful when choosing a rose as there are some roses that are the most beautiful yet can be dangerous and have many thorns. They can entice a man to lead him astray to pluck her sweet fragrance. But in the end one can get trapped and entangled. A godly woman is like a rose beautiful to look at and to be admired from a distance. She should give off a wonderful sweet fragrance in her actions and by her behavior. Her dress like the petals should be modest in adornment. You must be careful not to manhandle the rose as you will bruise the tender petals. When handled properly she will yield a great reward and blossom under tender and loving care.

A lesson I have never forgotten. I caught sight of MaryAnne then coming from the house she wore a yellow and white gingham dress with a white ribbon tied around her waist and Roman styled sandals. She was like a breath of fresh air. She didn't need any makeup, still doesn't as far as I'm concerned. I was smitten that very moment, all I could see was her in the soft summer twilight. Stopping at the entrance to the rose garden she called us to supper. Papa went first handing her a yellow rose that he'd plucked and had given his demonstration with. She had entwined the rose into the braid of her hair, tossing it back as if she'd done it a thousand times.

With certainty I can say each action was played out in slow motion, still does. Looking my way she smiled, it was a small smile used only for friends of friends, but for me a choir of angels rang out in song over my head, as a soft ray lit her from behind engulfing her in light. All I can say was that it was... magical.'

Then the woodland sprite in her did the unexpected after her father passed by her and her brother said something to her that I didn't quite catch. She stuck out her tongue at him and she turned and traipsed after Papa like the obedient little imp that she was. Maury was trying to get my attention, I was in a daze for sure. I asked him how old his sister was.

"She's eighteen today of all days, she wasn't expecting me to bring anyone home. I think she's a little upset with me that you're here. She may be a little jealous that you're here."

"Why would she be jealous? If you'd have told me I wouldn't have come. Perhaps maybe come a different day, this is time to spend with your family not with me, man."

"And where would you go? To some lonely hotel or wait out on the ship for transport? No, my friend, she'll get over it."

"But it's her birthday. We have to do something or go somewhere special for her don't you think? I don't want to ruin her special day, I mean eighteen for a girl is a big thing, what about taking her skating, she was just talking about that. I haven't in years but you know, it's like riding a bike right?"

"What are you insane? It's my baby sister you're talking about. My parents won't let her go on her birthday, it's a family day, we stay home and celebrate."

"Oh, I didn't know, my family is different. We always went out to do something different from the norm, for our birthday."

"Each family has their own way."

"Maury, what is her favorite flower? I can't go in empty handed, now that I know it's her birthday."

"She likes all flowers, but you can choose any color but red!" He was quite adamant about that. "Papa will not allow it. Red is for after she is married. Only then can she have red." So with his permission, I picked a bouquet of eighteen roses, one for each year. Ernesto had quite a variety, so I got shades of pink, a few whites, yellow and lavender. Maury kept urging me to come to dinner as the family was waiting.

Once we reached the dining room the table was set and everyone was just being seated, but I walked over to MaryAnne who had just sat down and I placed the bouquet of roses next to her plate. "I heard it was your birthday today, your brother hadn't told me and I didn't want to crash your party empty handed. If I'd known I'd have bought you a better gift."

She was so surprised then looked down the table to her father, who sat with his napkin in mid-air towards his chin. Looking down the other end at Mama, her mouth was agape. I was worried then, I had committed some sort of faux pas or offended them greatly. I started to sweat.

Maryanne found her voice and asked, "May I accept them Papa?"

Never in my life had I met a more conservative family. Ernesto paused for more than a heart beat looking at me as if reading my intentions. I sure stood up straight as if in front of a five star general, my intentions sincere and friendly. He finally replied, after he looked at me pointedly "It is only a gift from 'a friend,' he does not know our ways you may put them away before we begin."

Slowly I let out a breath and sat down, I was embarrassed, but determined to make it up to the patriarch, I said to Ernesto, as MaryAnne left the table for a vase. "I did not mean any offense or disrespect of any kind to you or your family, sir." I looked to Maury for help, but he was none. He just had a look like, "Boy your'e in trouble now," kind of look.

Ernesto replied, "Maurizio should have explained things, I am more disappointed with him," Maurizio hung his head, chagrined, "than I am with you, sir. He is supposed to look out for his sister" he gave his son a look of dis-appointment. I sure had a foreboding feeling that maybe the evening was going to be ruined by my blunder.

He opened his mouth to speak but then Maryanne came back in humming under her breath, placing the vase on the sideboard, she sat down and it seemed as if nothing had been said or that anything had happened. I understood they didn't want to ruin the evening for MaryAnne's sake. It was her birthday, and they would hold their words until later.

Holding hands to say grace, something I'd never done but with them it just felt right. As a family unit they were so different, yet I felt at home. Welcome. Like nothing I'd ever felt before.

"Destiny, predestination, whatever you call it, I was meant to marry MaryAnne."

"You really felt that way about her: Or are you saying that from looking back on it now?" Douglas asked.

"Well, perhaps, not in those exact words, but yes, that is how I felt. Still do."

"Wow, she must have really made such an impression on you, she must have been incredibly beautiful then. I mean she is a handsome woman now, you are a very lucky man."

"Douglas…, his eyes filled, 'it was more than exterior beauty more than the physical attraction," he cleared his throat, "I don't deny there was definitely that to be sure, but her soul was beautiful. She was simple and honest, her modesty, purity, her determined obedience to her parents. The fire of her lively soul to live life fully, in a godly moral way. A way that was pleasing not only to her parents, but out of a sincere devotion to her savior. I knew then and there I would endeavor to deserve her for I knew that I was undeserving of her affection should she choose to love me. I am a blessed man, indeed, not lucky. There is a difference, I was graced with God's favor."

"Undeserving? You mean to tell me that you felt that you didn't bring anything worthwhile to the "table," so to speak?"

"I am saying exactly that. No amount of riches or pride in myself or in my accomplishments, could win her to me. I knew that, I only had myself to recommend, and I felt lacking then still do. She is a treasure. Not just Ernesto's daughter, she is 'God's daughter.'"

"Lacking and undeserving? Those are some pretty strong words to think about one's self, don't you think?"

"Well, for me that is how I think of it, I feel I got the best blessing I could ever receive. I know I don't deserve my wonderful wife. God has been better to me than I have ever deserved to be blessed, when he gave her to me to love and to cherish for the rest of my life. Besides salvation, she is the best blessing that has ever happened to me."

"Which reminds me I told her I'd call her when we got in, and I haven't yet, if you'll excuse me sir, I'll go do that now. I'll clean up after I get off the phone with her."

"Don't worry about it. It's just two mugs, I'll take care of it. You go on and call your wife."

"Thank you sir, Good night then."

"Good night, Walter."

CHAPTER 25

SLEEPLESS NIGHT

Marie decided to take a luxurious bath before bed. With the candles burning bright giving off their sweet fragrance, mingled with those of the roses turning on the hot water in the soaking tub. Taking a rose from one of the vases, she tore it adding it to the swirling water. Walking over to the mini kitchen she served herself some sparkling cider, well chilled by now, taking a sip relishing its refreshing taste after their long drive from the city.

Taking her case, she unpacked as the sweet breeze fluttered the sheer privacy drapes that hung from above the partially open sliding door. Smelling all these lovely fragrances kind of made her hungry, so she searched through the cupboards and then the mini-fridge and to her surprise found several pints of her favorite B.J.'s ice cream!

"Did Douglas really know her so well? I'm not sure I know his favorite dessert!" Taking a pint out she decided to indulge a little. She found a spoon and took a bite, "Mmmm, So good.' Turning the water off she took the ice cream with her to her bath, turning off all the lights and bathed by candlelight. Something she'd never done and always wanted to do.

Douglas was so thoughtful, '...just like Robert.' Her heart felt unsettled, still. Why was that? It had been three years now since his death next month. How the time was slipping by, most of her friends had said "It's time to move on, you're still young only twenty-eight".

Chronologically she was young, but she felt as if she'd lived an age. First a wife, then a mother to four children, which was impossible and now a widow of three years. Life certainly hadn't turned out the way she'd thought. Though, even in all the tragedy she was blessed. It couldn't be denied. She was able to keep her home, she had work that she enjoyed, and happy children. 'Let's not forget a suitor..., who wanted to marry her!' She couldn't quiet yet call him her boyfriend, as sweet as he was.

Relaxing and satisfied with her ice cream it was having a soporific effect. Yawning, she needed get to bed before falling asleep in the water. Using droplets of water off her fingertips she put out all the votives. Dressing in comfy pajamas she decided to read the note Douglas had left for her one more time.

My Darling Marie ~

I wish to convey that I do not want to win your affection by monetary means, But it is also something within my power to "give". I want you to know that I was thinking of you and this is how I can "give" you something and I hope that you will accept my gift. I also want you to know that at this point I will be able to provide for you in the "for Richer," part of the marriage vows. Although we never know if there will ever be a "for poorer" event that may happen in future only the Father knows. That being said, I would be honored if you would allow me the privilege of taking you shopping tomorrow and purchase anything you would like for the reunion party tomorrow. I am hoping that you will allow me this honor. I also hope that this will be the first of many gifts to bestow upon you. You make giving to you very easy. I am in the hopes of making a fun memory for and with you on the morrow.

Ever Yours~ Douglas

P.S.~ If shopping can be said to be fun, I'm not sure. Lol :)

Sending up a prayer "O, God of my Fathers'-Please direct my path for right now

I am so unsure of where my feet are going, be the light unto my path." She knelt by her bed continuing to pray for direction when she finished she was able to lay her head down on her pillow and fall fast asleep being at peace.

Douglas on the other hand lay on his bed tossing and turning unable to fall asleep after his conversation with Walter. How his words reverberated throughout his brain ping-ponging back and forth.

"Lacking...undeserving...God's daughter..." again and again.

Pounding his pillow again trying to find a good position for sleep to claim him, closing his eyes only to have them pop open... 'Ugh!' *sigh* It was no use, he got up, turned the light on the nightstand on, sat up in his bed rearranging the pillows. He would do what he always did when he couldn't make up his mind about something. That was to write down the pros and cons of any situation and make a decision based on that. It didn't always work, but he decided to give it a try.

Pros - I am	Pro- She is
• Wealthy	~ Beautiful in every way
• Handsome	~ Lovely
• Intelligent	~ Smart in all things
• Proven Leader	~ Loving Mother
• Businessman	~ Charitable
• Respectful	~ Speaks no Evil, Eschews it
• Honest	~ Modest in dress, Righteous
• Giving charitably	~ Honorable & Honest
	~ Peaceful & Patient
	~ Compassionate

Looking over his list he realized he'd only written down things about himself that were about his work life, who he was within that realm. "Were there any other attributes or characteristics that he perceived within himself? He didn't know, his head began to ache trying to make sense of it all notwithstanding the lateness of the hour, the clock read 3:29am. 'Ugh'! I need some sleep.' Putting down the pad, paper, and pen, turning out the light and this time he fell asleep for exhaustions sake. Albeit was fitful and full of strange dreams.

CHAPTER 26

JUNE 25, 2005

"...Ha, ha, ha' 'Marie?' She turned and laughed at him, ran away from him, teasing him. Turning back around and called him to come closer with her finger, enticing him. He followed her, only to see her turn around and ran away laughing once again...'

Douglas awoke up with a start, panting, "What in the world was that about?" Not bothering to look at the clock, he punched the pillow and lay down again, attempting to still his beating heart, hoping to get some rest.

"...I'm so afraid Douglas... Help me Douglas... I'm so cold... Where Are you Douglas?"

"Where are you Darling?" The mist is so thick, I can't see you?"

"I'm over here, Douglas, can't you see me?" her voice was faint, sounding far away.

"Marie, where are you?" He called out, searching through the fog and mist to no avail. "He fell to the ground in despair, 'Marie!"

Jumping up from his sleep with a start, heart pounding a mile a minute, his chest, heaving. Walter, barged into his room, startling Douglas even more than he already was, "Sir is everything all right? I heard you shouting." Looking at him concerned. Panting hard and putting his hand to his heart to still it.

"Oh thank you God," he prayed. "It was just a bad dream. Woo, wow, I'm sorry to concern you Walter." He shuddered. "Did I wake you?"

"No sir I was just making the coffee, when I heard you call out. You're usually up by now."

"What time is it anyhow?" Rubbing his neck to work out the kinks.

"7:30 am, sir, Miss Marie is supposed to be over here about 8am to breakfast with you. So I suggest you hurry up and get ready now that your dream is done and over with."

"Yes, I'll do that, stall if you have to, please. Thanks Walter."

"No worries about that, Sir.' Walter left the room while he went to hit the shower. But before he did that, he knelt down, something he hadn't done in a long time. By his bed he prayed longingly and expectantly for forgiveness from a loving savior, for his wayward life up to this point, he prayed for and about Marie knowing He knew all the specific details of his situation. Yet bringing it all unto remembrance before him, asking that if she was "The One," that today it would be evident. He knew he shouldn't really ask for a sign, but he wanted to be absolutely certain that she was God's plan for his life, or 'was he the right one for her...,' that gave him pause as the thought entered his mind.

"Lord, please if we really are right for each other I'd like to have a fantastic day shopping with Marie, because you know how

I feel about shopping.' He shuddered at the thought, 'ugh'. And thanking the Lord for his diligent assistant, Walter. Thanking Him for sending him a faithful servant, who also loved the Lord. For the fact that he never had to worry about his personal or business life because of Walters' discretion and integrity. Lastly, thanking him for his faithfulness towards himself, Douglas ended his prayer. 'Amen'.

Saturday Morning

Marie woke earlier than usual but with a feeling of being rested, 'this bed is amazing, I wish I had one'. The word 'luxurious' came to mind. Sitting up she stretched and yawned, stuffing the pillows behind her back she took her Bible from off the nightstand and began to read her devotions for the day.

Afterwards kneeling next to the bed she for prayed for grace and strength for the day. To make wise decisions and not just good ones, but godly choices, not only for herself but for her family. Ending her prayers with Douglas in mind and the choices that could change her life regarding him. Also for Walter and his wife MaryAnne, who were such faithful servants assisting Douglas in his life and work. Whom also were becoming dear friends, Thanking God for their friendship. 'Amen'.

Rising she smiled and continued getting ready for a trip to the gym downstairs for a quick run, it was still quite early and breakfast was not scheduled for an hour and a half away at 8am.

Exiting her room, she didn't hear any stirrings from next door, so she took the stairs down to get a warm up for her workout it was only three floors down. As she opened the door for the lobby, Mandy was still at the front desk. She smiled to her, "Don't you ever go home? Though It's nice to see a friendly face this morning." She gave a small chuckle.

"Why thank you Ma'am. Yes, my relief is running late. Flat tire." She rolled her eyes and shrugged. "I'm glad I was here to greet you today. Is there anything I can help you with?"

"I'm looking for the gym, we got in so late last night I didn't get a run, in."

"Down this hall and to the left after the elevators."

"There's more elevators?"

"Yes, ma'am."

"I'll have to try and not get mixed up then."

"You shouldn't worry. It's impossible for your's is the only elevator that goes up to your set of suites. It's a private elevator only accessible with your key card."

"You're kidding right?"

"No, Ma'am," lowering her voice to almost a whisper Mandy said, "Mr. Fairbanks takes his security seriously and likes his privacy."

"Oh," Marie mouthed, astonished.

Returning to a normal tone Mandy said, "If there's anything else I could help with please don't hesitate to ask. I'll be here until my relief arrives. There's an intercom in the gym so if you need me just lift the hand set, it's a direct line to the front desk, okay?"

"Okay, Thank you Mandy." Marie walked off slightly dazed by all the information she'd just received. Mandy looked after her a little concerned, but just then there was a crash that came from the kitchen area, so she went to see what happened instead.

Brushing off the talk with Mandy to the back of her mind, she entered the now empty gym noting where the intercom was, as she saw someone heading towards the showers. Walking towards the treadmill farthest away from the showers, Marie began at a jog slowly working her way towards a full run which generally helped to clear any kind of worrisome thoughts from her mind, she jogged for about half and hour.

When the conversation with Mandy began to intrude into her mind, she didn't quite know how to take the information received. "Was Douglas so private that he was closed off, and one couldn't get close to him? Would marrying him like he wanted, lead to a lonely marriage? Would they be able to talk and have honest and open conversations? Or did he want to have his "affairs" private? Had he had other women here?"

That dart shot through her mind "Oh, my" she began to feel sick, as she faltered and her pace began to slow. "Was he a charming seducer? But why would she be a victim if that was the case? She had children who depended on her and he knew that! No!" that could not be the case, she affirmed. "Charming?" "Absolutely!" her thoughts went on. "Handsome? Devastatingly so! But certainly not deceitful, she didn't think so. 'No,' She didn't think it was possible. 'Could it?'

As the thoughts whirled about in her mind and brought confusion, she didn't realize until it was too late, that she stumbled off the treadmill. Marie walked like a drunken sailor as direct as she could to the intercom, lifting the receiver she heard it ring once, before Mandy picked up, "How may I be of assistance?"

"Mandy, get Douglas please." Then proceeded to faint sliding down the wall, then over onto her side. Leaving the phone handle dangling and knocking against the wall. Mandy heard the clunk of the phone.

"Miss LaSalle? Hello?...silence, 'Uh-oh, oh God, please help.' Mandy prayed, quickly putting down the receiver she grabbed a walkie-talkie and ran to the gym shouting into the walkie for Jim the valet on duty.

"Bleep" Jim, get Mr. Fairbanks, in the Presidential Suite, send him to the gym it's an emergency with Ms. LaSalle. Over. "bleep"

"On it". Jim left the valet office and entered the elevator nervously. Knocking on the main suite door, he waited. Walter answered the door with a questioning look, for they hadn't ordered anything and hadn't expected anybody.

"May I help you?"

Loosing his sense of thought Jim said, "Mr. Fairbanks...the gym... Mandy said,' then went silent knowing he messed up his words, 'dyslexia, argh'.

"Mr. Fairbanks is here not at the gym, son. There must be a mix-up."

Walter explained, just as Douglas came out of his room. Shaking his head to clear the thoughts. Jim explained.

"No, you don't understand, it's Miss LaSalle, something happened to her at the gym."

"Miss LaSalle!" both men exclaimed.

Walter huffed, "Why didn't you say so to begin with?"

"Let's just go!' Douglas stated, as he began to walk past Walter and Jim. He pushed the button for the elevator, then decided instead to run down the stairs, to run off his rising panic, taking two at a time. Just as he exited the door, the elevator dinged, he ran towards the gym while Walter exited the elevator seeing his boss's back he headed in that direction.

Mandy looked up just as Douglas entered the gym, looking worried and relieved, she suspected as he saw a medic with Marie. She halted his progress, holding up her hand so she could speak with him, while the medic saw to Marie.

"Sir, she's okay." Mandy said, just as Walter came walking in, he looked relieved too.

"What happened?" Douglas asked anxiously.

"Apparently a really hard workout…, and some pent up stress." Mandy's lips pursed as she tried to formulate the correct way to convey her thoughts, then decided her honest survey of the situation was best. "When I came to her, she was passed out on the floor here, when she woke, her thoughts were confused. At first I didn't understand what she was talking about."

"Confused? About what?" Doug's eyes stayed hooked on Marie, but when she didn't' look at him, he began to worry.

"Before I answer…, may I speak freely, sir?"

"You'd better, tell me everything. I told her I'd keep her safe on this trip. So I need to know it all, please."

"Well, earlier she came down we talked a little then she was looking for the gym, so I directed her here and let her know about the intercom. It looked as if she had a question on her mind but didn't ask it. And I didn't push her as I don't really know her, it's not my place."

"Then a few minutes ago, so…," she looked at her watch, "it's been about forty-five minutes since we spoke. I received the call on the direct line from the gym and she just said, "Mandy, get Douglas please," and then a clunk of the phone on the wall. So I had Jim go get you and then rushed over here. I found her where she's sitting now next to the wall and the intercom. I called Pete, she gestured towards him. "He's the medic on staff. Thankfully he was just walking in from outdoors. He's checked her vitals, which were normal."

Douglas felt and looked relieved, for now. She continued, "He put smelling salts under her nose to wake her and she opened her eyes. Upon seeing me she immediately began asking me questions about you." Looking at her feet then, clearly embarrassed, she continued, "Asking if you'd had other women here. I told her only once, and that woman had been your fiancee at the time, before the whole world found out about her indiscretions. I told her usually it's just you or your family, mother and sister. Only then did she really allow Pete to finish his exam to make sure she doesn't have a concussion or something."

Looking at Marie, he thanked Mandy for her help. Asking himself, "What has brought on these questions? Why now?"

Pete stood up and gestured him to come forward. Doug walked over, with Walter not far behind, so as not to frighten her in her delicate state. Pete helped her stand up holding onto her waist until she was steady before he released her arm. "How's our patient, Pete?"

Pete held out his hand to shake Douglas's and Walters. "No worse for wear," he drew near, "I suspect a little embarrassed". In a normal tone he continued, "She should see her regular doctor, just in case, but I'm sure she's good enough to continue her day."

"Most people forget to hydrate before, during and after a workout. Some people are more sensitive than others. I suspect that to be the case here. Especially since she was also exercising on an empty stomach. All she needs now is some TLC and a good hearty breakfast, I think." Pete took out a business card handing it to Douglas, "In case you need to contact me again."

Douglas held out his hand and shook Pete's, "Thank you Pete, for all your help, it is much appreciated."

"You're very welcome. It is my job, take care you two. I will warn you I think she may be a little emotional for a while, perhaps even a little anxiety." Pete took leave of them to attend other duties as did Mandy, when Douglas assured them he would take care of her." Holding out his arm for Marie to take, she continued to look at the floor, taking his arm anyway. He wrapped his hand around her small one at his elbow. His heart heaved a glad sigh that she was safe, but felt an ache inside that she wouldn't look at him.

Walter led the way out of the gym opening the door for them and leading the way back to their suite. He noticed she did not say a word, seeing her dejected frame, he turned to Douglas and asked, "If I may sir," interrupting their silence, "I will get the finishing touches on the breakfast I started. You could have a seat here, as you know they have an excellent coffee service, a quick pick me up?" He nodded directly at Marie showing he understood.

"That sounds great thank you, Walter." He turned to Marie and asked, "Is that okay Marie?" he asked quietly, he felt if he was any louder she would break down, so he remained calm for her sake. She acquiesced with a slight nod of her head. Douglas lead her to a quiet corner of the dining area. There were not that many people yet in the dining area for which he was grateful. He ordered them two cafe Latte's, it being her favorite drink, with sweetener of course. Keeping an eye on her, with her head still down at the table his heart couldn't help but ache at it. She looked so forlorn, he caught her trying to hide wiping a tear.

Turning his head from the scene when the barista called out their coffee order, he picked them up. Taking their coffees, he sat next to her on the bench setting hers in front of her. She reached out to take it with a trembling hand, but didn't lift it. He took her by the chin and pulled up her face to meet his. She kept her eyes closed the tears slowly rolling down, he couldn't help it he wanted to help her and hide her feelings of embarrassment.

So he did the only thing he could to take her mind off of herself. He thought to give her a quick peck on the cheek, but it landed close to her mouth. But once she opened her eyes in surprise, he set his coffee down, taking her into his arms.

Somehow her arms came around his waist pulling him closer, her head in his chest. Someone near by cleared their throat and both of them parted in haste. Her cheeks flaming as were his own. Douglas looked around and pinpointed an older couple seated nearby, he said, "Sorry, about that."

"No need to apologize young man, I know what it is to be a newlywed. Though it was fifty years ago." Giving them a wink. Doug was about to correct the man when his wife scoffed at him and smacked him on the arm. He ducked his head and chuckled, saying, "She remembers it too. She just won't admit it."

"Harry! Stop your nonsense this instant." Though she was smiling too.

"Mabel," he said firmly, then changed his tone to what could be described as cheeky, "You know you love me anyway, you can't get rid of me, we've been married too long." Wagging his eyebrows up and down. Mabel just shook her head at him, saying, "Eat your breakfast, Harry." Rolling her eyes as she said it.

Doug did not wish to embarrass Marie any further, so he took her by the hand and led her willingly away. "Fifty years, what a milestone, I'll send them some flowers." They walked to the elevator upon entering, she started to apologize, but he put his finger to her lips, "Shhh, don't say you regret coming with me, because I don't." Caressing her cheek, she looked into his eyes, while he confessed, "What am I going to do with you, 'Sweet Marie'. How you make my heart ache for you to be safe and happy". He thought, 'With me'. The doors opened, they entered when the doors closed, he pulled her close coffee and all. She did not cry, but just breathed deeply as if she found a measure of peace in his embrace. The ding from the bell at reaching their destination rung out, but they ignored it just holding onto one another. After a few moments Marie asked, "Douglas?"

"Hmm?" He didn't move or let her go.

"I would like to shower and change now."

"Do you..., now?" Continuing to hold her, her head under his chin.

"Mm-hmm." She said in the affirmative, sighing deeply.

"One more minute please," he relished holding her in this peaceable way.

"Okay, but I'm really hungry." Her stomach growled then.

"Oh, yes I'd forgotten." He released her but not before kissing her on the head. She blushed and went to her room slowly closing the door, watching him also go slowly to his own room. As the door finally closed, she exhaled gladly leaning against the door for a moment.

Douglas had watched her looking at him as she slowly closed the door. He smiled to himself, she had no idea what she looked like and how it made his heart stir. Her slightly tousled hair from her exercise. As he'd held her she was curvy and soft in all the right places he thought. There was such a wonderful charm about her, kind of like a young girl in the morning, all soft and cuddly, but certainly all woman. How he knew that he didn't know, but that was the image in his mind.

On entering his room, he saw Walter hard at work making the breakfast.

"Walter? Could the heart truly contain such strong emotions, that kill me?" *sigh* The coffee was percolating, a stack of French toast was kept warm on a hot plate, the bacon sizzled in the pan, Walter cracked eggs into a bowl.

"You're here aren't you?" he smiled at him.

"Yes, but if she doesn't take care of herself and keeps this up with the fainting spells, I don't know if I can take the strain. It's been so "emotional" lately.

"What did you expect? To go through the rest of your life untouched by natural human emotions? To not be affected by another person or their feelings or affection for you and from you?"

"I just thought...," he stammered, "I didn't think it would be so... so...?"

"Messy? Complicated?" Walter supplied.

"Yes, exactly so!" He pondered, "You know with Jessica or "Grayson" as she like to be called. Everything seemed simple." He shrugged, "she liked everything we did together and liked the same things I liked it was 'easy" you know?'"

"Yes, and look what 'easy' got you? She was never the one for you, she was a pretender. Thank goodness it was a relatively clean breakaway with that one."

"How can you say that? I was engaged to her. I loved her."

"No. I don't believe you truly loved her. As a father with two girls and a boy, you have to trust that I know what it looks like. I'm sorry to say, You had a very strong 'like' and infatuation for her, for who she was in the film industry, but as it turned out, and you know it's true," Walter admonished. "She was not the one for you. She had no real substance, her whole life is a facade. If you had observed her from my point of view, she was superficial, vain and prideful. I saw right through her, she wasn't in love with you it was all about the money, she held no allegiance to you or to our Lord. When you weren't around I caught her many times unguardedly speaking with one of her so called 'friends'. She was full of spite and venom. I'll have to say her best performances were around you, she definitely was an actress and played her 'part' very well."

"Why did you never say anything to me?" Doug looked incredulous.

"I hate to admit it but you were so infatuated with her that I could tell it would take something drastic, to protect you and turn her wiles away from you. So I did what I thought was best to 'break the spell' she seemed to hold over you. I hope you understand that my first job is to protect you, not only your safety but your reputation from scandal as well. If I can do it quietly all the better, yes?" He asked. Douglas nodded affirmatively.

"I have a friend Detective Slade, he's young but discreet. I had her followed; it only took him two days. I had him leak the story that you saw for yourself in the papers. I honestly hated to have done it, to have kept this a secret from you for all this time, but I didn't want to see you trapped in a miserable loveless marriage,

ONCE AGAIN

because I know you would have done everything in your power
not to end it, but she would have hurt you anyway, that's her way."

Douglas sat there absolutely stunned at what he'd just heard.
He didn't know where to begin, when they both heard a small
knock on the door. "Marie," they both said and smiled. The word
was light after the heavy conversation they'd just had. It brought
lightness to each heart for different reasons.

Walter finished the eggs as Douglas answered the door. There
stood Marie, meekly and like a welcome blessing. She looked
fresh, a summer breeze after a long hot day, dressed in a white and
yellow gingham dress with a yellow sash tied about the waist. Her
Mahogany hair loosely braided and pulled over one shoulder. The
sandals on her feet showed off her nail polish and ankle bracelet.
Looking refreshed, youthful. She held a small handbag.

Doug stood with mouth agape. Marie stood there nervously
as he did't let her in saying, "I hope this is okay for shopping?"
indicating her dress, with a look of uncertainty in her eyes, as he'd
stood there gaping at her.

"What? Oh, no, you're perfect. Come in, sorry" he got out of
the way and ushered her inside, smiling to himself.

Walter was setting down the serving dishes onto the table as
she walked into the dining area, he looked up to see an apparition
before him, he was shocked.

She looked to each man one grinning from ear to ear and the
other with a strange expression. Looking down at her clothes, she
said, "I knew this wasn't the right dress I'll go change my outfit."

"No. No, don't misunderstand the situation" Walter said, "You
my dear are a vision of loveliness." Walter came over and gave

her a fatherly kiss on the cheek. Blushing deeply when he said, "Absolutely stunning, don't you agree Douglas?"

"Yes, absolutely I couldn't agree more" her blush deepened. "Here have a seat" he pulled out a seat for her. She sat demurely, setting her pocketbook down, waiting for him to say grace so they could begin the meal. Douglas still sat mystified looking at her as did Walter. She then said, "Shall I say grace? I'd like to eat please and then you guys can tell me why you have silly grins on your faces."

"I'm sorry, yes, I'll say grace" She took Douglas' hand as she did at home with her kids. She had never done it before and it shook him to the core, he didn't know why, so he swallowed down the emotion and began. "Dear God, thank you for this meal of which we're about to partake. Thank you for the hands that have made it. Bless us all your children and may we be satisfied with those blessings you so choose to give and be content. Help us to be useful in your service. Amen"

As he'd prayed something in Marie began to burn, not quite knowing what it was but this particular prayer or rather the way he 'felt it,' was...sincere?"

Opening her eyes at his 'Amen,' she caught him staring at her again, blushing again at his sincere regard, feeling like a young school girl on a first date feeling awkward. She took sip of her orange juice. Finally she had to ask, "Okay, what is it? What did I do?" she set the glass down? "You two are definitely acting so weird." Both men burst out laughing and she was thoroughly confused. "Men!" she exclaimed, smiling and shaking her head at them.

Walter recovered first, "I'm sorry my dear" he said smiling, "It's just that last night Douglas and I talked. I was telling him the story about how my wife and I met," he began explaining, pouring her a cup of coffee. "The reason we're both mystified is that your dress is nearly identical to the one she wore. I guess we were both shocked and pleased," he said with a smile on his face.

"Truly, that's all there is to it?" Giving them an apprising look.

"Yes, truly, it is so." Walter held his hand to heart. Marie looked to Doug.

"Honestly Marie, you were exactly the picture I had of Mrs. Peters in my mind as a young lady when Walter told me their story yesterday. I was so dumbfounded that's why I could not give you even a proper greeting at the door."

"Wow, that really is quite amazing. But as I've noticed recently, everything that's 'old' is 'new' again when it comes to fashion. I'm definitely more a 'classic' girl. Good fashion never goes out of style.' Just then her stomach rumbled, they all chuckled, she said, "Let's eat, Please!" Sipping her coffee. Both men took a dish and piled the food onto her plate, causing her to laugh and so the morning passed talking, laughing and telling stories all the morning.

CHAPTER 27

THE SHOPPING TRIP

Douglas could not remember a time when he'd had so much fun shopping of all things! He thought it would be tedious going from store to store Marie trying to decide what was to be worn for his 20th High School Reunion. In past experiences it had been numerous outfits from the ladies he'd gone out with, not to mention the amount of clothing they'd purchased on his dime. They would try on each one turning this way and that showing off for him and most of the time he didn't care for their choices. Sure he was a man and liked a good figure as well as any man, but the extravagant showing off, was not his 'cup of tea'. Not to mention all the extra bits of accessories and shoes! "Lord have mercy", he prayed, when he thought about it.

"Ah, Marie." She was different. They strode hand in hand, a privilege she hadn't allowed him before, he was honored. She had looked at him shyly gauging his reaction when she had taken his hand. He brought it up to his lips kissing her hand in his. 'Ah,' his heart sighed at her pretty little blush and slight intake of breath. Suddenly she stopped. Looking through a shop window.

"Oh, it's so lovely!" Her eyes sparkled in delight at the dress in the window. Douglas noticed it for the first time, his eyes having been on her instant reaction. The gown was a pale blue tea length, ball gown, with a heart shaped bodice. The sleeves being sheer lace and chiffon. The skirt was of chiffon and organza, with silver sequins having been applied so it shimmered like diamonds glittering in the sunshine. "Let's go in and have you try it on."

"No, that's okay. I couldn't afford something like that. Plus where else would I wear it? It's not a practical dress. I'll get something that will be nice but that I can use again." She backed away from the window.

This woman! He shook his head in the negative, saying softly in a dramatic French accent, making her laugh, "Non Marie" You my girl, 'deserve' that dress" he emphasized pointing at "the dress". Then more sternly "We are going in there and you are trying on "that dress", because every girl especially 'my girl', he modulated his tone hinting mischievously, pulling her close and giving her a quick kiss on the forehead, "deserves a frivolous dress, besides I'm paying remember", he winked at her, "and if I want to buy you a dress that makes your eyes sparkle and dance like they are now, I'm getting it for you."

He took her firmly by the hand so she wouldn't resist he ushered her through the doors. Telling the lady who introduced herself as 'Donna,' he wanted the dress in the window for his girl to try on. She looked at Marie with a smile on her face.

"Right this way, Miss. A size 6, correct?" Marie nodded affirmatively, Donna found her size, headed back to the dressing area, with them following. Turning to Douglas, Donna said, "You may sit and wait there" pointing to a comfortable looking armchair, situated about five feet away at the viewing area near a full length staging mirror with three full views.

Marie entered the dressing room with a full length curtained 'door'. As she changed he called over to Donna, "Could you please find three different pairs of shoes perhaps silver or a pale blue to match the gown, I think she's a size seven".

Hearing him, Marie called out "Size eight, actually".

Douglas was surprised, "No way, your feet are so small."

"Compared to yours maybe they are, but not for a woman." She said feeling snappy because she didn't like her "big feet". She finished zipping her dress, she wasn't sure why she snapped at him, so she sat down on the little stool that was available, with a feeling of dejection. "Had she offended him?" She didn't hear him say anything. Beginning to worry her fingernail and not willing to come out just yet she stayed seated.

Until she heard a low chuckle and then a low rumbling laugh. Venturing a peek through the curtain, she saw a smile on his face when he saw her peeking out saying, "Come on out girl". Let me take a look at what I'm purchasing for my darling. Let's see if it's worth the price." Coming out from behind the curtain barefooted and beautiful. She stole his breath away.

"Is it okay? Or is it too much? I think it's too much." She said shyly and clearly embarrassed, about to retreat, until he spoke.

"You are absolutely stunning! There will not be another woman at the function that will be as beautiful as you are right in this moment." He mused "You know the theme of the reunion is 'Enchanted" and you my dear girl, are going to steal the show".

Marie blushed deeply, not having had someone compliment her in such a fashion for a very long time.

"I think I need a shawl or a sweater, I feel a bit exposed."

"We can do that, I don't want you to feel uncomfortable." He stood and slid his hands down her arms taking her by the hands saying "Let me see it all" then began twirling her around again and again like a ballerina until she laughed in delight and somehow ended up in his arms. Looking deeply into her eyes he wanted to kiss her, but refrained and kissed her on the forehead instead, pulling her close, 'perfect,' while she sighed her contentment being held in his arms.

Next he had her try on the shoes that were selected. Marie tried on several pairs to go with the dress and they finally decided on the right height for both of them. A pair that was comfortable for her to wear but allowed him the advantage of height so that he could look down into her sweet face and she could look up into his eyes or lay her head on his chest. Though neither party said such thoughts aloud. Douglas was so surprised that they had found everything that she wanted in the space of two hours. This girl was a fast shopper. He thought they'd be the whole day shopping, but she refused anything more. Deciding since they had time to spare, he'd find a new suit for himself to go with her new outfit. He asked, "Will you help me pick out a new suit? I don't want to look shabby next to you this evening."

"I thought you had one with you already?"

"I do, but with you and that pretty dress, it just won't do. I'd like to get something that would go with your outfit."

"Certainly not a new suit, but perhaps a new tie and shirt? Or perhaps bowtie and cummerbund?"

"Okay, we'll see, the shop I like is just around the corner." Taking her packages carefully wrapped by the shopkeepers, tucking it under one arm like a football player, he held her hand once again as they walked out of the shop.

Watching them go, Donna said to the cashier, Joan, "If my husband treated me like that man does for her, I would be one lucky lady." *sigh*

Joan sighed as well, "If only I had someone like that I would treat him like the prince he is. If she doesn't realize what she's got I hope he stops by again!" Both ladies began to laugh.

CHAPTER 28

THE REUNION

Walter parked the limo at the front entrance of the High School. He first opened Douglas's door quickly going around and opened the door for Marie. Taking his proffered hand, she exited the vehicle and instantly felt fifty pairs of eyes looking in their direction. Ducking her head in shyness, pursing her lips to get her emotions under control. She tucked her pocketbook purse under her arm as Douglas came around. He saw her obvious discomfort so lifting her chin to meet his gaze, "Courage, now my dear. They will love you, once they get to know you."

Searching his blue eyes she asked, "How can you be so sure?"

"Because they're all staring at you wondering, 'Who is that lovely woman?" His voice husky "Asking themselves, 'What is she doing with a guy like him?" he emphasized himself in the negative. Shaking her head in amusement at his self deprecation, she took a deep breath and blew it out slowly.

"I think you're wrong. I think they're saying. How did she end up with an amazing "Apollo" of a man. They will be jealous for you".

Shaking his head in resignation, he would not win this argument he could see. She was determined to self deprecate. She would soon enough see for herself.

"Okay I'm ready to be under the microscope." With that statement, he laughed taking her hand and kissing it. Then tucking her hand to his elbow, he escorted her to the reception area inside, while Walter parked the vehicle close by being on stand-by he parked, in a spot under a light, he opened a book set to finish it by the time they returned or he was called into service.

Once in the reception area they waited in line ready to be checked off the guest list and given name tags. Approaching the front entrance to the party, every guest was then ushered into the gym by a herald like a real Ball. They could hear shouts and whistles as people recognized names they hadn't heard in years. "Name please?"

"Douglas Fairbanks and the Lady LaSalle". There was momentary silence as they stepped through the main door, the spotlight then shone onto them from above flooding them both in light. How her dress did shine and sparkle and her beauty shone out when the herald mentioned their names and the shouts and cheers that rang out for Douglas was deafening. She could not contain her smile as she looked on at Douglas the apparent 'Hero' of the school body. Douglas just shook his head and made a slashing motion across his chest for them to "cut it out," instead they got louder.

Marie had to hold her hands to her ears. That's when the crowd began to settle down. He led her forward and then they were bombarded by his team-mates. As Doug greeted them all she could see the genuine affection they had for him and the obvious camaraderie amongst the guys. After the many pats on the back and handshakes, Douglas was finally able to introduce Marie, who'd stood next to him silently waiting and watching for introduction but also for her ears to stop ringing. "This is Marie, she is a very good friend and kind enough to come with me to this shindig." There were nods and a few handshakes.

"Wow, you guys sure know how to welcome a body. That was some kind of reception" her eyes crinkling, giving a full smile. Douglas had never seen that smile before. One of pure enjoyment and affection. "Wow, she was a stunner!"

"Yeah guys" Douglas interjected "I don't think you've ever been this, shall I say, enthusiastic before" he laughed with them.

"Perhaps" Harry said, "It's not because of you Douglas, but this beautiful mystical Princess that you have brought with you here tonight." Bowing magnanimously low before her. In turn she curtsied at the compliment, turning her head just so. Then as if on cue all his mates bowed to her, she returned the favor again. Douglas saw that as they all rose, they began to laugh and they loved her right then and there. "Wow," he knew it.

"Harry, you Shakespearean devil, you! I had forgotten you were always good with the ladies."

Giving a loud guffaw Harry said, "I've been caught you know, Ah, here she is now the love of my life, Scarlet." Scarlet walked toward them a very petite and largely pregnant woman with red gold hair and dove gray eyes, naturally pink cheeks and a pert nose. Scarlet handed him a cup of punch.

"Here you go love."

"Isn't she just amazing?" He kissed her passionately in front of everyone. Harry certainly looked besotted by his little wife, Marie observed. Little though she was, she packed a wallop and hit him full on embarrassed at his overt affections.

"Harry, not in front of everyone, you silly man," she giggled her face flaming, unable to contain her husbands affections toward her. While he just smiled, beaming a toothy grin, wagging his eyebrows unapologetic.

Marie initiated, "Douglas, won't you introduce me to everyone, I hope to keep them all straight" she worried her lower lip.

Patting her hand he encouraged, "I'm sure you'll do fine. This rogue here as I said is Harry Marxen, and his wife Scarlet. Fella's please introduce your wives if I don't know them."

He pointed next to him, "This here is Stuart and his wife Olivia. As you can see, yes, Stu is Harry's twin brother." She acknowledged them with a nod and shook hands with them both.

"Alex DuBois. Is your wife, Jilly, not here?"

"Powder room," he said in quotes, I think, you can meet her later.

"This is the 'Great Fred Grover". All the fellas let out a laugh.

She said, "I bet there's a story in there somewhere."

"Yes there is Ma'am, but I won't tell it now, Maybe later, once you get to know me before you believe these fella's lies." He gave them all a stern eye. They all burst out laughing.

Doug finally said, "Let's find seats so we can catch up better."

"Sure thing" Fred pointed "We have a table over this way." "Follow me," he led the way. As they began to walk that way, Scarlet sidled up next to Marie.

"May I say you are a vision of loveliness," *Sigh* I think you'll win some sort of prize if there are any to be had." She said honestly.

Blushing at the compliment Marie thanked her, ready to reciprocate, "You look wonderfully healthy too, when are you due, if I may ask?"

Scarlet blew out a labored breath "Ach, any day now dear." Taking Marie by the hand like old friends and patting it saying, "My due date was two days ago, but no such luck as yet not even a hint of contractions. So here we are, I didn't want to come, but Harry wouldn't come without me. I did want to see everyone, so here we are, but let's not talk about that now..." they continued chatting as Douglas caught up with his friends as well.

"So what have you been up to Fred?"

"I'm in sales and marketing at the local plumbing supply. My father in law owns, it's in the family so it works out anyway as long as my wife is happy I am too," he grinned.

"Stu, what about you?"

"If you can believe it I teach here, high school math and I coach my boys' team."

Alex piped up then, "I bet they don't know how good they have it. You know if it wasn't for Stuart helping me out with my math back then, I woulda' never got off the bench to play ball." Alex looked at him then saying, "If I never said it before, 'Thanks

Stu for all your help, man."' Stu grabbed him around the neck and gave Alex a noogie.

"No worries buddy."

"Hey" Alex got out of the hold. "You'll mess up my hair." Everyone laughed. "So what is it that you do, huh, Alex."

"I'm a construction contractor. So all that math has actually paid off, I've put it all to good use everyday."

"That's great" Douglas said, 'Everyone has a different...' Harry interrupted, pointing, "Hey look who's coming everyone! I think it's Tish Mallory." Harry shouted out to her. As per her usual exuberant self she tossed her head back in a loud laugh, smiled coquettishly giving all the "boys" a hug and 'air' kiss. She was dressed rather scantily in a short cocktail dress too short for her height. She stopped in front of Douglas and patted his cheek instead and sighed.

"If Only" with puppy dog eyes suggesting something had been between them in the past. Marie wasn't jealous, not really, she had no right. These were his people, his intimates in the past...' Looking on at the exchange. Being seized from behind, Marie yelped. Douglas's eyes zeroed in on her, seeing a man turn her quickly around, her arms flying up over her head and landing squarely on a man's shoulders, who looked vaguely familiar but Douglas didn't know why. Marie's hair spun around, her soft curls landing back in place except for one errant strand that lay across a cheek. Taking it off her face the man then proceeded to kiss her cheek, reverently.

Douglas saw red, with a capital 'R'. He didn't care who this man was, he stood up and was about to go over there and drag him out by his ear if necessary, just as quickly the fuse was struck, out it went when he saw Marie flash a sign of recognition, smiling in unbelief, mouth open.

"Marie, my dear! I never expected to see such a friendly face at one of these functions." Unable to contain himself, kissing both her cheeks, holding her at arms length, he exclaimed, "Let me look at you". He twirled her around. "Ah, Que Bella" he kissed his fingers, exclaiming, "So much more beautiful than I remember, so lovely, divine."

"Franklin, you sneaky devil! How good it is to see you! My word, it's been ages and ages" she said kissing his slightly rotund cheeks in return.

"What are you doing here? I thought you were still in Texas? And what a surprise to find you here." He hugged her again he was so excited, and she reciprocated laughing to see such a friend. Everyone was stunned at the two, seeming to be in their own world, especially Tish and Douglas.

"Ahem". Tish cleared her voice protesting loudly, saying, "Honey? Are you going to introduce us?" Frank finally noticed his wife and the consternation he saw on her face.

"Oh, My dear, come and meet my friend Marie. Goodness I haven't seen her in...' he blustered, "How long do you think, Marie?" he redirected the question to her.

'Goodness..., probably not since college, it seems ages ago," she gestured laughing. Spying Douglas out of the corner of her eye, because she'd been faced away from him. The emotions that registered across his face held a mix, confusion, anger, jealousy, and hurt? 'Oh she didn't like that'. Her heart hurt to see that look on his face. Or the fact that he held all those in at a low simmer. Her desire to be a peacemaker, and calm his mind.

"Franky, let me introduce you to my good friend and benefactor for this evening. My Lord Douglas Fairbanks". At this sign of respect she curtsied and held her hand directed towards him.

Douglas took her proffered hand, pulling her to himself, holding her to his side, as if to say "back off, she's mine." Acknowledging Frank with a nod of his head and not a handshake, saying as politely as he could, "How do you do?"

"I'm fine now that there are two familiar faces" he said jovially. Tish came to stand by her husband, not to be outdone by this girl, this usurper, she took her husbands hand then, "So how is the food my dear?"

"It's fair considering it's a buffet, but of course I could have done better."

"So are you a chef?" Harry asked.

"Honey?" Scarlet questioned him "Don't you know Frank Oliver when he's standing right in front of you? She turned to Frank and Tish, "I'm sorry."

"Oh my Really!" He smacked his head, "No, you're not 'The Frank Oliver' from that cooking show 'Oliver's Offerings," are you?

"Yes, I am." He stated rather proudly mildly offended.

"Wow". It's just I didn't recognize you without the beard," he remarked. Mollified for the moment, Frank said, "Like Marie says, I am 'a sneak". I was hoping to be incognito so I wouldn't be harassed by the general public. Being a celebrity sometimes can be quite tiresome." Douglas heard a waltz begin to play, as the others were talking with Frank engaging him in conversation, asking him questions about his life.

He took the opportunity to gently pull Marie away to whisper in Marie's ear "Shall we dance?" She turned to him looking into his eyes, seeing a fire burning there for her attention, biting her lip.

"I suppose, I just hope I remember the steps from the class." Douglas excused them and just like that Frank Oliver was forgotten. He kept her on the dance floor waltzing to several songs He knew he was monopolizing her time, but couldn't help not sharing her with anyone else. They talked, about nothing and everything, she was having a wonderful time with him floating her across the dance floor. You could hear her delighted laugh across the room if you paid attention to it. He caused her to laugh again and again, loving to hear the sound of it. Then Stu caught their attention waved them over, it was time to dine.

Scarlet had saved them both a place to sit since she was winded after the first few minutes on the dance door. Scarlet sat with Harry and others who didn't want to dance. Harry was undoubtedly excited about this baby he had made sure his dearest was completely comfortable and brought everything to her like a servant. Though she could hardly hold very much down, she was so large, she said, "There's just not much room to spare anymore". To which the table laughed.

"I would like to have some cheese cake, oh, and milk if they have it. I know I shouldn't but I have had such a craving ever since I saw it." Saying it sheepishly. Marie patted her hand, having sat next to Scarlet.

"I know the feeling! With my last one I couldn't get enough milk, I must have drunk a gallon a day and forget about the last month! I ate a pint of B.J's ice cream every night!" she laughed at herself and the remembrance of feeling like a whale.

"You have children, really? I wouldn't have thought you had any children at all, you are so slim and lovely." Scarlet declared.

Marie blushed at her praise, "Thank you for the compliment, I am blessed."

"May I ask how many children you have?" Everyone at the table seemed to hold their breath awaiting her answer listening to their conversation. No one had suspected she'd had children as they knew Douglas had never dated anyone with children before now.

"I had four, three boys and one daughter." Not looking at anyone around her as she'd said it looking down into her lap at her empty hands. Douglas saw her distress, and reached for her hand under the table, comforting her. She looked up at him and smiled her acceptance.

Scarlet continued with questions oblivious to her new friends' sudden shyness. "What are their names and ages?" Marie held on tighter to Doug's hand as if to fortify herself. It was not always easy to speak of the son she'd lost. So she omitted him usually. Sethy is six and a half, he just Kindergarten, little Lizzie is five, she's a little firecracker who's completed K4 and Sam is two she finished.

Tish hadn't missed the discrepancy of the children she'd named "I thought you said, you had four? You only mentioned three?" saying it in an accusatory tone as if she'd lied. Douglas squeezed her hand, when Marie's eyes flashed daggers quite quickly at Tish's accusatory tone. He interjected for her calmly.

"Marie's oldest son Robbie and her husband Robert died tragically in a car accident a few years ago."

"A Widow!" Tish exclaimed horridly, her hand going to her chest.

"Tish!" Frank fairly shouted at his wife with a tone of disapproval, intoning she'd gone too far. She sat chagrined. He generally didn't mind her attitude of general disdain for most people, for most were fools, in his opinion, but Marie was none of those. She had always been special to him. Had always encouraged him when no one else believed in him. Apologizing to Marie offering condolences, "I'm so sorry Marie, I hadn't heard about Robert or Robbie. Your husband was a very special man indeed."

"Thank you, Franklin, I appreciate it."

Scarlet becoming teary, touched Marie's forearm sending her comfort by the motion. Marie looked up briefly "He was very special. There was none like him." Not looking at anyone else at the table she rose and excused herself from the table. Realizing she'd excluded Douglas by her comment.

Almost everyone turned fiery flashing eyes at Tish, when Marie had walked away a distance, they being in dismay as she alone had caused the hurt in the eyes of their beautiful new friend. It only added to the mystery and allure of her strong quietude. Tish looked back glaring at everyone in turn, "What, I only asked what everyone was thinking! I just asked her a simple question". Pursing her lips she defended herself, crossing her arms over her chest. Frank sat unbelieving at his wife. That she could be so unfeeling.

All the while Douglas's eyes followed Marie. He knew she hadn't meant to exclude him, at least he thought not. Robert was her husband, he would always hold a place in her heart. He just hoped she would give him a little slice of hers. Giving her a moment to herself, when he saw her look back at him, making sure that he saw where she was going, he then knew she understood he still had a need to protect her on this outing. She sent him a silent invitation to wait a moment before following her out. Then she walked out of the side door that led towards the football field.

Scarlet had followed Doug's gaze, when he excused himself from the table, weaving his way towards where Marie had exited the building. She sighed quite happily saying, "Besotted, he is."

Harry smiled at his wife, "You are quite the romantic." He kissed her nose. "Finally, someone worthy of his love and attention."

Lovingly she looked at her husband, shaking her head "You've got it all wrong, my love. It's the reverse." Quieting his protestations with a kiss that brooked no argument.

"Oh Puh-leeze, get a room!" Tish exclaimed disgusted at their blatant display of affection for one another. Both giggled like children caught with their hands in the cookie jar with crumbs already on their faces. They didn't care one wit what anyone else had to say about their affection. Harry lifted Scarlet to her feet, "One last dance, my dearest love?" She nodded her consent a happy smile wreathed on her face.

As Douglas walked out into the night, he noticed the stars as they shone out brightly. All a body could see was the manifold witness of God's greatness in his creation. He spotted Orion, Ursa Major and several other constellations, not a cloud was in the sky above, as clear as day was the night. The moon was full but waning in its circuit. Breathing deeply of the fresh air, he surveyed the surroundings looking for Marie. Instead he spotted Walter standing within a short distance that if Marie was in any danger he would be close to hand.

Walter had turned at the sound of the door when Doug had stepped out. Since it was him, he'd jerked his head in her direction. Not wishing to disturb Marie by the sound of his voice. As Douglas drew near he whispered asking "How does she seem?" He watched her sitting on the grass a handbreadth out of the circle of light, just as Frank had described her, "Lovely and divine". She had let down her hair. It flowed over her shoulders cascading like a shawl down her back. She looked like a flower, her dress surrounding her like petals on a flower in full bloom, she'd taken off her shoes and they lay to one side. He thought about what Walter had told him the lesson Ernesto had given to him.

Walter broke into his thoughts, "She's strong that one. I saw her come out and asked if there was anything that she needed, because you were not with her. She told me "I just need to speak with my father," I attempted to hand her my phone, she gave a small laugh, amused. "No" stilling my hand, "not that one, the one who sees me here" pointing to her heart. Then only used my arm as a brace to take off her shoes and went and sat on the grass out there. Looking up into the clear sky a moment silently calling to him to hear her, then bowed her head in prayer. She must have just finished, for she's lifted her head now, but I haven't heard a word from her since". They both looked on.

Shifting her position she sat up knees bent, laying her chin on them, looking out into the dark starry night. She didn't turn as she heard Douglas approach, she felt him lay her shawl about her shoulders. "Thank You". He smiled but didn't look at her, as he sat down next to her one knee drawn up one arm extended from atop his knee, the other stretched out behind her. Wanting her to feel he was near but not obtrusive. Not wanting to encroach upon her thoughts, he remained silent. After a time she said, "Is dessert ready?"

That through him so off guard he laughed heartily. Then said, "And here I thought you were contemplating the deep mysteries of the universe." He could not contain his smile, laughing once again.

She gave a smile at his own enjoyment, then turning her head towards him, looked serious, and leaning her head to one side, "I was, but I'm done for now and at peace. She smiled mischievously, her eyes sparkling. "But you know with all that thinking, it's made me kinda' hungry." She crinkled her nose at him playfully. Suddenly time stood still as he looked into her luminous eyes. There was no sound, no breeze, no people, just the two of them. Right then and there he knew inexplicably for the first time in his life that he was truly in love.

His hand reached out of its own volition and cupped her face, it was as if he was watching himself doing this from afar. He kissed her softly on the cheek. As he pulled away, she took his face in both hands and she kissed him on the lips. He felt as if an explosion of fireworks was set off inside of him. "Wow, wow, wow, glorious". He pulled her back, to make sure this is what she wanted, but she turned away clearly shocked and embarrassed at her impetuous behavior.

"Stammering she said, '..I...I...I don't know what...what came over me. I'm sorry.' Tear filling her eyes.

"Don't be sorry, because that means you regret it and if you regret it, then how am I going to reconcile with the fact that I'm in love with you." There he'd said it, he laid himself bare for real this time come what may. Marie choked back her tears, biting her knuckle.

"...In...in love with me?" She searched his tear filled eyes. He shook his head affirmatively. "Oh Douglas!" Throwing her arms around him she began to cry, he pulled her close into his bosom. Not for the last time he kissed her on the top of her head feeling a keen sense that he'd never felt before. "It must be true love". His heart soared into the heavens as did his eyes, he looked up thanking God above for this love He'd put into his heart. He was feeling so light, yet as deep and strong as a current in a river. He laughed towards the heavens, his heart full. Nothing else mattered except this to be with her if she'd allow him to marry her and they could be together.

From his position Walter watched over them, witnessing the silence of companionship, the laugh of friendship and the look that fanned the spark into a flame. Followed by the tender kiss that unlocked the door of love. He'd felt it a great privilege to have been a witness of love's first kiss. Thinking to himself that the Lord was indeed very happy that two of his beloved children had found one another accepting his grace and acceptance, hopefully of their coming union.

In that moment Harry and Scarlet came out quietly, seeing Walter, Harry asked, "May I help you in some way sir?" His guard went up because he'd been observing the couple on the lawn.

"No, sir. I believe you're, Harry, am I correct?" he held out his hand, when Harry hesitated, Walter said, "I'm Mr. Fairbanks personal assistant."

"Personal assistant?" Harry questioned.

"Yes, it sounds more snazzy than, 'bodyguard,' doesn't it?"

"Oh, yes. But how'd you know me?"

"The yearbook photos in the gallery, it's my job to know people and remain vigilant. I'd say except for a few extra pounds you look pretty good for thirty-nine." Drawing attention away from himself and back on them. "I'm guessing this is your lovely wife, Scarlet, is it?" taking her hand he kissed it, "You are quite lovely my dear, if I may say, you've done very well indeed young man."

Blushing deeply she said "I know, you're just being kind, but I don't look or feel very lovely at the moment, but thank you for the compliment all the same."

Walter admonished her gently, "Any sensible man is never more in love with his wife than when she's carrying his child. His love for wife and child grows exponentially, when it is a love like yours. A love for God and hearth and home." He winked at her, making her blush once more. Harry beamed at his wife confirming the statement, while she got all teary eyed.

"Oh look what you've gone and done. With these wild hormones, you've gone and made me cry." She wiped at her quick tears, Harry offered her a hanky.

"Only stating the truth, besides they are happy tears, are they not? Never to be regretted ma'am."

Marie sat against Douglas, her tears having been spent. Enjoying the feeling of being held by a man who declared his love for her. She hadn't realized how she'd longed for love to return unto her. She'd kept it hidden in the recesses of her heart for fear of hurt not only for herself, but that of her children, if things didn't work out between herself and whomever she'd gone out with. But now her children would be loved by a father figure, if not a father, then at least a good friend. She had no doubt they would accept and respect and even possibly love him should she decide to really marry him.

The wind picked up causing her to shiver and bringing softly the voices speaking in the background. Douglas saw her shiver, so he shifted himself to block her from the breeze. "You're cold. We should head inside and get you all warmed up."

"I'm a mess though, aren't I, from crying?" she wiped at her eyes, sniffing then looked up at him for his disapproval of her looks.

"No, you look even more beautiful now than ever before," he wiped a stray tear from her cheek. She smiled unbelieving.

'You've said that to me before, 'Liar'. She winked at him, "But thank you for thinking so all the same."

"Marie, I never lie, honesty is always the best policy." Reaching into his pocket making a swift decision, he produced a small box containing the ring he'd been waiting for the last two months for just the right time to give it to her. "I think this will show more than my words can convey, to you that I'm no liar and how serious I am, about us." Taking her right hand, not her left, he slid the ruby and diamond princess cut ring on to her forefinger. She looked at him quizzically.

"In Jewish tradition the ring is placed on the forefinger of the right hand signifying it is the prominent digit, that all may know you are promised to me. When we marry, it will be placed on your left hand because that vein, that runs from the your ring finger directly to your heart," her heart skipped a beat, he continued, "now the Jews believe a simple gold ring should be used, so that all may see a determinable value, thus how much you are worth as a bride."

He paused a moment collecting his thoughts, "But you, my dear Marie, I believe with all my heart are a virtuous woman, and 'Your price" is far above rubies. I see how you fear the Lord wholly. Therefore I want all the world to see that you, 'God's daughter' as such are valuable. You have great value far greater than a simple gold band." His heart soared and filled him with the truth in his words challenging even himself to be a better man than he was for her sake.

Sitting in silence, she was looking at the beautiful ring how it glittered and shone. Not knowing what to say at all. "You don't have to give me an answer right away, like I said before. I just wanted you to know that I am in earnest, wanting to win your heart."

For not the first time she caught him off guard by asking, "So... you're Jewish?" He laughed as he stood up and pulled her to her feet.

"No, but I have a Jewish friend or two and I ask them lots of questions. Because How can one know Christ without knowing his customs and culture? Well, at least understand a bit more about the day and time he lived in."

"Hmm. I'd never thought of it like that. Do they have books about it that can be recommended I read?"

"Do you like to read?"

"I love to read. My perfect day would be spent by either the lake in summer or a fireplace in winter cuddled up reading a good book. The subject doesn't matter. I try to read one "broccoli" book tempered by a "sweet" book." They walked hand in hand, her shoes in her other hand.

"Okay, I need to know, what's a 'broccoli book?'"

"You know one that you 'need" to help you grow in your life spiritually or emotionally, it's good for you even though you may not like it at first. So obviously a 'sweet' book is just something fun and short, but doesn't require a lot of insight to be nourished, its just "a treat".'

"Oh, I get it."

"Are you a reader?"

"I guess you could say so, I'm more a broccoli book guy. I took up speed reading long ago; I read two or three books a week. There's no other kinds for me because I'm always trying to stay ahead in my business. I have to keep up. All work and very little play time."

You put me to shame. I wish I had or could make the time to read so many books. But I have to ask, do you really get a lot out of it? I mean with the speed reading?"

"Well, most of them are business minded books, and many authors repeat key virtues of how to be a better business person or whatever the case may be, but real truth is universal, so you chew the meat and spit out the bones. Anyhow I didn't imagine you had much time for reading, having to take care of kids and working and all the millions of things mothers have to do."

"Did you mean, 'How can a mother of three rambunctious children possibly find any time to read at all? Especially, with dating a man who has been thoughtful, honest in his intentions, warm and caring and most of all makes her laugh and cry on the side?'' She giggled at that, he smiled.

"I'll tell you when I find time to read. I actually carry a book with me everywhere I go. The children also still have an early bedtime, so once they've been tucked into bed with prayers said for the night I have a few hours to myself. I often prep for the following morning, but once that's done I have time for myself. I try not to watch television, I find it to be such a time waster a distraction I don't need. I'd rather occupy my mind with a good book, even one that pricks my heart and helps me to change for the better. There's so much wrong with me. I don't know if I'll ever be good enough." *sigh*

"You know you shouldn't be so hard on yourself. What you glean at your own pace is given no matter when the impact is made. It was meant for that time and place. That I learned a long time ago". He stopped walking and caressed her cheek knowing he would never forget her.

"There's so much wrong with me. I don't know if I'll ever be good enough,'" she sighed heavily.

"Are you always so hard on yourself? Please don't put yourself down it's not healthy."

"Maybe, I am I wouldn't really know. I think I used to be more fun, but with the pressures of being a widow, a single mother, sole provider, I suppose I expect a lot from myself. Being both mother and sometimes 'father'. I have to be tough and not let the kids 'run wild' or run all over me." She shrugged, deflated. "Don't get me wrong I love being a mom, but there are times, not often mind you, when work does get in the way. I try not to let it and since I work for my Dad, I kind of can get away with things now and again. I don't try and take advantage of his good graces, so I try to work extra hard for him while I'm there."

Douglas thought to himself, '...she works for her dad? Who is her dad? Did he work at Dean and Perry, too?'

"My parents often admonish me to take all the time I can because the kids are young and need me now to help develop and shape their lives. So what they see me do and how I behave will help them in their future. Time right now is so precious, I won't have them to hold onto forever."

"You are a good mother you know." Holding up his hand seeing she was about to contest him, he paused them in their walk. "That was a statement not a question." Taking her by both hands, he looked into her face. "When we are married your life will become a bit easier. You will not have to be both mother and father. I am hopeful that the children will allow me to be their father and I can help take that burden off of your shoulders. Then You'll be able to see yourself in a singular role again, as it was meant to be, a good mom to your kids. You may also choose not to work if you don't want to, or do work if you so choose. I won't stand in your way either way. But I hope that you take not working into consideration."

He kissed the top of her hand, she shivered, for it was growing chilly, and she held her peace for once. Feeling rather giddy as if a burden that she bore on her shoulders were slowly beginning to lift at his kind words. She kissed the top of his hand as well. Seeing movement, Douglas saw that they were now not the only ones out and about. Many people began to filter outside for some much needed fresh air. Harry caught his eye giving Doug a lopsided grin with a wink to boot.

"How about a quick game of ball, for old times sake? I'm sure I could round up a few of the fella's. I could get the coach to turn on the lights, huh...huh..?" Nudging him with his elbow when he came to his side. Harry lifting his eyebrows up and down in quick succession, like when they were kids and about to get into some "fun trouble" he used to call it. It was always fun, but they always got into trouble.

"I don't know Harry…, we're all dressed up and I haven't played since college." He hedged.

"Hey Stu, Doug says "He's too old" he air quoted, "to play a game of ball. I don't think he remembers how to play."

"Too Old!" Douglas gesticulated, "Now wait a cotton pickin' minute…!"

Stu chimed in, '…Nay! He's just gotten too fancy for the rest of us, doesn't want to mess up that fancy thousand dollar suit of his, that's all."

"Hey, that's…" Douglas wasn't allowed to finish the statement.

"No, no, no, it's not that." Fred chimed in, "He just thinks he'll make a fool of himself in front of his girl, 'The Fairy Lady LaSalle".

"Since when did that ever stop him" Tish cried out, egging him on.

Everyone was smiling, even Marie, at their joshing him. She held an amused smile on her face and a silent challenge in her eyes. Would he give in?"

Douglas looked to Walter then. He was absolutely no help at all as he held out his hand for his coat and phone and anything else he wished to hand over. Knowing his pride was on the line more than anything else. Letting out a frustrated sigh, he bellowed "Fine"!

Everyone cheered, Harry whooped, 'All right! Stu, turn on the lights!' He exclaimed as he threw his tie into the air. "I'm gonna go get more fellas." Harry sprinted towards the gym leaving his wife with Marie.

Beginning to undo his tie, Doug also decided to take off his hundred dollar shirt he just bought. No sense ruining it with grass stains. Marie held out her hands feeling slightly guilty, telling him, "You know you really don't have to do this? They really won't hold it against you, you know?" She looked at him seriously and a little guiltily.

He placed the cufflinks in her hands, curling her fingers around them, these are important, they're my fathers, keep them safe. He took his jacket off draping it over her shoulders to keep her warm, "And you are kidding right? I will never live it down if I don't do this. Anyway it should be fun to see if I've still got "the touch" he winked at her. He sat on the bench to take off his shoes and socks.

"I'm sure it'll be second nature for you. Your mind and body doesn't forget, just like riding a bike, right?"

"We'll see, I guess, especially when the aches and pains begin to hit full force tomorrow." He laughed, rolling up his pants to his knees. Marie giggled, when she saw his feet and legs. But attempted to turn away. "What, are my feet that ugly?" he asked with arched eyebrows.

"No, it's just a girl thing, you would't understand." Before he could ask what she meant, he stood up. Someone threw him the football, he saw it was heading towards Marie, he caught it just in time before it hit her, without thinking. She gasped at his speed, then smirked, 'Second nature,' winking at him in return, he kissed her cheek, and walked off. Marie turned around and began walking to take a seat on the bleachers as a mob of guys descended around him dressed as he was in their best trousers rolled to their knees, white under t-shirts and barefooted.

CHAPTER 29

JOHNNY AND SCARLET'S STORY

As the men picked their teams and loosened up older tired muscles, Marie smiled at men playing at being boys. Scarlet who sat next to her, also wearing her beloved's coat, took Marie's arm in her own in a gesture of friendship, like old girlfriends would when sharing secrets. It endeared her all the more to Marie to know that she was accepted by these kind people, friend's of Douglas's, touched her deeply.

Douglas gave a final look in their direction before the game began. Noticing also that Walter stood within a quick distance should either party require his assistance, yet far enough away to give them some private space, especially Marie. The game began, men running, the snap of the ball...

Scarlet broke into her thoughts, "You know besides my Harry, I've never seen a man so in love before." She nodded her head towards Douglas.

"Do you really think so?" She questioned.

"Personally, I judge a man by his actions and his friends. How do they treat him and vice versa? What is that man like when he thinks no one is looking? How does he treat his enemies? Or better yet how do they treat him...? Look, do you see that man that Douglas is helping up?"

"Yes, that big burly red headed one?"

"That's Johnny McTavish. Harry told me that he never really liked him, partly because he always seemed to have a chip on his shoulder. He seemed to get into fights regularly and brag about it in Jr. high school...

'...It was their sophomore year in high school when they all found out by accident that, the fighting "off campus" was not the real story." Scarlets gaze wandered off.

"What is the real story?"

"Johnny was defending his mother and little sister against his Fathers' rages. So all the black eyes were borne by him, all the bruises from being kicked and knocked down were felt all by him."

"Everyone had just assumed he'd been fighting other kids in the neighborhood. But he was really defending the defenseless, from a drunken father. No one ever even suspected because Johnny's dad was a well dressed and well respected businessman in town. He was always kind to other people, but it didn't run deep. Once he came home and got to drinking he became a different person altogether."

"Harry and Douglas only found out when Doug had forgotten a book he needed from his locker, they had turned back to go get it, when they heard crying behind the bleachers. No one else had been around, so they went to investigate and found him there holding his little sister, she was about ten years old at the time. Her arm was badly broken and bruised.

Johnny hand't heard them coming to see what it was all about, when he did see them, and their obvious concern for his sister. All the tough guy attitude left and he pleaded for help, because this was something beyond his scope. Douglas had sent Harry for his Dad, who was the town doctor. Here was John a six foot plus teen built like a steam engine, falling to pieces over his little sister, thinking she might die, she was so battered. He'd seen her come running to the school through the back wood of the property and had collapsed in his arms.

Harry's father had come and got her stable enough to transport her taking her in his car personally to the local hospital, working on her himself.

In the meantime the sheriff caught up with Johnny's dad and arrested him for child endangerment, then they went to the home and found my mother dead. Whether she was pushed or had fallen down the stairs we will never know. He was eventually charged with manslaughter and sentenced to seventy years in prison once the state also realized Johnny was being beaten regularly. "That was the worst best day ever."

"You're Johnny's sister then?"

"Yes, red hair can't you tell?

"I would have said your hair was auburn, more reddish brown".

"I dye it brown sometimes, but the red still comes through". Then rolling up her sleeve so that Marie could see the scar. "I don't usually tell people how I got this." Scarlet revealed the length of her arm. Somehow I thought you might need to know what kind of man Douglas is, even when he was a young man. I also trust you won't hurt him. He's very special to all of us, even though we don't see him that often."

"I'm very sorry for the loss of your mother. A mother is precious to have to lose and in such a way so young."

"It was for the best". Don't take me wrong, I know God could have worked things out differently, but my mother didn't know until it was too late that she'd married an unbeliever. A few months after their marriage his non existent faith began to show along with his ugly side. Poor mother. At the time of my mother's death we had no living relatives or ones that would deign to take us in. So instead of us being turned over to social services and possibly be separated. Douglas had entreated his mother and father to take us in until other arrangements could be made.

Douglas though just a teen along with his mother, had looked and asked around for potential caretakers for us. They found us a home with an older childless couple. We had seen them in church before, so we sort of knew them.

Dougray and Sue Thomason. They'd been married about twenty years and had tried to have kids and even attempted adoption, but it didn't work out for them. I think God allowed it because he was waiting to give us to them".

"What a lovely way to see it."

Scarlet smiled "The Thomason's loved the Lord and when we came along they just loved us right away. I'd never been enveloped in such loving arms. Johnny was a bear for a while you can imagine, he couldn't trust their love for him. I'm glad they stuck it out. On a particular day he'd been particularly boorish, but they said to him

"Our love for you and your sister is unconditional. It wouldn't matter what we did or even said about them, they felt in their heart that we were theirs to take care of no matter what, so that's what they were going to do. We were a gift to them and they wouldn't squander that love, because we were given into their care". That night I saw my brother come to terms with his own bad behavior and really his own sin, by being angry at God for all his suffering. He realized he needed a savior because like Jesus, Dougray, showed unconditional love towards him. He was saved by God's amazing grace that night as did I rededicate myself to the Lord. From that point forward they truly became the mother and father that we needed. We called them Dad and Mother. Because they were our parents.

"Isn't God so good? Sending us what we need just when we need it?"

"Yes, he is. When Johnny went off to college on a football scholarship my father was transferred to Scotland, of course I fit in and Johnny spent his summers with Doug working in construction or on the farm his parents had, before they moved to Montana.

"Douglas's parents own a farm? I can't picture it, or construction for that matter. He's so posh."

"He surely did as I'm sitting next to you. His plan was to have the understanding of the building process from the ground up. To learn the trades as best as possible and become a successful business man not taking 'the little guy' for granted. Paying fair wages to his workers."

"How do you know all this?"

"Well, I listen and back when I was in Scotland, I yearned for letters from home. I was a pen-pal with Douglas for many years along with many of their friends. At one point I thought I loved Douglas, romantically. I later realized I love him like a brother, since his own sister isn't here to protect him, I guess I am. She chuckled, by the way, He passed the test."

"What do you mean, 'He?' I thought I was the one under scrutiny. Nah, we girls have to stick together. There's less of us and way more of them." She laughed, something that Marie would call "cute".

She continued her story, "So anyway, in High school I was able to come back home. I had met Harry again and at first I hadn't recognized him. He was a college guy then and had a scruffy beard."

I'll never forget that first Sunday back in church, he was in town for winter break with his parents. He brought me a bag of Hershey's kisses. He said they were to remind me. At first I didn't understand what he was talking about. It took me a couple of days actually."

"What were you supposed to remember?"

"To remember to send a kiss to my mother and be thankful that I was alive, even though she wasn't here I could still have sweet reminders of her kisses."

"That's so sweet."

"He told me that way back when I'd come out of surgery and he'd brought me a few kisses. He said that "One of God's kisses towards me was to send me a new mother and father who could show us how to have a real loving family, because God could do it." He had such faith on our behalf. She smiled at the remembrance.

We were married after I graduated High school and he finished college. I was eighteen and he was twenty-four. God has blessed me so much over the years. God is good."

"Yes, God is good. Thank you so much for sharing your story with me. I feel as if we can be real good friends. If I may I feel as if we've been friends all our lives. Isn't it neat how the Lord knits our hearts together as believers."

"True Christians are like that, as are small towns like ours and a thriving church community."

"What time are services on Sunday? I was hoping to attend."

"Sunday school is nine-fifteen and regular service is at ten thirty in the morning. The evening service is at six in the evening."

"Really, that's great. I have heard of some churches not having an evening service, can you believe that?"

"I know, especially since the Bible clearly states, David's words proclaimed in the Psalm 134:1-2, 'Bless ye the LORD, all ye servants of the LORD, which by night stand in the house of the LORD. Lift up your hands in the sanctuary, and Bless the Lord.'

"Isn't it wonderful that the Bible has an answer for every situation?"

"Yes, I...Oooh. I mean yes, I...Oooh." she doubled over.

"Scarlet what's the matter? Is it the baby?" Giving a look of horror and then amusement Scarlet nodded, yes, beginning to laugh, then stopped. Ooh...'

"Walter"! Marie yelled, "Get the men!" He looked from one woman to the other and the look on Scarlets face made him realize the situation, he had been so engrossed in watching the game. Douglas was a really good quarterback. Marie, snapped at him when he hesitated a moment too long, "It's the baby."

He sprang into action at her insistence, trotting onto the field so that he could be in Douglas's purview. Doug snapped the ball, right before he was taken down by one of the opposing team. 'Oh,' Walter thought, "that's going to hurt tomorrow."

Harry helped Douglas up off the grass as the play ended. "Hold on a minute guys" Douglas did a 'T' with his hands indicating a time out. What's the matter?"

"Douglas, Harry, you'd better come quick. The baby's coming, uh, now." Harry looked over to the bleachers and saw Marie helping Scarlet who was somewhat doubled over, down the steps and towards the parking lot. Harry turned around and yelled "Games over fella's, I gotta go, I'm going to be a Dad tonight!" He whooped. All the men whooped and cheered for him, as the three men walked off the field.

CHAPTER 30

PAPARAZZI

At the hospital they did not have to wait long as Andrew Dougray Marxen, entered the world at 11:05 pm. Just two hours after their arrival. Marie was so relieved and tired as she felt the adrenaline begin to leave her body. Knowing that most anything could happen. Today had been full of high emotions all around. It was a wonder her body hadn't given out yet.

Next to her Douglas had been beside her the whole time nervous as a cat. For his friend would be a new father, but this was his own first experience having to wait for news, his faithful friend and assistant Walter waiting "in the shadows" should they require anything.

Harry finally emerged through the double doorway, looking as pleased as punch, saying 'It's a boy'! Congratulations were shouted all around as others had trickled in, some had come and gone knowing it may be awhile but lending their support all the same by their presence.

After all the congratulations, most began to wander home. Doug stayed around seeing what he could do, if anything. Harry pulled him aside, 'Scarlet would like Marie to come and visit tomorrow, if possible. The poor dear could hardly keep her eyes open, he was a big boy for her to get out. She could barely keep her eyes open to feed the lad,' he beamed.

"How big was he then?" Marie asked.

"An eight pounder, bless her. She did it though."

"How wonderful, I just love chunky babies!" She squealed in delight. "I'll come by if that's okay, Douglas?" she turned to him questioning her request.

"I think that works out, I have a meeting that will last until noon, I didn't want to leave you alone all that time, but it's something I can't avoid resolving tomorrow. I'll be busy until noon? Does that give you enough time?" Doug asked.

"That's perfect, I don't want to tax her energies". She turned to Harry, "so I'll come around ten in the morning and stay until about noon or so?" She wanted him to give the okay time wise.

"Sounds great to me, see you then." Impulsively he gave her a kiss on the cheek and a hug. "I'm really glad to have met you." His eyes danced in amusement. "Now to call all the relatives…" he chuckled as he shook Douglas's hand "See you later my friend," then walked back to his wife.

Doug and Marie watched him walk away, not realizing that they had been naturally holding hands drawing and giving comfort to one another by that simple action. "Shall we?" Douglas gestured toward the exit with his other hand.

"Yes, let's get out of here." Suddenly realizing where she was and all the emotions slamming into her, stole her breath. She coughed, trying to hide her discomfort at being in a hospital, but she'd done it for Scarlet. "Baby steps"

"Are you okay?" Douglas asked.

"Yes, fine" She lied, "just a dry throat". She cleared her throat. "I'm glad I got to be here for her, my new friend". The adrenaline began to wear off even more so covering her mouth she yawned. "Oh, excuse me." Without a word he put his arm around her waist, guiding her out to the car. She didn't protest but put her head on his shoulder as the car was not very far away, but it was quite chilly out, being so late in the evening, she still wore his coat draped over her shoulders. Walter had gone ahead and brought the car around, he was waiting with the car warming, so Douglas opened the door for Marie, she got in and closed it herself as he came around the other side and sat next to her. She'd tucked her feet under herself and was arranging her shawl about her shoulders to get warm beneath it putting his coat over her legs like a blanket.

"Getting comfortable, I see."

"Why not? It's a ways to the hotel, so I may as well take a little nap, so I can walk to my room and you won't have to carry me" she teased.

The image that produced in his mind made him smile. He would love to have the privilege of carrying her..., over a threshold.

"I haven't been up this late since our ladies retreat last year, and I didn't make it past midnight." She covered her mouth to hide a yawn, "Oh, excuse me".

"Hey, don't do that"...'yawn'... "it's contagious, you know" he managed to say through a yawn.

"I'm sorry, but"...'yawn'... "I'm so tired". She began to giggle.

"What's so funny?"

"Nothing".

"What do you mean,"Nothing"? Something made you laugh." Giggling again, saying through the giggles, "I'm sorry, sometimes when I'm really tired, I find everything funny and it doesn't even have to be anything a normal person in their right mind would find funny at all. It's all 'fair game.'"

"So if I made a funny face at you..."

"Oh please don't. I'm going to close my eyes now so I won't have to see whatever it is you're doing." She giggled closing her eyes.

"But you can't resist taking a look at me...I can wait you out you know."

"Stop it Douglas, I can feel you watching me..., stop..." she laughed.

"I am doing no such thing." He said with a smile in his voice.

"Oh yes you are! I can feel it." She said with eyes closed, then she gave a peek and he was close by making a silly face, she laughed out loud, exuberantly, then clapped a hand over her mouth to quiet the sound. "Please stop" she asked, once she gained control of herself.

"I can't promise that, now that I KNOW your secret." He wagged his eyebrows at her. All mirth and color drained from her face looking mortified. His look grew concerned and then from somewhere deep inside, she burst out laughing again, his shocked expression made her laugh even harder. She tried to speak, "I'm sorry,"...hahaha...,I...,hahaha,...can't...hahaha,...stop...it... hahaha, now...hahaha," taking a deep breath...,'A-hahaha, hahaha".

At that point she just couldn't contain herself and laughed no matter how hard she tried to stop it, she laughed until the tears streaked down her face. Douglas had caught the bug and laughed with a deep resonant laugh that tickled her on the inside and so she laughed at his laugh, which then caused her to give a snort and stopped for a moment, but that made him guffaw and so she laughed and the cycle began once again.

Upon reaching the hotel, they both had spent plenty of tears from having laughed so hard. Realizing where they were, they both began to take deep breaths to calm themselves. Marie reached for the tissue box, wiping away the joyful tears and the mascara that was bound to be streaked across her face.

After she cleaned up, in a more calm tone "Laughter is good for the soul, Don't you think?".

"Then he asked, 'Yes, yes it does, Ready?"

Blowing out a calming breath yet again, "Yes, I'm ready". She handed him back his coat, he donned it then took her hand in his, kissing her hand, just as Walter opened his side of the door and she scooted over to exit his side. "What a beautiful evening this has been," she said standing up out of the car. I really enjoyed meeting some of your old schoolmates. Harry and Scarlet are such a lovely couple. I would like to do something special for them, soon."

"You are a special woman," he took her face with his free hand and kissed her cheek. Suddenly they were surrounded by dozens of flashes from cameras.

"Douglas? What's going on?" She became afraid, hiding herself in the back of his coat, as he tried to shield her from view.

"Oh, no." He vented, calling out, "Walter?"

Walter, pushed people aside, giving no regard to them. "Right here sir, a pack of wolves, these are." Meaning the paparazzi who had descended upon them. Taking off his coat quickly, Walter and Douglas, covered Marie as best they could telling her to run with them to the elevators, because these people were not allowed in the hotel. Seeing their opportunity, when Mandy came to see what the commotion was about. They shoved their way to her and Mandy urged them on when she saw that it was Mr. Fairbanks. The security force had arrived just as they'd made their way through the lobby doors, heading straight to the elevator, once they got on and the doors closed behind them, they took off the coat shielding Marie.

Douglas let out a yell, and pounded the elevator wall in frustration. "How did they find me?" He growled in protestation. Marie was startled and visibly flinched as he shouted his discontent having never seen him this upset and angry before now.

"SIR!" Snapped Walter who was upset with him, as he held Marie, who was now shaking visibly. "Take hold of yourself, young man! It's not all about you."

Upon seeing Marie so visibly shaken, he pulled his hand through his hair. He immediately deflated placing his hands in his pockets to let her know he wouldn't ever harm her. Then stated in a more calm repentant voice, "I'm so sorry Marie," he leaned against the opposite wall away from her. "Not just for the press, but for shouting and letting my emotions get the best of me. I was really hoping to spare you any undue publicity."

She paled considerably more, "Do you...," she swallowed hard, "do you, mean to tell me that I'm going to be in the papers tomorrow?" She stepped out of Walters care facing him down.

"Quite possibly, I'm sorry Marie. They'll probably be waiting for us in the morning too," he looked chagrined. Marie fainted, just as the elevator reached their floor and the bell dinged. Douglas caught her on the way down, Walter helped him reposition her and he took her in his arms and carried her to her room. This was Not how he envisioned carrying her over a threshold. Walter took the key card and opened her door. He went and pulled down the bedding.

Douglas lay her down on her bed, gently arranging her head on the pillows. Taking off her shoes, he then covered her up to her chin with the duvet. "Shall we call the medic, Jim?"

"I don't think so sir, no, I think she's just had a great fright. As you can see she's breathing normally now. She never hit her head because you caught her."

"This certainly wasn't what I expected of her. She's so strong, I didn't think anything would phase her."

"Sometimes there are things that can overwhelm us, but we never know what that might be, until it happens to us. She is a woman..."

"I know that..."

"Sir, if you'll allow me to finish..." Douglas nodded, "what I was going to say is that, they are more genteel, even when they show strength, it's quite possible this situation was beyond her own abilities. Therefore her mind has to have a 'reset,' if you will. We are admonished in scripture to honor women as 'the weaker vessel." I do think someone should be with her, but not you sir, it wouldn't be proper. I could call my MaryAnn and have her here soon.

"No, please don't disturb your wife. I'll think of someone here in a minute, I just want someone to be here when she awakens. I know that she's had fainting spells before, but this was different. I saw total fear on her face. What could she possibly be that afraid of, I wonder?"

"I'm not certain sir, but whatever it is, has to do with her picture being in the paper. I hate to say this, but I think I should discreetly find out 'why,' "if only for your protection sir."

"How could she possibly be hiding something, anything, for that matter? She's a widowed working mother carrying a big load."

"I don't know sir, but please let me do this, as your friend. If I find nothing, you'll be better off knowing it isn't anything. But if it is something...I'd rather you be prepared, than blindsided, in light of what occurred the last time."

"Okay fine, but these inquiries better be absolutely discreet, I don't want her to think I'm spying on her for nefarious reasons."

"She will never hear a whisper of it, that I can promise." Leaving Douglas to mull over the situation, he'd return soon if he couldn't find someone to keep watch over Marie.

"Before you go, can you bring my notebook over, it's on the nightstand, I have some thinking to do."

"Sure thing, I'll be right back." He opened the shared door behind him then walked out the front. Douglas, pulling a chair close to the side of the bed, bowed his head and prayed. He soon heard Walter leave the notebook by the table and left quietly. He'd never thought he'd pray so much in all his life or that he would have a need to.

"God- I feel so lost at sea. I feel in my heart of hearts that no matter if this business plan fails, I would like Marie to be in my life. I want her to become my wife. I love her. This is something I've never felt before now for anyone. This love that I feel is so strong, it is an ache within me, to feel her pain, her fright..., what is that kind of love about Lord? How am I to be responsible for this woman and her children? Will they...Can they love me? Will they treat me with respect?, all of these thoughts went up in his prayer. Most of all Lord, How do I protect them from the evil of this world?'

Pondering his own prayer and staying silent, 'You cannot,' he told himself, 'but I can Trust in the Lord.' He must trust, leaving doubt at the alter, the Lord could handle it. He felt a peace and knew whom he needed to call, who would be discreet and watch over his beloved, Marie, in privacy.

CHAPTER 31

PLANS

Marie opened her eyes to a warmly lit room from the softly draped windows. A warm breeze stirred the curtains and the smell of coffee roused her from slumber. She rolled over onto her side and was surprised to see Mandy sitting by the table with a book in her hand thoroughly engrossed.

'Yawn' "What are you reading? Marie stretched. "It must be really good".

"Oh, Ma'am. I hadn't realized you were up. Would you care for some coffee?"

"I would, but may I ask what you're doing here?" Pinching her nose between her eyes at the mild headache that pounded there.

"Oh" she said surprised, "you don't remember what happened?" Mandy poured the coffee readying the breakfast tray also with creamer and sugar. She brought it over as Marie sat up in the bed ready to receive the tray.

"No, I don't remember what happened. Obviously something not good, because I'm still in my evening clothes."

"Mr. Fairbanks told me that you fainted in the elevator because of the onslaught of paparazzi that converged on you all last night. So he sat up with you, or actually for you last night, until I could arrive, Walter was in and out too. She indicated the access doors between the rooms. I had to go home first and explain to my parents and keep everything on the down low. Plus I really wanted to change out of my work clothes."

"Mr. Fairbanks called me asking me to be discreet about the whole situation, even telling me how to get in the back way into the building. Today was supposed to be my day off. But he wanted me to stay with you, just in case a woman was needed. You know he offered me triple my wages?... I told him no way! It was an honor to be of service, it's the way I was raised, you always help a friend in need." Taking a sip of her own coffee, and closing her book on the table while Marie fixed her own cup of coffee.

"Since you were here all night, did you sleep any?"

"I did sleep a little, so don't think I stayed up all night. I slept out on the sofa in the other room. It's actually really comfy, I was surprised. But my internal clock is now set, so I couldn't sleep past four this morning, I dozed until about five, then it was no use. So I got up. If I smell coffee it wakes me up, I didn't know if you were like that either. I didn't want to wake you with the smell of coffee that early, if that was the case so I waited until now."

"Thank you for your discretion Mandy, and thanks for not waking me with the smell of coffee that early either. I may have had a worse headache than I do now. She sipped the hot liquid,

"Wow, this is yummy." She smiled thanking the Lord for his care and the hot brew. "The coffee's helping the headache though."

"When you've finished, would you show off your dress to me. I had to leave before you came down so I didn't get to see you." Feeling a bit self conscious she demurred.

"I must look like a wild person, I bet my hair and make-up are a mess."

Mandy gave her an assessing look before she answered. "Nah-not really. You kind of look like a girl who just woke up too early in the morning. Your hair's a bit messy, but nothing a few strokes of your hand can't fix. Your make-up's a little smudged, but not horrid or anything, no raccoon eyes, I promise," she smiled.

"Oh, all right." Rolling her eyes playfully, smiling. Mandy came and took the tray from her. Marie stood up, twirling this way and that to show it off. The effect was achieved that Mandy imagined. "You are the prettiest woman I've ever seen, you could be a model." Marie brushed aside the compliment.

"You're wrong, but thank you."

A strong deep voice said, "She's not wrong" Startling both women who turned to see Douglas in the open doorway, '...when one not only sees the physical beauty but that which lies within, you are breathtaking."

Marie's blush went straight down to her toes, she grew shy being barefooted, so she put one foot over the other and curled in her toes. Douglas noticed but said nothing. He thought she looked very like a fairy princess, the only thing missing was her wings. Their eyes met and Mandy swore she saw sparks fly between them.

Trying to leave them silently, thinking they needed a bit of privacy, she walked slowly away. Douglas noticed, turning towards her, stopping her, "Thank you Mandy for helping us out. I won't soon forget, if you ever need anything you let me know." He took out a business card handing it to her. "This is my private line, I never break a promise, anything, you hear me." Sounding like a big brother he looked at her pointedly, "okay".

"Thank you sir, and just so you know I saw paparazzi, still hanging around downstairs. I'm sorry."

Douglas's features changed. Leaning up against the door jamb, he ran a hand through his hair, bringing it over his face and rubbing it in frustration, but doing his best to hold it in, for Marie's sake. He crossed his arms, one hand tapping his nose thinking. Finally he asked Mandy, "Do you know of someone whom you can trust, who is about my height and build. He doesn't have to be exact, but just tall enough for someone to think it's me?"

Mandy lit up, "Like a diversion so you can get away?"

"Yes,' something like that."

"Ye-ess', she fist pumped, 'I'll be back soon, I've always wanted to do some-thing like this. Don't you worry Mr. Fairbanks, I'll handle everything, she began to back away from them. It'll be the best task I've been given. I'll call you, she held his card up, she stopped suddenly, "Do you mind paying for a party?" She asked unsure, but smiling hugely.

Chuckling, "Whatever it takes, Mandy" laughing now at her enthusiasm. She backed out of the doorway, "When I've got everything set and ready to go. I'll let you know, this is gonna be great!" she squealed as she practically ran out the door. Marie chuckled.

"The exuberance of youth."

Putting his hands in his pockets, "Yes, indeed" he felt a bit shy, "Feeling better?"

She didn't understand his reserve, she thought "It must have to do with last night. Why couldn't she remember?" Looking down at her feet she nodded, 'Mm-hmm.' Then he was there lifting her chin like he always did when she tried to hide from his magnetic, piercing blue eyes. "I'm really sorry about last night, my behavior was deplorable, but won't you speak to me? This is killing me." Asking softly he released her chin, resting their heads together, holding her arms loosely.

Her memories of last night in that moment went a hundred different directions as they came flooding back they began to overwhelm her. She fell out of his arms, sat on the bed in a rush, like a balloon that was deflating rapidly. The voices of the past and present intruded in her mind. The headlines that read "Local Teen ...," "Found Near ...," "Young Teen ...". It stole her breath to think about it. No! She wouldn't think of it, but...what will he think of me if he finds that out? Dear me, I hope he doesn't find out!" She looked at him, unable to say a word.

"You love him" her heart spoke softly.

"I do'?" She turned away from him.

"He needs to know the truth about you, the truth shall set you free." Her conscience urged her to tell him.

"No, I mustn't tell him. I can't, I'm afraid." She crossed her arms to protect herself.

"Then what have you been doing these last few months dating him, if not to tell him and move on with your life? You know 1John 4:18 says'... for there is no fear in love". Her heart cried out urging her to tell him about her past.

"I don't know...?' She put her hands to her mouth to silence herself. Douglas was concerned for her, he could see the wavering desperation in the look of her eyes and countenance. The war that raged on inside of her but for what reason he knew not.

"Let me get you some fresh water, you look peaked".

"Thank you" her voice sounded hoarse even to her own ears. Walter walked in and could immediately feel a brooding tension in the air. He went directly and sat next to her on the bed. Taking her hand as a father would.

"It's been a long and exciting night for you hasn't it?" Feeling comforted by his fatherly presence, she placed her head on his shoulder.

"Yes it has, indeed" the words were weighted.

Douglas was suddenly struck with jealousy. Thinking to himself "Why could she speak to Walter and not to me?" They sat and spoke quietly amongst themselves, as he spoke to himself.

"Because you were an dolt". he answered himself.

His conscience whispered, 'You let your anger take over your emotions. Proverbs 15:18 crossed his mind, 'A wrathful man stirreth up strife: but [he that is] slow to anger appeaseth strife'.

"O' God, that is what I've done!" He confessed in his heart praying, closing his eyes swallowing hard he pinched the bridge of his nose as he acknowledged his anger. Continuing to ask the Lord for his forgiveness right there, to guide him in his next steps to heal the breach he'd caused with Marie. Hearing her sigh audibly, he came out of his own introspection hearing her say, "Scarlet will be so disappointed that I can't visit her today."

Walter comforted her, "She'll understand my dear, anyhow, you could always call her, you know."

"I never got her number." She looked disappointed. Finally noticing Douglas, who had come out of wherever his thoughts had taken him. She had noticed he'd gone somewhere mentally, feeling some sort of chagrin or shame?She sighed, "Maybe, who knew his heart, she certainly didn't."

Walter announced, "I'll find her number never you worry, but I think that we can safely visit her without all the hubbub. Besides, who would care about a regular mother having had a baby just last night."

"No one but friends and family" Douglas interjected, handing her the water.

"Perhaps, but you are friends of theirs, Douglas." She took a sip, "Someone will be waiting there, in the shadows, even if most are here trying to get a glimpse of you. You do see that don't you?"

"Why don't we call and find out, I may still have Harry's number." Taking out his cell phone, he located Harry's number and put the phone on speaker. It rang five times.

"Listen, I said, NO COMMENT! Don't you people understand? Stop calling, I said to "Leave us…." Douglas interrupted.

'… Hello Harry? It's Douglas, what's going on?"

"Oh, thank goodness, it's not another reporter, How is it possible they got our number? My phone's been ringing off the hook since seven am! I was about to turn it off when it rang in my hand."

"I'm so sorry, Harry, we're getting a plan together, so that you can be left alone. I'm leaving town today. So that should help you and Scarlet get some peace and quiet." His face downcast, wanting to see his friend again, but not like this.

"Thanks, buddy. I'm sorry about it too. I really wanted to catch up with you, it's been too long my friend."

"Don't I know it, I'm sorry about that. Look when things calm down, I'll send for you to come and visit me at my home, we can get together in a more private setting. You'll have to bring Scarlett and the kids too, when she's up for traveling".

"That sounds like a plan, I'd like to see you too, buddy."

"I'm going to hand you over to Walter, I'd like to get your address, so that we can send you a gift without it being so public, if that's okay with you."

"You don't have to do that, we're pretty set, we have all the things we need from the previous kids."

"Fine, but I'd still like to send something, say for Scarlet instead, Okay?"

"Oh, she'd love that, a surprise. Perfect. Thanks Douglas."

"Glad I thought of it." He chuckled, while Marie was asking with her eyes about her invite, with Scarlet. "Also please let Scarlet know, Marie is quit upset she couldn't come for a visit."

"All right man, I'll let her know, she actually figured that may happen since she found out about the reporters. She's upset about it as well. We'll talk soon, though and get together, all right man. Don't be such a stranger, okay?"

"I'll try not to be. Here's Walter...' he handed off the cell.

Walter walked to the adjoining room to give them a moment of privacy while he spoke with Harry, that was his excuse anyway.

"Would you care for a warm-up on your coffee and maybe some breakfast?"

"Coffee would be nice, but I don't think I could eat." She felt nauseous. Taking her cup from the tray, he went to the kitchenette, poured the coffee then asked, "Cream and two sugars, right?"

"Yes, thank you." Surprised he remembered, he handed her the cup, she took a sip. "Perfect thanks." She gave a tentative smile. He was giving her a worried expression, he didn't know how to broach the subject of them leaving.

"You've got something on your mind Douglas, tell me." Somewhat surprised she could read him so easily. "We should head back, to home. I know we were supposed to spend a few more days here, but I honestly hadn't counted on the paparazzi getting ahold of where I was. I mean really who cares about a twenty year reunion? I wasn't going to come, if you weren't interested." he ran a hand across the back of his neck, exhaling, frustrated.

"We're going back." It was a statement. "I don't want to get caught with you". To Douglas, It felt like a slap in the face. "I'll have to answer questions that I don't want to tell. I will not put myself through that...' she caught herself before she said, 'again'. "People asking inappropriate things, she shook her head, no. 'NO'. She rocked herself back and forth without realizing it. I want to be with my children and put all this behind me. I don't know what I was thinking agreeing to this, to come here." Rubbing her forehead in worry.

"Come now Marie, it hasn't been all that bad, has it? Please put things into some sort of perspective."

Becoming upset and hurt, "Perspective?...Perspective!" She fumed, "You may choose to and be able to have people chasing you all around the country getting into your 'business' for all I know you may even like the attention! I just can't, I will not pay that price again! I Can't," crossing her arms, then pulling the ring from her finger she calmed down when she said in a whisper, "I'm sorry Douglas, I can't do this". Tears rolled down her face when she opened her palm for him to take the ring.

He gasped, "No". he said firmly then, his heart breaking at the set of her jaw. She would not back down from her resolution. "The ring was made especially for you, my dear Marie. It was meant only for you. The symbol of the ring is true to who you are, I had it made especially for you, it was always meant for you." He closed her hand around the ring with both his hands. "You do understand that all this fuss will go away, what they say doesn't matter, it is all chaff, it will blow away in time."

"I don't have the luxury of time, for the sake of my children, I can't take that chance. Please don't make it harder than it has to be." She attempted lightness, "Let's chalk it up to be two friends who had a 'jolly good time" together for a day. We can forget the other bits."

Saddened by her words, "If it's all the same to you I will not forget my first real love." Brushing her hair back, he kissed her lightly. Inhaling deeply, he would never forget her.

Gasping at his remark 'First Real Love' and the tenderness with which he'd said he loved her. Made her heart quiver. 'God help me,' she uttered a quick prayer, vexed, yet thinking she must hold fast.

"I suspect he always has". Unshed tears in his eyes, "I know that I want to spend my life with you, Marie, my love". A tear slid down his cheek. "I will be a gentleman, one you've come to know, I suspect love, yet are afraid too. When you decide to change your mind, I will be there for you." Leaning over he kissed the top of her head, as was his way. He left her then closing the doors between their rooms as if shutting the memory of her away for safekeeping.

How forlorn she felt without him near. Life would not be the same without him in it. She threw herself onto her bed and cried. Feeling abandoned for who would come now to be a voice of reason, to comfort and reassure her that she had made the correct decision?" Thinking "She was making the right choice, wasn't she? For her children's sake, she protested."

Her mind played traitor... "No, you're just using them as an excuse to not move forward, you're choosing the cowards way out".

Douglas's heart rent when he heard Marie sobbing. He was about to go to her, but Walter stopped him. "No, don't sir." he stated firmly.

"But she needs me" he said emphatically. He reached for the doorknob. Walter held him by the arm, 'Yes she does, but not right now and not this way. Marie is a strong woman."

Looking puzzled himself and as if Walter had lost his mind, "Of course she is, what's that got to do with anything?"

"I believe, sir, she is the kind of woman who needs time and space to figure things out for herself, and lots of time to pray over a situation. I fear, she feels she jumped without considering the consequences of her choices and is now unfortunately regretting her lack of prayer over the situation."

"She's regretting being with me?"

Thinking before he spoke. "One of two things will happen, if you go in there and try to 'Rescue" her. She may give in but later rebuff you and come to regret the decision over time, since you backed her into a proverbial corner. Neither of you would be happy. It wouldn't be or feel the same as it had.

Doulas asked. "And number two?"

He sighed. "This one is tougher, requires more from you." Walt ran a hand over his chin back and forth. "Let her be and in her own time she will come back to you. I have no doubt. Circumstances will bring her back to you, she just has to move past what's holding her hostage. Although it may take more time than you may want to give."

"I don't care about the time it will take, I just want to love her. To love her and her precious children. Is that asking too much from her?"

"Maybe for her but not for the Lord. Put all of this in his hands won't you sir? And in the meantime Detective Slade, my friend, will find out what the barrier may be to stop her from accepting you and hurting her further because it surely seems to be something extraordinary for her to react as she has. Then we can do battle in prayer against the enemy of her mind, 'Fear.'"

"I never thought of it like that."

"That's why I'm older and wiser, and what you pay me for, my wisdom." Walt smiled. "I'm sure you don't want to sacrifice everything you've built up in this business with speculation, uncertainties, and certainly not a marriage."

"When you put things in that perspective, it won't hurt to find out any useful information. You my friend are my Solomon. But it doesn't hurt any less, to feel her suffering."

"No one with any sort of feeling or compassion would dismiss her turmoil. Yet sometimes, there are some things that need to be faced head on and alone. No one can do 'the work' we're supposed to do for ourselves. Though not really alone if you have Christ. Don't forget, she has those who love her and pray for her, us too, but mostly, if she'll allow him, the Lord himself can help her fight those battles."

"I guess this is one of those times, isn't it, Walter?"

Nodding his head. "Yes, I really think so. Come, sir." Pulling him away from the doorway and had him sit at the counter. "Have some coffee, I'll get started on breakfast, I'm sure by the time I'm done, she'll be spent and come around. We need for Mandy to come through with her plan. We'll be needing our strength for whatever comes next."

"I'm not that hungry, Walter, don't make anything extravagant like yesterday. He choked on the words. "Excuse me" he fled to his room, crying out in prayer, to his God.

CHAPTER 32

THE RUSE

Over the next few hours Mandy had outdone herself. She had called in favors and cajoled vendors in the area to drop what they were doing to have a big shindig at the hotel all at Mr. Douglas Fairbanks' expense. Some had questioned her about it, never having had the hotel call in such favors, but when she told them to name their price, within reason of course, giving them his expense account number, they were right on it, as many in the town were tightening their belts feeling that there would be a downturn in the economy.

Mandy had to direct the set up of the party, since it was yet early and she had called everyone personally, she wanted to set things quickly in motion, so that the trio upstairs didn't have too much time to fret about getting out of town. She set the party up for One O'clock, it would be held between the pool and gazebo areas. She had invited all the hotel guests. It would showcase the famed Frank Oliver who was also staying at the hotel, (it being the only five star hotel in a three star town, that employed a large portion of locals). Frank would be doing cooking demonstrations for the guests and locals, even the reporters had been invited and allowed on site this once but not before one pm.

This party was passed around by word of mouth mostly and created such a buzz locally, that many had called in friends from nearby areas in the county.

Just as Mandy hoped for they came pouring in to see the celebrity chef. And perhaps catch a glimpse of their town hero, Douglas Fairbanks. Mandy was so happy her diversion was really beginning to take shape. Things were moving along about forty-five minutes into the festivities, when she felt the mood was set just right for the diversion to begin.

Her long time friend Henry, who'd been hidden away in the back office earlier in the day, sat up when she entered. "You all set Henry?"

"Yeah, Mandy, you know me, all up for some fun, but you owe me big time."

"No, I asked a friend for help, which you accepted, without preamble I might add." Wagging a finger at him.

"Well, I've been thinking, since I've been sitting here so long" she rolled her eyes, 'wait was he sweating?'

"What is it Henry, we don't have a lot of time, the mood is just right, now?"

"I want a real date with you out of this, take it or I'm outta here." He folded his arms across his chest. He was so cute when he got all ruffled, but she kept her face straight feigning, surprise.

"A Date!"

"Shh, not so loud. I thought we were going to be quiet? Anyhow, is that so terrible?" He asserted. Pretending to think it over, she squealed inside.

"Oh, alright." she said with feigned pretense of being put upon "It's a date."

Smirking as if he had one over on her, "Are they ready?" he looked up as if he could see them through the ceiling.

"As ready as they'll ever be, I'm sure." She said, 'The media and paparazzi are too busy getting pictures of Frank Oliver, they hadn't expected him to be here. Let me take a final check before we head out."

Taking her walkie from her belt loop she called, "Bill?"

"This is Bill, over."

"All set for the Grand Finale?"

"All set over here".

"All right, Let's kick the tires and light the fires!" she mouthed. "I've always wanted to say that!" She laughed.

Henry said, "That was so corny, but cute. Let's get this show on the road then."

Mandy, went onto the patio, that was near the golf course, but in view of Frank Oliver giving him a general "Whoop" when her hands went up with two thumbs up, which was the signal. He nodded, in a general way, showing he got it. He lit the 'Banana flambé'. "Oooh"…All eyes were on him and his demo as the flames took hold keeping the audiences attention.

Suddenly on the golf course's main lawn, a helicopter landed with the Fairbanks logo emblazoned on the side. Someone shouted, "Wait, Mr. Fairbanks!"

Mr. Fairbanks and Marie, followed by Henry who ran after them shouting, "Wait...wait...Mr. Fairbanks! I just want to ask a couple questions..." The couple ran for all they were worth towards the helicopter. All pandemonium broke loose as the media broke from the crowd at the demonstration. The cameras were heard clicking away, as reporters and cameramen ran after them shouting, "Mr. Fairbanks, Wait...Who's the lady with you?...What's her name? Mr. Fairbanks?"

When Mandy saw, that the media crews were nearly to the copter, she called into the walkie, "The sparrow is taking flight." The only response. 'Copy'.

Walter looked at the two of them, "Ready?" he set down the walkie. Marie nodded, as did Douglas after he saw her nod. Silently they walked down the three flights of stairs, Walter having previously taken the luggage down. Once at the bottom, Douglas went behind the stair case to a door marked as "Janitor". Taking a key from his pocket, he opened the door revealing what was as you'd expect a Janitors closet to look like.

Marie said nothing, but watched as he moved a cleaning bottle from the shelf and felt behind until you heard a 'click,' she was mildly surprised. Douglas pulled on the shelving and the entire wall moved, it was ingenious a secret door-way. As he opened it fully, the stairway went down one flight and was well lit from above.

Walter said, 'Let me go first, sir. He took their valises and headed down. At the bottom the lights automatically came on. He commented, "It's been a long time hasn't it sir?"

"Yes, yes it has. I'd hoped to never use this again, but I'm glad it's here for our safety. Life throws curveballs every so often." As

Marie descended last in the lineup, her foot caught on the hem of her skirt at the bottom. She was propelled forwards by inertia, straight into Douglas's arms as he'd turned around just at that moment. She gave out a small cry of fright.

When he caught her, he held her just a moment kissing her cheek, thanking God and Aristotle for the law of inertia. Just setting her on her feet, made his heart race, he pulled her arm through his so he could walk her through the underground tunnel. It was about a half mile long, he wanted her to see he still cared. He wouldn't leave her not matter what. Leaving was her choice.

No one except for Douglas, Walter and an out of town contractor knew of this exit that had been labeled at the time "service entrance," but after that contractor had gone, Doug had "repositioned" the kitchens and service entrance. No one was the wiser or had known that this existed. Douglas had also had the plans changed in the main city blueprint, architectural renderings had been replaced with a new set, not a "revised" one. So no one would ever find out about it except family.

Marie did not protest when Doug took her arm because she didn't like narrow places, bringing her a measure of comfort. As the walkway began on a rise up, Doug whispered in her ear. "You can put your sunglasses on, it will be bright here in just a minute." She did as directed, silently, in truth she barely spoke, she either obeyed his directives or nodded her responses.

They came out into a potting shed. Walter took the first look around outside. He came back saying, "I see the truck sir and no one else is around the area." So Walter proceeded to lift a pot and took out a key.

"Good. When you get it started we'll come out okay."

Walter took off towards the old truck that was nearby, he attempted to start it, it failed the first time. They both looked at each other, her in fear, he in worry. Then it dissipated as the truck rumbled to life on the second try. She sighed audibly.

Trotting back through the leaves Walter came back taking the valises and stowing them in the back of the truck. He motioned for them to come out and get in, being grateful to whomever owned the truck. It was clean, immaculately so, yet with a well used look about it. 'Thank you God, for small mercies', she prayed. Marie quickly ran through the foliage, for it was particularly dense through here. Douglas was hot on her heels matching his pace to her smaller one, as they reached the truck, she got in first being the smaller of the two. He climbed in after and patted the side of the truck, the window having been rolled down, as he closed the door.

Pulling out of the old dirt road, onto the byway, he went past the speed limit, as no one was around and trying to gain distance from the hotel, just in case. Once outside city limits, he slowed his pace to match the speed limit, not wanting to get caught speeding and draw attention to themselves. There was very little conversation, the only sound coming from the radio and the wind, except for fast food orders and rest stop breaks on the four hour drive home.

Mandy was so proud the ruse had worked and Mr. Oliver had received more free publicity, while Mr. Fairbanks made a clean getaway. 'Not bad for a few hours of planning,' she thought to herself. She was quite thankful, her brother Bill had been about the same size and build as Mr. Fairbanks, he even had a similar hair color, but she had him wear a baseball hat with the Fairbanks logo, so that he wouldn't be detectable with his signature styled sunglasses in place.

The clothing wouldn't matter, no one would notice. Thankfully Bill's girlfriend agreed to help them out too. She looked nothing like Marie, but no one really knew that. They put a large sun hat on her and large sunglasses, with a brown long haired wig, as she was a blonde. Bill was excited to help for other reasons, this would be the perfect opportunity for him. On the mad dash he held his girl's hand hopefully not for the last time.

On the ensuing flight to the local airport as they laughed nearly hysterically at the fun of it all. Bill had sobered enough and proposed to his high school sweetheart, mid flight.

She emphatically gave him a resounding, '"Yes!" When he produced a ring and slipped it onto her finger, he would be forever grateful to his baby sister, for helping to make it happen and Mr. Fairbanks of course, for the use of the copter.

After dropping off his moon-eyed young charges, Ed Jensen headed back to his main hub in Madrone Valley, to await the arrival of Mr. Fairbanks. He flew over the highway and spotted the vehicle he'd been told about, he did a slight flyby letting them know he was on his way back to base. He saw the flashing of headlights, letting him know they saw him and he set off as the crow flies.

Ed thought about his checklist for the flight to Montana to visit with Douglas's parents. It'd been awhile since any of them saw the family. It would be nice to see Miss Christy again, she made the best apple crisp he'd ever tasted. That put him in a chipper mood for the rest of the flight.

CHAPTER 33

BACK HOME

Somewhere along the route Marie had fallen asleep on Douglas, he'd put his arm along the back seat when he saw her starting to nod off. When he felt she'd finally given in, he pulled her gently to himself and let her sleep, whispering sweet nothings in her ear, hoping beyond hope that her soul would hear if not her logic.

Sleeping peacefully for about an hour, when the driving pattern changed, for they were no longer on the highway, she must have sensed they were near home, for she opened her eyes to find Douglas smiling down on her.

"Oh,' she exclaimed and sat up. His smile faded and pulled his arm to himself. She sat up straight trying not to touch him, dashing any hope by turning away from him for she was ashamed.

Ashamed and angry at herself for letting this all happen to begin with, a tear escaped, wiping it as covertly as possible. She should never have agreed to come, let alone date him the last few months. So discreetly, her father didn't even know and she

241

told him everything. This seemingly simple act, just complicated everything, she didn't need complicated right now. She had to face facts.

Fact one: She was a widow and needed to remain so.

Fact two: She was a mother.

Fact three: She loved Douglas.

"Wait, no, no, no, no, no" her eyes filled again.

Turning down her street, she saw her house, sitting up straighter she couldn't wait to see her babies. Douglas saw her face perk up and a sparkle in her eye or were those tears? A mothers' love is quite powerful, it made him feel it too.

As they turned into her driveway Mrs. Hawkins from next door came out of her house to get the mail and looked at her strangely but waved anyway. So Marie waved back. The boys seeing a car they didn't recognize they came running out to see who'd come to visit. Marie practically climbed over Douglas in her haste to get to her children and feel their comfort.

'Momma...Momma...,' they cried out jostling for the best position, "you're home. You've been gone ages and ages" Seth declared hugging her about the waist. While Sam wanted into her arms, so she brought him up snuggling him close. Inhaling that little boy smell.

"I missed you also my darling boys. Where is your sister?"

Seth said, "She fell again, Gramma, is fixing her knee. But she'll feel all better now that you're home." He turned around suddenly "Who's that Momma?" he asked pointing at the men. Turning her head she looked straight into Douglas's eyes, 'Lord,' she hadn't meant to do that. She swallowed hard. "That's uh-that's uh-...".

Douglas saved her the trouble of having to explain who he was to her. Holding out his hand, he said, "Hi, I'm Doug, a good friend of your mommy's."

Seth grew suspicious. "But mommy doesn't have any friends" She paled. Then Seth clarified, "Who are boys. Are you my Mommy's boy-friend?" Leave it to a child Marie thought. Swallowing hard, waiting for Doug's answer.

Clearing his throat a few times, Douglas finally answered, "Um, I work with your Mom, so yes, I'm a friend who's also a boy." Douglas clarified carefully.

"Oh,' That seemed to satisfy whatever curiosity he had, "Nice ta' meet ya" And he shook his hand. Douglas was impressed.

"Nice to meet you too, Seth."

"Hey! How do ya' know my name?"

"Well, uh" Marie stammered, unsure what to say.

Again Douglas to the rescue. "I saw a picture of these handsome boys and this beautiful little girl in her office, so I asked her who they were. And to my surprise she said they were her kids. Well, I couldn't believe it, so she asked me to come on over and see for myself and here you are the two finest looking gents.

"Can I tell you a secret?" he knelt down to their level speaking man to man. Sam got down from his mother's arms to listen in too. "I'm good at keepin' secrets ask anybody." Walt snickered, somewhere behind him, covering it with a cough.

Doug had to control himself from laughing, instead he said in all seriousness, "You boys look a lot taller than you do in the picture, definitely taller" he winked at them, shaking his head assuredly.

"Wow you really think so?" Asked Seth all surprise.

"I'm big too" said little Sam.

Doug stood up, "Yes you've really grown too." then ruffled his hair, "Your mom should get new pictures in her office, don't you think?" They enthusiastically agreed. Can I get a picture of you boys? I'll send it to your Mommy on my phone.

"You can do that, Mr. Doug?"

He was shocked at them giving him a nickname already. "Yes," he cleared his throat, "Yes, I can. Is that okay Marie?"

She nodded her head. Marie wasn't shocked that they accepted him, because Seth was the only one who would really remember his father and the male bond and companionship that they had together. She watched as Doug snapped a picture or two of the boys together.

Sam strutted to his grandma and sister, "I growed big Gramma" he exclaimed hands on hips and nodding his head up and down. She chuckled from the doorway, waiting to be introduced. Watching everything with a mothers' keen eye. "I can see that."

Upon noticing her mother, she was afraid her mother would ask them inside for tea or something. Noticing her distress Walter walked past them and dropped the valise next to the front door next to "grandma". "Ma'am" He tipped his hat and was walking back towards the car.

Marie stopped him and hugged him fiercely,"Thank you for everything Walter." Nodding meaningfully at him. "Come boys" she took each one in hand tossing a final "Goodbye Douglas" over her shoulder, how it cut deep. "Oh Lord" she prayed 'help me to forget him and follow your plan for my life.' as she walked into her house and didn't look back. She knew it was the worst, the rudest thing she could have done, but she didn't want to raise his hopes.

She closed the door behind her as she ushered everyone inside. It was all just a dream...a really nice dream. Now it was over. Back to reality.

CHAPTER 34

BATTEN DOWN THE HATCHES

To keep the media's attention off of his mystery woman and his subsequent disappearance Douglas had his office assistant and Walters' wife, MaryAnne. Inform a mutual friend at a reputable newspaper, to use a stock photo of Douglas, no mystery woman photo was needed, nor would it be given.

Asking them to let the 'general public' know in their society column that he left the party early without interviews because there was an unexpected issue that had come up at his family's compound in Montana it needed his immediate attention he was needed there post haste. By himself, she emphasized.

His female friend from the party, was a family friend and did not wish to be involved in his life. It was a mutual friendly gathering, she would not like to be seen or heard from in the papers, she was helping out a friend, out of respect for the family friendship, that was all.

"Come one MaryAnne, throw me a bone, 'Who was she?'"

"A family friend, that's all I'm saying Neil, so you can stop asking."

"Okay, okay, but one of these days you'll owe me big time."

"Perhaps', She smiled to herself. "Neil, just print what we've asked and you'll be the first to the presses, I'll give you half a day before I call anyone else."

"Fine, fine. I'll do it, you sure know how to twist a fellows arm."

"Neil, I've seen your other work. Why don't you stop this gossip nonsense and do what you've been called to do, what really matters out there in the world." He sighed, "I will one day, Miss MaryAnne. It's a tough business."

"You should at least think about it seriously. Now, I don't want to hear from you anytime soon."

Chuckling, "Yes, Ma'am. Ta-ta, for now."

Hanging up the phone she sighed. She hated these kinds of phone conferences, but they must be done, to protect Douglas, but in this instance, Marie. Whether she knew it or not. This was the only way to keep the dogs at bay. Poor Douglas. She had never seen him so upset, frantic to keep Marie out of the papers. He had gone so far as to say "Batten down the Hatches," MaryAnne. I want absolutely no breaches of any kind. There will be No "Story" if we get ahead of this thing. Anything that they think they have, will fall on deaf ears, they didn't get any pictures of her face, I'm certain. She hid her face before I even knew what was happening. I don't know how."

That was yesterdays conversation from the hotel room, they'd left the hotel, and she was still running interference ever since. Turning in her office chair to look out the window, she mused, 'the most worthwhile woman, got away'. Doug hadn't said much after about the situation, but was doing his utmost to keep her out of the limelight. This single action told her that he cared for her deeply, 'if only she had realized it in time or maybe she did, who knew?' Being a big romantic she sighed at the current situation, she had such high hopes on his behalf. Walter was walking into her office when he heard her sigh. He came over and kissed his wife on the cheek. "What's the matter hon?"

"The usual, you know I dislike making those phone calls. She shivered, "It feels akin to lying, though I never do, I just omit information."

"Do you need me to handle the next call?" He asked as he sat on the desks edge, kissing her hand. She playfully whacked his arm.

"No, siree! You have no finesse! Don't you remember what happened the last time, I let you?" He gave her an innocent until proven guilty look, "They came banging on the door looking for a pound of flesh. Never again, my dear! I love you truly, but stay away from the publicists."

Looking mildly offended by her tirade, he asked. "Who me? All I said was that there was no story."

"Exactly, that's like blood in the water to a shark, and some of them must be related, that or to mosquitoes. The blood suckers."

"Dearest! Being on the phone doesn't agree with your sweet disposition, usually, please come take a lunch break with me."

"Half and hour more, my love, then I promise to have a better attitude, after I've repented a few hundred times."

"Not a moment longer. Mind you, I will come hang up that phone, even if you're on with the President of the United States!"

"That's why I love you! Give me some sugar, to sustain me through this." *Smooch* "Is that better?"

She sighed, 'Ah, yes for now. Now get along." She shooed him out. He acquiesced. Mary watched him go with purpose, there was never any wavering with him. 'Dear God, how I love that man. Thank you so much for him.' She prayed quickly then sighed, returning to work.

CHAPTER 35

ONE WEEK LATER-JULY 3, 2005

Douglas Jr. came towards his son, "Douglas?", calling out to him as he sat at the kitchen island dressed in blue jeans, a t-shirt, and workbooks that he kept here. Specifically, for the farm work he helped with when he was "home". Easily falling back into the familiarity of the work life here. It always grounded him when life through him a curveball.

"Yeah, Pop?" he didn't look up from the laptop he was perusing.

"Artie?" Intoning his voice with quiet questioning, using the nick-name he'd been given as a child by his mother. Using his middle name to differentiate between the three Douglas's on the homestead when he was a kid. Catching his attention, "Sorry Dad, what's up?" Looking up from his laptop, partially pulling down the screen to better see his father with. Showing he was paying attention to what he had to say, not wanting his father to see that once again he was looking for any sign of news about Marie in the papers. He trusted his household staff, but money or debt was a lure to some looking for a quick fix to their situation. So far not a peep, for which he was grateful. The Lord had protected Marie, for which he was truly grateful.

"I'd like for you to come and take a look at one of my tractors, you know you were the best mechanic I had around here. Always fixing things, I can't seem to figure this one out." Douglas knew, this was one of his Dad's tactics, if you couldn't figure something out, you worked at something else until the answer presented itself.

"Well I did learn from the best."

"You've got that right!" Doug Jr. playfully shoved him off the stool, "Come on now, let's go. The day's wasting away." Closing the laptop completely before they walked out of the house. Walking side by side to the barn Douglas noticed his Dad's steps were a little slower paced, there was a touch more grey mixed in with the brown. How had he missed his Dad aging this much. He needed to come back 'home' more often.

As usual his Dad cut to the heart of the matter. "Any news son?" asking the question that was on Doug's mind so he slowed his gait more so they could talk.

Putting his hands in his pockets, "No, thank goodness."

"You love this woman". It was a statement not a question. "So why don't you go after her son?"

"It's because I love her that I can't. It's complicated, Dad."

Dad gave him a quizzical look. "Complicated, huh? I don't see what's so complicated about love? It's the most uncomplicated thing I know. In my day, If you loved a girl, you went after her and that's all there was to it. If she ran away it just went to show you how much she loves you. The further she goes, the more she loves. Sometimes, it's the fear of love or rather the fear of being loved. I suppose in her case she's afraid of starting over; loving another. 1John 4:18 says, "perfect love casteth out all fear." Fear Kills love every time, son. She needs to see "Perfect love" in you and through you."

"So, I haven't shown her "perfect love"? Is that what you're telling me?"

"Only you know the answer to that question. I have't seen you two together. I haven't met her, but that's besides the point. The real question is 'How do 'you,' he pointed at his chest, show perfect love or express it in a way she understands, from a biblical point of view, not the worlds. What does her inner self need from you? What's missing from the picture of her heart? What does her heart need the most? Understanding? Truth? Honesty? Compassion? All of them?"

Douglas's expression carried a deep frown as they reached the barn. His dad showed him the tractor momentarily distracting him, "So what's wrong with it?" Douglas asked.

"Not quite sure, just doesn't seem to run right, I figured I'd get a second opinion from you. She probably just needs a little lovin' and compassion," he wasn't just talking about the tractor either. Dad winked at him, when one of the farm Hands came calling over to his Dad needing his attention, he let Doug get to work on the tractor leaving him with his own thoughts.

Starting the tractor known as 'little blue,' a favorite of his Dad's that he tried to keep in top shape, Doug began to trouble shoot. Dad used it in the Fourth of July parade in their town and that day was tomorrow, so he got to work.

A few hours in, his mother Dorris, came to check on his progress but also to call him in for lunch. "Douglas?" she called out as she neared the tractor and found him deep inside, wrench in hand. He was oblivious to her presence, so engrossed was he in the work, it felt good to see him using his hands instead of his head every once in while. Smiling at her son watching him work, "Douglas?" she was at his side.

Shooting up quickly banging his head on the hood. "Ow". He rubbed at the spot, "Wowz, Ma, don't sneak up on a body," easily returning to his country roots.

"I was not sneaking. Let me take a look, hopefully you didn't cut yourself."

"I'm fine, Ma." He shied away from her probing hands.

"Alright, all right." She held up her hands in surrender. "I did call out several times." Looking at him with motherly concern. "Lunch is ready, if you are ready for having some?"

"Is it that time already?" he looked at his watch, that he'd taken off while working. "Whoa, I guess so". He wasn't hungry, his thoughts hadn't resolved.

"Are you coming?"

"I'll be along, as soon as I wash my hands." He held up his greasy paws. "I was just finishing tightening the last bolt. Why don't you start her up. Let's see if I've still got the touch," he chuckled.

She climbed up gracefully and gave the key a turn. It started right up and seemed to purr. "Excellent, you always were mechanically minded, a true gift. Your Dad will be so excited. You know how he loves to be in the parade, showing off." She giggled like a young girl. It was nice to see his mother so excited, she looked youthful for her age. He didn't know how to take her compliment, so he just closed the hatch and buttoned her up. Wiping off any smudges of grease from his hands, he went over to the work sink and began to scrub up.

Mom turned off the tractor walked over to him and just watched her son as he washed up, not saying a word. She took the towel off the hook handing it to him after he rinsed. Looking on with motherly concern.

"You love her, son?" Not one to beat around the bush, his mother asked.

"Yes, I don't know Mom, honestly," he sighed, "She's been through so much. I was just hoping to ease her lot in life, and somehow I made it more complicated". Throwing the towel onto the counter after drying his hands.

His mother, took the towel and put it back onto the hook. Letting him talk it out for himself. She knew that about her son, It wasn't just the thinking, but many times the solution needed to "breathe" to be expressed in words to find a solution. She knew from experience that sometimes you needed the Lord to work things out on your behalf and just wait patiently. Harder said than done. Sighing, running a hand through his hair, a crooked smile etching his face.

"You know, she's a lot like you Ma....She is loving and kind, generous. She dearly loves her children and just wants to protect them, I understand that."

"Every mother does, even when they're your age," she smiled. "But do you really understand her need to protect her children? Perhaps even herself. Your life is so public son. She could really just be afraid of all that publicity and what it would mean for her and her kids if she doesn't want to be in the public eye.

Constantly being judged for your actions that are seen when you go to the grocery store by yourself or you just want to be 'normal'. Like going to the mall or out to dinner. It's like some fun way for your life to be plastered all over the magazines for someone like you, it's just an adventure.

But for her...it seems she doesn't want any part of that. She doesn't want to live under a microscope. I can't blame her. When you were on the cover of that fancy magazine a few years ago, everyone wanting to know who you were and where you came from. "Small town guy makes it big". They came knocking on the door. I finally posted signs to keep them out. I even met a few with good ol' Matilda. It was the name she gave her favorite Benelli shotgun.

You know sometimes we just have to let go and trust the situation to God's care. He can handle any situation, even this. Either you give up the 'limelight'. Or she comes to adjust to the idea."

He rested against the counter, opening up to his Mother, taking all she'd said into consideration. "I asked her to marry me..."

"Oh, Douglas," clapping her hands, she momentarily got excited, but then saw the expression on his face. "What happened?"

"She turned me down, Ma...it hurts real bad, I can't go after her for her sake and the kids," blowing out a frustrated breath, "I thought, foolishly, that if I took her to meet some old friends of mine, quietly under the radar, where no media or paparazzi presence would seek to follow me. I thought it would be nice, you know "An innocent outing," she could get to know me better.

We've been quietly dating for a few months, per her request with no hint of media presence."

"We've noticed, but we thought you were still brooding over the previous one. Don't look at me like that? You never hinted or said a word, we haven't seen you in nearly a year Douglas."

"What? No! Grayson was done and dusted well over a year ago," he gave his mom a distasteful look. "I just don't want the 'dogs" going after an innocent family should things have not worked out between us. So far so good," he sighed in resignation.

"We'll keep praying the Lord will work things out in His good time." She pulled on him, "Enough jawing, let's go have lunch, I'm starving I've been up since four am, my stomachs knawing on my backbone." Laughing. Hilda made your favorite so, cheer up."

"She made lasagna?"

"Well, no I guess, it's your second favorite, then... Bleu cheeseburgers, with homemade onion rings and her special pickles.'

"Oh, stop, you're making my mouth water," he sucked back in an attempt to stop his drooling. "That makes me hungry now."

"That's the spirit. Hard work'll do that to ya" She laughed pleasantly taking him by the arm and out of the barn. Once outside, she stopped a minute to survey all of the Lord's blessings, the sunshine, the grass on the lawn with the tick, tick, of the sprinkler, the birds chirping in the trees and bushes. 'Ah,' "Bless the Lord O' my soul" she praised the Lord, "What a beautiful day".

Turning to Douglas "Listen to your old Ma' now"...

"Ma' you're not "old". He protested rolling his eyes at her.

"Hush, now and listen to what I've got to say. On the one hand, your so called "success" in the eyes of the world does not define you or "who" you are or "whose" you are, I do mean the Lord. You are the Lord's and not this world's, or have you forgotten? Never mind that for now, all they see is the outward appearance. Now the Lord, he looks in the heart. I have some questions for you to think on.

One : "Is all that you've accomplished in this life, all the monetary gain, all the 'success," is that 'all' you hope to accomplish in this life?"

Two: "Is that all that's in 'Your' heart?"

Listen now, or there's the other hand, to want 'True Riches'? Riches that last, and that cannot be taken away, the ones that are undefinable to the logical human mind and heart? Something that is only felt by the soul?

"You know, all the riches that your father has attained, many people say he is a success, and he is. Riches are not what define him, or his character. He is only as successful as the people he loves around him and he is surrounded by those who love him and have a deep respect for him. That my son, is true riches.

"Think of it this way if you will. If something terrible were to happen and we lost this place and God allowed it, we would still be rich indeed. Because we have our God to guide us. We have our health and each other, where we live or what we do doesn't account for much, only our faith in each other and a mighty God who is always looking out for our best interests and if he deems the ranch to go for our benefit, then so be it. God is always good, always kind. It is his goodness and mercy that keeps us going strong each and every day.

"If Marie gave you a chance, 'what is it that you want from her? And why?" Do you just want to have a marriage of convenience because it'll look good on your resume? Or something true and honorable in the sight of God and lasting, something that sustains you in the summer of your life and the cold dark of winter, because those times will come, when the storms breaks, the wind howls and beats on your door, but then a soft gentle voice breaks through and brings you inside out of the storm setting you by a roaring fire of their love bringing you back to life, "till death do you part?".

"Is she that kind of woman? Because whatever pain she's trying to hide from you or shame or guilt or whatever it is...I don't think she's learned to forgive herself. She has a great amount of fear I sense from what you've told us. "You know, 1 John 4:18 says, 'But perfect love casteth out fear: because fear hath torment.' Think about that". She finished her monologue as they were now on the back porch.

Entering the house, "That's exactly what Pop told me."

"Great minds think alike," she chuckled. "He is a wise man and he does have compassion for your plight, he did after all come," she pointed at herself, "chasing this fearful girl and I'm grateful everyday of my life that he did."

CHAPTER 36

DORRIS'S STORY

Douglas stopped short, shocked at this new revelation. "What were you afraid of Ma'? I've never heard this one before." Sitting down at the kitchen table.

"You didn't need to know before and now you do. Simply put I was afraid of love."

"How is that possible? You are the loving-est mom around and I know Dad thinks you are the "cats, meow". She laughed in spite of herself, then sobered, twisting her water glass.

"Before I met your father, I was in an abusive relationship. How I let it happen, I don't know, maybe because he charmed me, even now when the devil attacks my mind, I still can't say why I let myself get into that kind of situation. I knew I wanted out, I just didn't know how."

Douglas saw the remnants of pain cross her face. His lovely mother abused, his heart ached inside. He touched her hand consoling.

"Your father came into where I worked at the Feed store one day. He was kind and there was something different about him. It ate at me until one day I asked him about it, "Why was he kind and different, he wasn't just being nice?""

So straightforward, your father, "It's because of Christ in me," so simple and yet profound, for a sinner like me." Douglas couldn't imagine his mother being a "sinner," he'd only ever seen her a 'saint,' who sometimes sinned. Like when she got mad from time to time.

"I was shocked, when he told me he'd been praying for me. In the end I accepted the Lord as my savior. Eventually I got out of the abusive relationship, because I wasn't married to the guy only dating him when I told him I got saved, he beat me, that's when I knew for certain I had to get out, I reported him to the police, the rest is history."

"I thank the good Lord and your Dad for rescuing me. It took him two long years of patient waiting for me to realize that he truly loved me for myself and no other reason. But that revelation scared me and I ran away to an Aunt in Ohio."

Her thoughts went there remembering, a far off look on her face. Douglas waited for her to return. He smiled when she did focus on him.

"My aunt was the one who convinced me that your father was the one for me, for he found me two weeks later. She was a strong prayer warrior and had prayed for me that if he truly was 'God-sent' for her young niece that he would show up on her doorstep at exactly two o'clock in the afternoon, the next day."

"Obviously he did." Chuckled Douglas, wondering at the miracle.

Smiling, "Yes she admonished me before he brought me back home, to accept his love, because the Lord approved of him as my future husband, not only that but to accept was the only way I would grow in Christs love. I am a testament to your fathers' faithfulness and unfailing love that I would in kind learn to be a better christian. We married within the year.

Slightly dumbfounded, Douglas sat at the table marveling at the work God had accomplished in his parents lives. He'd witnessed only the love his parents had for each other never realizing how deep that love went and how it impacted their lives and those around them. He himself came to Christ as his savior because of their deep love for God and each other. He could never in his life ever have imagined his mother being abused the thought revolted. How could anyone harm such a lovely caring woman. He'd only ever thought of her as loved, protected, cherished.

Knowing then, he wanted that kind of love for Marie, he wanted to be that man for her, to love, cherish and protect. To guide her towards the love God bestowed on them all. He choked on the tears, when he realized he was not that man. He would have to change and rearrange things in his life in order to line them up with the Lord's example. Like his own father had done.

Wanting to be like his Dad for the first time in his life. Who now became a real hero in his eyes a true picture of Christ, a true believer, a "little Christ," walking this earth, showing and giving out the love of God freely. This would take time and perseverance on his part to make the changes necessary, a lifetime.

For now time was on his side, as Marie would not accept him at the moment, but giving over the situation to much prayer, he'd never felt anything so strongly before, it was overwhelming.

Douglas felt his Dad's presence enter the room, he'd sat down behind him, a while ago, as he'd been facing his mother. Doug turned to see tears glistening in his eyes, for his bride, having to share painful parts of her past, with their beloved boy. His "Darling Dorris," as he called his mom everyday of their lives. Moved to prayer as they stopped speaking, Dad held their hands asking Hilda and Ed to join them at the luncheon she'd made. They joined hands, he began his prayer:

"Dear Heavenly Father-
We thank thee for this blessed meal provided graciously by thine own hand. We thank thee for thy love and for the family that you've given to each of us. We thank thee for your love and faith unwavering and thy grace unending. Grant us thy wisdom in the face of uncertainty and for grace to see us through the future that thou hast ordained for us before time began. You thought of us... (he paused, clearing his throat for his emotions overwhelmed him)...We love you Lord and thank thee for thy many blessings. (He paused again) If I could ask one thing Lord?... Please give Edward the courage to ask Hilda out on a date. Amen."

Everyone's eyes opened immediately, both Hilda and Ed's eyes were as large as saucers and went blushing deeply to their plates. A burst of happy laughter ensued as the two shyly looked at one another, in mutual acceptance.

It was good to be home.

CHAPTER 37

DOUGLAS'S LETTER -
FRIDAY, AUGUST 19, 2005

A manila envelope arrived from Montana by signature mail on Friday morning. Marie was surprised when the worker had rung her doorbell and asked for her to sign. She hadn't purchased anything and she knew no-one in Montana, she didn't think so anyway.

The insert had been typed so there was no telling who it came from other than Heaven's Peak Ranch, Montana, as the return address.

Pulling the tab, taking out a single sheet of paper, her hand stopped mid-way out of the envelope. Her hand shook as she looked at the bold handwriting. Douglas. '... I was afraid to send this sooner...' She couldn't read this now, it was the first week of school and Sethy needed to be on his way. Pushing the papers back inside, she quickly ran upstairs and threw it onto her desk for later...much later.

"Seth, are you ready for school?, we've got to head out now."

"Mom, I can't find my shoe, I think Sam hid it again." Sam just came out of the bathroom, saying, "I did not! Mommy he's lying!"

"Well, you hid it last week!"

"But I didn't this week."

"Boys, Boys!" She shouted! "Stop this, this minute! Now you both go look in your rooms and under the beds, everywhere you can think of upstairs. I don't want to hear anymore arguing out of either of you until that shoe is found. We'll be late if you don't, now move it you two." She pointed up the stairs.

Lizzy casually walked out of the kitchen peanut butter smeared on her face from her peanut butter toast, shoes on the "wrong feet". Marie chose not to say anything other than, "go wipe your face Lizzy and brush your teeth please".

"Okay, Momma," she skipped to do the job.

Seth yelled from upstairs, "I found it Momma!"

"Where was it?", she asked as she got her own lunch together, zipping lunchboxes as she went.

He mumbled under his breath, "un__ th' b__...".

"Please Seth speak up, enunciate your words."

"Under the bed," he shuffled his feet.

"You should go apologize to your brother then, right?"

"Yes, Momma."

"I know it doesn't always feel good to humble oneself, but we must be right between God and man, that includes your brother." He nodded his head "Good boy" he shuffled along slowly to find his brother.

The words striking a chord in her own heart. She almost broke down crying, 'Wasn't she behaving as Seth was with his brother, as she was with Douglas? Blaming him for...for...Loving her? How ridiculous was that?' She would have to deal with this and soon, but not now. These kids needed to get to school and she was headed for work, too much to do and no time to do it.

Story of her life.

July 31, 2005

Dear Darling Marie,

I wanted to thank you for the best weekend of my life. It has in turn changed me for the better, I hope. To see the world around me in a different way thanks to you. To feel blessed, to know that I am blessed by God, to be grateful for every experience whether good or bad. To recognize God is in control of it all. I do not know of another way to thank you for helping to open the eyes of my heart. I think you stole it some time ago. I have also come to realize although you may not feel the same as I.

I must tell you that I love you truly with all my heart. I will never love another like I do you. You have captured my heart and my imagination. I try not to think about you, but it is a fruitless endeavor. How can you stop the sun from shining? How do you stop the flowers from blooming? Can you stop the stars from shining so brightly in the night sky? If there is a way I have not found it.

If you cannot love me, then I will not ever be loved by anyone else. Foolishly I had declared that I would not wait long, that I would move on, I had thought to myself. I was wrong. My affection for you is such that I will wait for you, because I realized that I have waited for you my whole life. I find that as I pray for you and the children on a daily basis, my love grows stronger and deeper. My faith in our Lord God grows greater each day.

Since it is within my power at this moment to do so, I ask you please to allow me to continue to write to you or at least to the children. I would like to get to know them better, to hear even one word about you would be enough for me. No, I take that back. I want you, all of you. To be with you, to spend time with you is my greatest joy, next to my love for our Lord. On the other hand if you do not wish to keep in contact with me, I understand. This letter as I review it does seem a bit desperate. I have no other defense for myself than an honest desire to always be there for you, 'in sickness and in health, forsaking all others'.

Only, If you so wish it, Please know that there is a man who will continue to love you until his dying breath. I have lived my adult life never having said, "I love you" to any other woman. I have only ever and will continue to love you truly, deeply from the bottom of my heart. I would gladly alter any part of my life, even my business life, if you would one day consent to be my wife. I have asked you once. I will not impose on your good graces and ask again. But if your feelings for me have changed and grown to have any form of affection for me, Know that I would cherish them and hold them dear unto myself.

I want more than anything to help you raise the children with you in the nurture and admonition of the Lord. I want so desperately to ease your burden, to yoke up with you. To truly love you as you so deserve to be loved, as God's daughter should be.

I imagine that you shine brighter when love is in your heart for another, the one your soul desires. Please know that wherever I am in the world, you my darling, will never go unloved by me. Allow me the privilege to love you for the rest of my life.

Ever Faithfully Yours-Douglas Arthur Fairbanks, III
Heaven's Peak Ranch, Montana

The tears streaked down her face the night she received the letter. Sitting in her bed, the pillows piled behind her back. The children finally in bed and down for the night. She waited an extra hour before reading it, because there was always the occasion to delay bedtime. Tonight she was blessed with obedience.

"How can he love me? It's just business," he'd originally even proposed in such a manner. "A marriage of convenience," he'd said. She and the children would be cared for and he would have the prestige of having a wife, 'a ready made family'. It's because of that fantastic, yet frustrating weekend. I let him 'take care of me' and somehow he had mistaken it for love." She had to nip this in the bud for he truly could not love her and she could not allow this to go on any longer. Knowing she had to be strong for her boys and daughter, she couldn't let him 'love' her. She wasn't worthy of him.

"Then why is your heart breaking?"

"My heart is deceitful above all things, who can know it? (Jeremiah 17:9) My heart is trying to deceive me into believing it's the right thing when it's not. I'd better hold on to logic, it's the only way."

"What does logic say? That it's okay to raise boys without a father?"

"Yes, it can be done. The Lord shall be my helper and my guide." Her heart went mute. "Who can fight against God, and win?"

"I'd better write that letter before I forget."

CHAPTER 38

SAM'S DREAM - AUGUST 20, 2005

Saturday morning she went through her morning routine of getting ready for the day. Just because it was the weekend didn't mean that she could slack off. There was always laundry to do and chores around the house that hadn't been done during the week so she did them first thing.

On her way back upstairs after having fed the kids running through a few chores downstairs, she saw the mail truck across the street, which meant he would be at her house in about half hour, just enough time to get that letter in the mail.

Finding Sam sitting at her desk with all of his crayons out. "Sam what are you doing in here?"

"I'm colorin.'" He sat dangling his feet in the chair at her desk, wiggling and smiling as he colored.

"Yes, I see that, but why are you here, at Mommy's work desk? You have yours in your room. Why aren't you there?"

"B'cause I needed the special paper. You said you used it to send to special people. So I am too."

She had to think, "Who did Sam think was 'special,' her mom? Perhaps his Sunday school teacher? "Okay, who are you writing too, grandma?"

"Nu-uh." Shaking his head, in the negative. Was he playing a game?

"Um, Ms. Levy, your Sunday school teacher?" She knew he had a crush on the pretty red headed teacher.

"Uh-uh." Sam kept wiggling in his seat and drawing.

Frustrated she sighed, "Then who?" She put her hands on her hips.

"Your boy friend, Mr. Doug."

Marie stood there stunned, "Why...why do you have to write him a special letter?" She looked closely at his drawings, they were getting really good for an almost three year old.

"B'cause," Sam kept drawing. "I had a dream about him last night playing ball with me, so I want to send him a picture of us playin.'" Sam continued to refine his drawing adding details like grass to the picture. Marie looked at the picture and in it Sam, with a moniker pointing to 'himself,' and one for Douglas, while his sister and big brother were sitting watching them play sitting in chairs. Then he began to draw people up in "the sky," in the clouds. Curious about that. So she asked, "Who's that, Sam?'

"Oh, that's Daddy and my big brother, Robbie, the one who went to heaven to be with Daddy and Jesus. They's watchin' me play ball from the clouds and they are cheerin' me on."

A sob caught in her throat, she put her hand to her mouth to quiet the sound. Tears filling her eyes. Sam was engrossed so he hadn't noticed her distress. When she could calm herself enough to speak, she asked, "Why is that Mr. Doug and not Pa-paw?" As the kids called their grandpa.

"B'cause, I like him. I want him to be my new daddy. So I want'a tell him all the fun things we can do together. Like play ball, fly a kites, make a fort, I want a fort to play in Mommy, but I want to make it Sethy can help me' n' Mr. Doug too." Sam took a deep breath and then he can read me stories too, at night. I might let him read to Lizzy, but that's be okay 'cause he could be her dad too. I think I'd like that lots."

"But I read stories to you and we do many of those things together and Pa- paw plays ball with you."

"Yup, I know dat. But Pa-paw can't always come when I want to play. And maybe if Mr. Doug was my daddy, then he can live at out house and play with me all the time, when he's not workin'. Sethy says, 'Daddy's hav' ta work, then they can play, he knows he goes to school.'"

Taking a deep breath how did she let down her son and tell him Douglas couldn't be his father. She'd messed that all up. Kneeling down to his level on the chair, she began "Sam honey, I don't know if Mr. Doug can be your daddy."

"Why not? We don't have a daddy and we need one." Looking confused.

"It's just not the way things work when you're a grown up, he's a very busy man and I don't think he can be your daddy."

"You can ask him. I know he'll say, Yes, cause you're the prettiest Mommy and you make the best-est homemade Mac' n' cheese and apple pie."

"It doesn't work that way Sam. I would have to love him to marry him and I don't think I can."

"But why not Mommy, he's a 'good guy,' I can tell he'll be nice to us. You have to love him." He said emphatically as only a little boy can trying to get his own way. His lips pouting.

"It's complicated, honey."

"Whats' that mean?"

She sighed resigned that he wouldn't stop until she answered all his questions. "It means that there are too many things that are in the way, for it to happen."

"Well, why can't you just move the stuff outta' the way so he can be my daddy". Wise Sam, shrugged his shoulders throwing out his hands, "See it's easy."

So Simple in the eyes of a child, "Out of the mouths of babes" she thought, "and yet, so hard to do." Sitting next to him more confused than she was ever before. "I don't know if I can, Sam." The tears stung her eyes, then rolled down her cheeks. Tears welled in his eyes looking resigned to having no dad, but an idea struck his own little head. "Can I send him the picture anyway, please Mom? I want him to 'me'member' me." He said sniffling.

Marie relented not willing to completely break his heart, which she may have done already. "Yes, you may. Finish it and then I'll send it today in the mail. Hurry though I saw the mail man a bit ago, he'll be here soon."

He brightened some. "I'll hurry, I'm going to ask Sethy to help me write the letter, he can write faster than me. Thank you, Mommy." He took off from his chair grabbing his papers and crayons calling out for Seth. How she wished with all her heart that life were as simple as a child believed it could be. She found no solace within herself, being torn to give in and put her trust in God. To allow him to have control in her life. To submit herself under the umbrella of God's authority and Douglas's as the "man of the house". As was His intention from the beginning of time.

She knew that "Submission," in todays' world is as good as a four letter word, but she knew it to be a false sense of empowerment in todays feminist movement. She worked yes, but only out of necessity.

When she had married Robert, yes, he had wanted her to be at home with the children in their formative years, but if she so desired, he had told her in their many conversations as husband and wife that she was free to return to work. Many women in the Bible were examples of "working women".

If she had an idea that she could work from home and have that "home-based-business, he was all for it. Because it kept her and the children in the safety of his covering. They wouldn't have to hire babysitters for her to work, only for going out on dates or special occasions. But she had decided that she wanted to stay at home for as long as possible with the kids. She had not regretted that decision.

But when he died, all of that changed, and she had to juggle motherhood and work. She did not like having to leave the kids in the care of another until they reached school age. 'What was a widowed single mother to do?' She sat down in the chair that Sam had vacated, spent even though the day had just began. 'Could she love Douglas and let go of the past? Also her present, could she turn it over to the Lord?' Putting the "Do Not Disturb," sign on the knob of her door before closing the door to her office, she needed to pray and seek the Lord's answers to the many questions floating around in her head and heart.

"Dear Lord, Help me!"- at the moment it was all she could utter before her eyes welled with tears and allowed herself to cry. She cried for Douglas, for the hurt she was causing him. She cried for her children for the hurt she was causing them as well. And lastly for herself for the love that she had lost and felt she could never regain ever again.

A soft breeze blew in from outside the open window caressing her cheek. "But haven't you?" Her conscience prodded.

"Haven't I What?" She asked herself.

"Found love once again?" Her conscience prodding her to examine her heart carefully.

"How can I bear it, Lord, to love again?" She prayed in the quiet.

"Why are you looking at love as a burden to bear?" She asked herself.

"Because I'm afraid." There she'd finally said it, to herself, finally admitted it. she was afraid.

"Why are you afraid of love?" Her heart asked.

Ah, 'the heart of the matter is always a matter of the heart,' pastors sermon words came back to her then.

"I'm afraid to love him because if I do... I may lose him like I did Robert and I don't know that I could handle it if he died. It would hurt too much, it would kill me too." She admitted the fear that was keeping her hostage. She felt impressed to open Robert's KJV Bible to Ecclesiastes 3, it was some of Robert's favorite verses, he would read them right before bed, for as long as she'd known him.

Ecclesiates Chapter 3:

To every thing there is a season, and
a time to every purpose under heaven:
2 A time to be born, and a time to die;
a time to plant, and a time to pluck
up that which is planted;
3 A time to kill, and a time to heal; a time to break down, and
a time to build up;
4 A time to weep, and a time to
laugh; a time to mourn, and a
time to dance;
5 A time to cast away stones, and
A time to gather stones together; a
time to embrace, and a time to
refrain from embracing;
6 A time to get, and a time to lose;
A time to keep, and a time to cast away;
7 A time to rend, and a time to sew;
a time to keep silence, and a time to speak;
8 A time to love...,

Marie paused there, her eyes full of tears spilling over, she continued...

...and a time to hate;
a time of war, and a time of peace.

She jumped down to two verses Robert had highlighted. Verses 11 and 14.

11 He hath made everything beautiful in his time; ...

..., so that no man can find out the work that
God maketh from the beginning to the end.
14 I know that, whatsoever God Doeth, it
shall be forever: nothing can be put to it,
nor any thing taken from it: and God
doeth it, that men should fear before him.

Marie realized she was having a 'lightbulb' moment. "The Lord, was confirming in her heart that he had been at work in all of her life that he was the one orchestrating all of these events to happen."

Choking back sobs, "So, 'It's time for me to...' she choked on her tears, 'for me to move on with my life and love again."

"...a time to heal..., a time to plant..., a time to build up..., a time to laugh, ...a time to dance, ...a time to embrace..., a time to love, ... a time of peace..."

Marie allowed the words from scripture to wash over her, "Okay Lord, I give up". The tears rolled down her face freely as she surrendered to his will. No longer was there confusion or frustration, only peace and joy, she laughed as the cleansing filled her soul. And experiencing His goodness and grace bestowed upon her.

Knowing in that moment His thoughts for her had never been to cause her misery, they had always been a way to work good things into her life.

"For I know the thoughts that I think toward you, saith the Lord, thoughts of peace, and not of evil, to give you an expected end." Jeremiah 29:11 floated to the top of her mind.

She alone had been the one fighting against her savior's perfect plan for her life. Right then she asked for his forgiveness for her waywardness, for not trusting fully in his goodness or his plan for her and her children. "Lord, help me to make amends with Douglas. To repair the breach". I will mail the children's letter and go from there. The plan was tentative...tenuous at best. But some leaps were best taken one step at a time.

"Baby steps".

CHAPTER 39

THE CHILDREN'S LETTER,
MONDAY, AUGUST 29, 2005

"Douglas!" Dorris shouted to him, as he was packing for his return trip home to Madrone Valley. "There's a letter for you". She said in a sing song voice.

"A letter?", he was expecting an envelope by courier. Perhaps that's what she meant. "I'll be down in just a minute," he zipped his bag closed then headed down the stairs, with the valise.

Dorris waited for him at the bottom, smiling and holding the letter. "Hurry and open, it I want to see." What had gotten into her? She was never this excited about mail.

He took the letter from her hand realizing it was not the letter he'd been expecting. It was addressed in a child's script, 'There was no return address. Strange?'

Opening it he took out the thick stationary. Folded into thirds were three sheets. Taking it over to the hall table he set down two of the three sheets, the top had been a Childs drawing.

He took time to study it. There was himself in a baseball cap and the shirt and jeans he'd been wearing on the day he'd met Marie's children, albeit 'accidentally'. She hadn't allowed him to meet her with the kids before, the baseball event had been a ruse on his part, but the kids were half asleep, so he knew they couldn't have possibly remembered him, could they?

This boy was talented. Including himself in the portrait catching a ball. Dorris's voice caught as she looked from beside him, seeing Dad and Robbie sitting in the clouds watching them play with smiles on their faces. "Oh, Artie." Always reverting to his childhood name when she was emotional. Tears stung his eyes as well.

Hope began to stir in his heart as he put down the drawing and picked up the second letter, in child script, but rather nice penmanship.

August 20, 2005 Saturday

Dear Mr. Fairbanks,

Mom says, that's your last name. Sam wanted me to write to you a letter for him. Sam says, He really likes you even though we only met you once. But I know it was twice. I remember you from after the baseball game we went to for the first time. I'm sorry I was cranky. I never said, sorry. That night wore me out, I was little-er then.

I remember seeing my mom kissing your cheek and I hoped after we might see more of you. But we didn't. I was sad about that. I miss having my dad around.

Sam thinks you could do a good job at it, but mom says, it's complicated. Whatever that means.

Douglas could hear the eye roll over that statement...

I think she's just scared that you'll die in an accident just like our dad did.

Lizzy likes the way you smell. (Girls) she says it's the way a daddy should smell. I said I don't think so, she got mad at me and punched me cause I didn't want to write it, but she won, so I had to write that to you. We all hope that we can write to you again, if mom lets us.

Always your friends-

Seth, Lizzy and Sam LaSalle (Marie's Kids)

Thankfully his mother had a seat there he had to sit down after that letter. His legs would have given out at the emotions that were rolling through him. He was bewildered that these children whom he'd only met twice in fact would open their hearts to him. He handed the letter to his mother to read. His hand shook as he reached for the last letter. Marie's letter.

August 20, 2005

Douglas-

The Lord has been working on my broken heart with a vengeance recently. When I received your letter yesterday by courier, I honestly didn't know which end was up. Please read Ecclesiastes 3:1-8, 11 & 14, also Jeremiah 29:11. It explains better than I can put into words what is happening in my heart.

Love-Marie

P.S. Thank You for the Lovely bouquet.

Douglas sat with shaking hands, "Ma, where's a bible?"

"Right here, what's the matter?" pulling out a drawer from the hall table and producing the Bible. He handed her the letter to read for herself.

Taking it he looked up the passages reading them all, twice over. After reading he looked up to his mother who was reading the last letter. He said, "I think she's trying to tell me that she's ready to...' he swallowed hard, 'to... love me, at least to think about it."

"She is, but like her boys so astutely said, 'she's afraid," afraid of the future. Now is the time for God's Word to go to work through you, show her what 1 John 4:18 is all about. You must show her that no matter what is in her past, her present or the future. God will be that perfect love for her and you can only be a conduit of His love. You will fail, you are a man after all and 'man' has failings. But you can help her, with his help to guide her towards that love she longs for."

"Yes, I think I understand that now Ma". Thank you for praying for me for us, I know you've been praying the situation to be resolved in his way and in his timing."

"As a mother, it's been difficult to watch you go through this, yet it was necessary for your pride to be broken. To come to a place of brokenness before him. So that you could be an instrument that he could use."

It was true he realized. Kissing his mothers cheek, "my relationship with my savior has been put to rights. I hope you know that it's not just a passing thing for me anymore or my walk with Him to be taken lightly. I'm in it for the long haul."

"Good, you're gonna need it, it you plan on raising those kids. I just want the best for you all, I love you son."

"I love you too, Ma.'"

"Now get out of here and get that girl and bring her and those kids to us, so you can get married. Soon! I'm ready for those grand babies to start running around this house."

"Mother!"

"What! I'm not getting any younger and I want to see you happy and finally settled."

"She may not want to get married right away."

"I've been praying that the Lord gives her a good shove towards the alter," she laughed in glee, clapping her hands in delight. "Yes, Lord!"

Douglas laughed with her, "To everything there is a season..."

"Don't you sass your Momma, boy. The Lord and I have an understanding and I promise you it will be sooner rather than later. Now go get your things I can hear the helicopter landing out in the field."

He rose up and hugged his mother tight. She reciprocated and made sure he had a snack in hand as he headed out towards the helicopter and towards home, and to Marie.

CHAPTER 40

DOUGLAS'S ACCOUNT - AUGUST 30, 2005 TUESDAY

Sitting in a club chair, Douglas waited for Mr. Perry to be done with his previous appointment. He was running a bit late. Which was unusual but he understood things happen. Mostly he was wondering how he would react if he ran into Marie here. It was possible, but not unlikely either because she was the finance manager on his project, unless she passed it on to someone else. He hadn't kept up faithfully with this project, just 'okay-ing' things over the phone or by e-mail.

His leg bounced in nervousness. A coquettish voice interrupted his musings, she tossed her fine blonde hair when she got his attention with a bat of overworked eye lashes. "Would you care for some coffee, while you wait?"

"What? No…, uh, Thank you." He tried to resume his thoughts when she interrupted again.

"It's no trouble at all really." She brightened her smile a mile wide.

He brushed her off with a final and firm, "No, thank you. I'm sure you have other tasks to do than to have to wait on me."

Visibly she pouted and was going to speak again when Mr. Perry's office door opened. Douglas stood. Mr. Perry exited with an older gentleman who's hat and clothing had seen better days, but was well kept.

"I'm so thankful Mr. Perry. God bless you, sir."

"He has already, Roy, tell the family I said, 'Hello'. I'll come by later this week." Roy, with a sparkle in his eye and a grateful heart put his cap back on his head saying to them all, "That be a good man!" Walking out with a brighter smile and a quick step.

Douglas smiled at the man. Mr. Perry saw him standing there," I'm sorry to keep you waiting, Mr. Fairbanks, but we had a "little emergency". That's dealt with now, come on in." He gestured for Douglas to enter the office, turning to his secretary he said, "Please hold all my calls for the next hour. Thank you". Before she could inject herself he closed the door.

"Well, Mr. Fairbanks, I hope you know all is running smoothly with the project and you are satisfied with how things are coming along. Stan said this as he unrolled the blue prints of the project onto the architects table. Except for the delay with the windows, everything is coming along quite well I want you to know."

"Yes, I'm quite satisfied, I drove by there yesterday. It looks so much better than I thought actually, having been away from it for the last two months. I never dreamed restoring a historic home was going to involve so much red tape and hoops to jump through." He sighed thinking about all that was involved.

"That's why you have us to help you jump through those hoops. I'm sorry about some of the unnecessary delays that occurred. But I think we're back on schedule once the windows were approved by the historical society."

"I'm blessed I have the means to take on the project. I couldn't imagine any one who doesn't have the means to do it, could really get into trouble restoring a historical home. But, when I'm not in residence, I'll give the key to the historical society and they can "show" it on their "Historic Homes" walk that they do."

"I think the council was pleased you would be willing to let it be seen once restored."

"I'm sure they did. I think I could see dollar signs in their eyes, from the revenue that 'historic walk' makes for the city."

Both men laughed at that.

Stan gestured, "Lets take a look at these final things that are left to do and see if we're on track and on budget with the revisions the historical committee had us implement with the landscaping." Seeing a change come over Douglas of apprehension and doubtful excitement? Why was that? The project was a long daunting one, understandable given with such an undertaking as this home was. He sensed there was something more going on. "Let, me call my finance officer Ms. LaSalle, she can go over the numbers with us." At the suggestion Douglas hesitated. Stan put the phone back down slowly.

"What's the matter?" Douglas asked as he saw him lower the phone without calling anyone an odd expression on Stan's face.

"You love her." Stan stated solemnly.

Douglas was confused at the change in topic. "Who...? What do you mean?"

"My daughter Marie, that's who." Stan felt chagrined, "I've seen the signs of something going on with her but I dismissed it. Until now. Tell me I'm wrong." Stan challenged him, his tone tight, his jaw clamped, then softened as if hit.

"Marie is your daughter?" Astonishment written all over his face.

"Yes, she is my only daughter. Now tell me if I'm wrong."

The pieces finally fit together, all the little things that Marie either said or omitted saying, like when she hinted at working for her father. It all made sense now. Douglas confessed, "No, sir, you are not wrong." Running a hand through his hair. "I didn't know she was your daughter. You have different last names, I never suspected, because she's only spoken of you as "her boss" and spoke of you by your title, "Mr. Perry". She never gave a hint of who you were to her. Doug sat down in the nearest chair, deflated of all energy at the revelation.

On the other hand Stan remained standing. "Do you know she has three children to care for? I won't have anyone toying with her emotions and especially those of the children, he stated firmly with conviction of fire in his voice and eyes. Using his steely blue eyes for emphasis and his former Marine training brought to fore in his stance.

"I'm astonished Marie has not told you, her parents, anything. I mean I thought she would have talked things over about us, at least to her mom. What daughter doesn't go to her mom about her dating life?"

"She hasn't let out a peep. Marie usually tells me everything. Tell me the truth, about everything, I won't have anything less." He stood rigid in front of Douglas hands to hips.

Douglas was not intimidated, he just felt sorry that Mr. Perry had been in the dark about their relationship. He could understand that she didn't want to be involved in the media, that often came snooping around for a 'scoop' of gossip. Yet, to keep it from her family, he could not comprehend her actions. 'Maybe if she didn't tell them it wasn't real? Who knew where her thoughts lay'. He set it aside.

"Shall I start at the beginning?"

"I should think so." Stan decided, since Douglas was sitting, he'd better take a seat as well, so he sat in the club chair opposite him, it looked to be a long involved story. He had to admit to himself that he was hurt by his daughter. 'Why wouldn't she come to him? They always talked about things'.

"When I met your daughter over a year ago at that impromptu luncheon, I thought she was beautiful. I never intended anything to come of the actual meeting with Robert, or you. I knew Robert must be a busy man, but I made the attempt anyway. I figured at least I could get an appointment onto the books for sometime in the future. I had nothing but time to see this project through as it was something of an unknown for me. And I have a home elsewhere."

"I'm going off track..., the luncheon at Demitrio's' set my path. When Nonna made me apologize with the bouquet of flowers. I had found her across the street at the park making a list. I had interrupted her. We chatted and I must say that I was intrigued. Marie was unlike anyone I had met before. She politely declined any advance I attempted. Just so you know I just asked her on a date.

We weren't an 'official couple'. We just went on dates, we mostly talked about work and the renovations, as I think about it she didn't say much about her family life. We probably had a date twice or three times a month, some because of traveling that I do for my business. But she wouldn't allow more than that. I would sneak in a date or two when I would come to check on the progress of the project. I would "bump" into her here and go out to lunch with her to talk about what I observed with what was going on.

Stan chuckled here, "No wonder I've missed her for lunches! She's been with you, and here I thought she was running errands or something, here she is being courted. Ha!"

Douglas was glad Stan was not more antagonistic, that gave him a dose of courage. That is partly true, I would go with her on some errand or other. Dry cleaning, etc. Other times I tried to get her out, but she would always be 'busy' and wouldn't allow me to join her. I can charm a girl usually, but she held firm."

"I should hope so, for the kids' sake."

"The thing is, Marie didn't tell me about the kids until this past May and shared her story about her loss with me. I was really shocked to say the least that she was a mother. But I didn't think it was a deterrent to having the occasional date, I was so intrigued by her, I didn't see a problem with it. I asked her to go out with me again as "friends" for my 20th High School Reunion. I didn't think she would accept, but I figured I'd ask any way, since it's a few hours away. And I said we'd stay the weekend at my hotel. With separate rooms. Doug clarified, holding up his hand to suppress any argument. "To my surprise she accepted."

"What?" When was this?" Stan was shocked.

"The weekend of June 24th. We had dinner with her that Sunday, how could this be, she was home? I don't understand."

"I have to confess I asked her to marry me that weekend."

"What?" Stan sat forward.

Douglas held up his hands in surrender, "Whoa, wait, wait, let me explain."

"You had better, I must say I am so shocked! I don't even know what to do."

"Yes, I asked her, but she declined me, by the end of the weekend she walked away from me and didn't look back."

"But you still love her?"

"More than anything. Yes, I still do. I'm just afraid that if she rebuffs me again..., well I'd rather not run into her."

Stan was sitting back fingers steepled drumming them together, inhaling deeply, and letting it out. He closed his eyes a moment before he said, "If I may, I think the Lord has sent you into her life for a purpose. Perhaps to help her fully heal from her loss. I would love to see my daughter whole again."

"I want to help her, love her, but she has to want my love in return, I cannot force her to love me. Even though I know that I could love her all the days of my life."

"There is something that I need to know for certain before we continue with this discussion."

"Anything, sir."

"I need to know your testimony of salvation, because without it I cannot give my consent for a marriage, were there to be one in the future. I know my daughter is a grown woman but I'm still her father. "How can two walk together except they be agreed?"

"Amos 3:3" Douglas answered, "I understand your apprehension, because it seems this has just been sprung on you. A year ago, I would not have advised a marriage between us. But ever since our relationship has grown bit by bit and then her refusal actually helped me to return to the Lord first."

"As for my testimony of salvation, I was quite young perhaps five years old. My father is a farmer, so he used to teach me lessons about the Lord through the farm lessons about sowing and reaping. One night we had a campfire going, we were set to make some s'mores. I was burned, nothing serious mind you but it was enough to scare me about burning in the lake of fire forever. That night my mother talked to me at bedtime I had many questions but in the end I trusted Christ as my savior."

"That's wonderful, how is your relationship with the Lord now."

"I will admit now that I had been backslidden for sometime, even while I was with Marie. Nothing immoral mind you, I just want to be clear in that regard. I was a prodigal son to him for a while. I dated the girls of the world, with abandon, and didn't think anything of it. The Lord had become a stranger to me. I had chased the 'gods of wealth and status, power even'. For whatever reason He has blessed me with wealth, but perhaps it was to bring me to my knees. I had foolishly thought in my pride, "Who could refuse me, 'I'm Wealthy'".

"My Daughter."

"Hmm, yes, Marie. She certainly put me in my place, rightfully so. Rather the Lord used her to bring me back to himself."

"How so?"

"I realized when she had refused me that I was consumed with myself and my selfish desires. I was empty with frivolity chasing things that weren't needful for a truly fulfilling life. She made me realize I needed a helpmate, someone to help keep me in the ways of the Lord."

"A helpmate can keep you grounded. Anything else, you want to share?"

"I know now I can't be in control of every situation. All of my so called wisdom is nothing compared to what God has for me as his child and I need to trust him and not doubt his intentions for my life. The Father knows what is best for me even when I don't."

"How is your devotional life now?"

"Much improved. I start my morning at five in the morning, I read my Bible and pray for an hour. I go for a jog after that, so I can continue to meditate on what I've just learned or read about. Then I get ready and start my day. Either at home or at the office."

"So you would be able to be home some days, working?"

"Yes, usually Tuesday or Friday's on rare occasions, both".

Stan pondered that for a while. Chewing it over in his mind before he spoke.

"So you would be home sometimes?"

"Yes, I wrote her a letter recently telling Marie that I would change it all just for her. I'd be willing to change my occupation, for her. I've only received one letter from her, it just arrived yesterday."

Blowing out a sigh, "...but she's refused you?" Stan asked, pulling at his chin as he watched Douglas.

"It's here, you may read it." Doug pulled it from his breast pocket the note looked read and handled much.

Stan took the letter and read his daughters words. There was no need to read the verses. He had been praying these verses over his daughter from the beginning of her mourning and sorrow. That the Lord would somehow bring an end to it, and she would have a time of joy once again. Right now it was looking as if he was answering those prayers. Tears came unbidden into his eyes. Wiping at them, he cleared his throat a few times.

"So tell me Douglas. I know that you say that you love Marie and you know that she has children, but are you willing enough to care for her children and call them your own? What if, when you are married you cannot have any of your own? Will that change your attitude or perspective?"

That stopped Douglas, he'd never contemplated that scenario. The truth rose to the surface, "At my age, to be honest even though Marie is young I don't expect to have children. But should the Lord will, and bless our marriage in such a way. Rest assured that I will not treat Roberts children differently. They would all be mine to care for. If we are married. I would be receiving a gift in them and I will not trample on the Lord's gift towards me."

"If I may ask, what is your age, Douglas?"

"I'm thirty-eight come November. I know I'm a bit older...' Stand held up his hand to stop him. "Age is of little consequence to me. I'm seven years older than my own wife. In the Bible, Abraham was older than Sarah by ten years and they were still blessed with a son in their "old age". What truly matters is your love for Marie, because the children will one day grow up and be gone and it will only be the two of you."

Douglas pondered this a moment and did something he'd never imagined he would do. Rising from his seat he humbled himself before this man of faith, saying "Sir, it would please me very well and be a great honor if you gave me your blessing to continue courting your daughter in hopes that one day she will marry me if she so chooses."

Stan was immediately struck with a love for this boy, nee, this man who loved his daughter. It was what she needed now. A man. That in itself was a miracle in his eyes. Laying his hand on Douglas's bowed head, he said, "Yes, I consent." He prayed,

"O' Lord my God hearken unto my prayer. Now be pleased to bless the house of your servant, that it may continue forever in your sight; for you O' sovereign Lord, have spoken and with your blessing the house of your servant will be blessed forever.' Lord keep these children under the mighty shadow of your wing, guide them unto all righteousness and truth. Holy Spirit indwell them richly and show yourself strong in their lives as they live out their faith before you. May they be forever faithful to the house of the Lord. May they live out their purpose before you. To love you Lord God with all their heart, soul, mind, and strength, together. In Jesus precious name. Amen"

Both men were full of emotion and freely allowed the tears to roll for there was no shame in weeping for joy. Each man pulled out a handkerchief and mopped the tears from their eyes. Standing, Douglas only felt it right to embrace Mr. Perry, his hopefully, soon to be, 'father-in-law'. Stan accepted and embraced him as a son. A squeaky turn of the doorknob was heard, fumbling papers were also heard giving each man a moment to compose themselves. Marie walked in slightly frazzled. Wearing a light cream top with cap sleeves, black pencil skirt, black pumps and her hair piled on top of her head in a messy bun with a pencil going through it. Her only make up that he could tell was a magenta lipstick, maybe a hint of mascara. She looked so lovely he could hardly breathe.

"I'm sorry for being late Mr. Perry, no one told me that Mr. Fairbanks was here to go over, to review the budget."

"Please calm down Marie dear. You're unnerving me with all your bustle." Stan admonished her in a loving tone, which in turn made her stop in her tracks.

"I'm sorry sir," she laid the folder down at the table it landed in a haphazard manner. There was something different about Douglas. She couldn't explain 'why?', as she looked at him for the first time in almost two months. Her heart betrayed her by stopping completely, then beating like a mad drum it hurt physically to look at him. He was so handsome in that black suit. 'Was it the same one he wore to the Reunion?' Her heart sighed at the sight of him. Rubbing her chest, to stop it from hammering so, to slow it down. She had to talk the nerves away, her hands sweat, so she ran them down her skirt. "I hope everything is... is..' she stopped.

Father and Douglas were looking at her strangely, one smiling, the other one with a wistful expression on his face.

Stan said, "I'm glad you're here Marie we were just talking about you...'

She interrupted, "I know. I'm sorry. I'm late it's..."

Stan interrupted her, 'It has nothing to do with work."

"Then what is it?" Her eyes grew as large as saucers. "Oh no." she said whispering to herself.

"You've been caught red handed, Marie. Douglas told me his side of the story."

"Have I? Oh, has he." She tried to evade his look.

"Yes, Douglas and I have been discussing your, uh- courtship. As was or is? Marie quickly thought, 'My Dad's calling him on a first name basis? Uh-oh.'

"My Courtship?" She swallowed hard, eyes looking like a cornered rabbit.

Douglas felt sympathy for her. Her breathing became erratic. "Yes, Douglas and I have had a long conversation about the two of you... I think you need to have a talk of your own. Just so you know," he stood up in front of his one and only precious daughter, rubbing her upper arms. "I have given Douglas my blessing to marry you." He hugged her, squeezing her tight. "I would not consent for a less worthy man, my dear." He kissed her on the forehead, releasing her.

Douglas gulped, now understanding the new yoke he would have to embrace, should Marie agree to marry him. "Take my yoke upon you and learn of me: for I am meek and lowly in heart: and ye shall find rest unto your souls. For my yoke is easy, and my burden is light."-

The gentle words from Matthew 11:29 whispered to his heart, he decided to find rest in His grace.

CHAPTER 41

THE TELLING

Stan turned to face Douglas, his daughter tucked into his arm. "There is something about Marie that you should know before you go on further..."

"Father, NO!"-a look of terror filled her face and tears immediately filled her eyes.

"Yes, my dear. You have to find a way to tell him, let him know. "The truth shall make you free..." Daughter, you will never be free to love him until you tell him all. I suspect since this whole business has been kept a secret that it's been hindering you from moving on and moving forward in your life, or at least part of the reason, isn't it?"

Marie nodded and wiped the tears rolling down her face. Stan kissed her head releasing her and just walked out the door, but stopped before he closed it saying, "Please tell him daughter. I love you always and always."

"I love you too, Daddy."

Douglas had not understood their cryptic talk, but could see that she steeled herself for what was to come. Waiting patiently for her to speak, hopefully an answer to this riddle would soon be forthcoming. He attempted to reach out to her, but she turned away. His heart plummeted.

Suddenly she sounded strong and in control of herself. "Douglas please sit." She paused a moment. "What I have to relate to you I can only do if you don't look at me." His hand reached out to her but fell to his side. As she shook her head side to side, telling him, 'No,' by her actions. He couldn't sit this felt ominous so he stood waiting for her to begin. She felt his presence so near. "Please Douglas," she whispered as she went and stood by the glass wall, that was over looking the greenway and woods beyond. Her posture stooped, her head hung in, 'shame?'

He finally sat to where he could see her reflection in the glass. She shivered but it was not from the cold. She crossed her arms, rubbed them slowly. He wanted to go to her, but he knew she would not allow it. There was a great silence that filled the room between them, then she began her story resigned to tell it.

Sigh

"When I was fifteen I was a volleyball player at my high school. At that time we lived about a mile away. So most days I walked or rode my bicycle to school on non-practice days." She shifted uncomfortably, comforting herself, hugging herself.

"One day I couldn't ride my bike back home because of a flat tire. So I decided that because I didn't live that far, I'd leave it and come back for it later. There was a wooded lot I always walked past on my way home...', she swallowed many times before she could continue. "Someone came up behind me, I was hit in the head, so

I never saw my attacker. I was then dragged into the woods and 'forced...' you understand?" The pain etching her sweet face, was torture to him.

Swallowing, "Yes" he said unbelieving yet comprehending, feeling her hurt.

She spoke in a voice not her own, as if this event happened to someone else. "I was severely beaten and I was actually shot. I don't know why, but I was left for dead. I don't know 'why'? maybe the person thought I would bleed out before anyone found me." She shrugged, shook her head not understanding. "Generally I was home about the same time everyday, so my mother thought something was wrong when I didn't show up at the usual time, she waited half an hour before she started making calls to my friends and their parents. It was a small town so everyone began to look for me.

A neighbor found my backpack on the side of the road by the wooded lot. I was found around dusk that night. Only by God's mercy and grace did I pull through. I didn't want to of course when I finally woke up, I just wanted to die, I was so ashamed, embarrassed, severely depressed." She gave a harsh laugh.

"Then a reporter somehow got into the hospital and without my parents consent or that of the staff, he came in when I was dozing and began taking pictures of me. When I woke because of the weird noise I'd heard. I told him to get out. I had to scream bloody murder before he took off. They never found out who the guy was but my pictures ended up all over the papers even national ones the following day."

'So this is why she is afraid of the media. Poor girl, no wonder.'

"I was so distraught, I don't know if my parents thought I could ever recover. I just wanted to die. They took me to psychologists to get me help, put me on meds the whole bit. I wouldn't cooperate with them. I felt my life was over. Robert had been my boyfriend at the time, we'd been friends for years before then. I told him I never wanted to see him again. He did honor my wishes for a time, but after a few months he showed up and wouldn't take no for an answer. He just sat with me. We never talked. He came everyday. He did that for months, just come and be with me without saying a word, after work, after school, after church. He would pray silently, I could tell. We'd known each other a long time, I knew him.

Then one day, he just started praying aloud and then just shared, what he'd learned during Sunday school or church, bit by bit. He didn't always talk much he didn't have to. I couldn't stand a lot of talking back then. I didn't eat, so he began bringing some of my favorite junk foods. You see I went from a healthy one hundred and twenty pounds or so, to a wraith. I was about eighty five pounds before my comeback to living life again.

Slowly, step by step, he tempted me to live once again. The treats at first were freely given, but then he would "charge" me for a favorite memory or something benign, like what was my favorite color or favorite movie..., before he would give it to me. He was smart that way, you see in a way God used him to bring me back to life, to the land of the living. Now can you understand why I'm terrified of reporters?"

Douglas nodded, 'Yes'.

"And why it's been so difficult to let the memory of Robert go?" Turning back to face Douglas now, she conveyed passionately, "Robert was there for me, in my worst moments, always silently loving me, praying for me. He was everything to me. So when he died, I just fell apart. My 'idol' was taken away, I only kept going for the kids sake. I couldn't even stop, to grieve properly. I was so angry at God. 'How could he do this to me?' I felt betrayed." The grief shone, plain on her face.

"I went through the motions of going to church only because I knew it was right, but I didn't feel anything from the preaching. I didn't allow it to nourish me." Marie paced the room now as she let her aggravation out.

"Then I met you and things began to change within me. Recently a guest preacher came on a Sunday, basically his message was about letting God be God, no matter what happened in your life. There was a plan and I shouldn't get in the way of His plan. Because then I would be hindering His work in my life."

"Talk about getting hit with a metaphorical 2x4." Giving a small laugh. "Realizing that all this time I've been trying to put a cork in His work in my life because of my insecurities and pride." She stopped pacing and faced the window again.

Douglas, sat in silence he absorbing all that she said and the implications of what happened to her, 'She survived still..., wow, what an uncommon woman'.

His silence was too much for her, she wouldn't be surprised if he just walked out the door never to be seen again. She wouldn't blame him, never. She was too broken for most men to have to deal with. She spoke softly, "I would understand if you no longer wish to see me". Taking off the promise ring he'd given her, she laid it on the desk. Being embarrassed about wearing the ring, with all the rubies and diamonds, having hid them underneath towards her palm, with only the gold band showing, so with a quick glance no one could see what she wore. Had they looked at her hands.

Rising when he saw her lay the ring on the desk for him to take back. He walked over to her, standing behind her. "Marie?", he asked gently, "Will you look at me?" His voice quivering.

She turned around slowly, looking at the floor. Not wanting to see pity or disappointment there. 'What could have been between them, ruined,' she thought.

Putting his knuckle beneath her chin, he was getting used to doing this now. "Please look at me." Shaking her head, "No" Bringing her chin up a little, he asked, "What are you afraid of? Are you afraid of me? or of what I may say?"

She couldn't answer. Her heart beating faster, unsure of the outcome. Douglas could hold back no longer, he had to show her how much he cared for her, but gently, he didn't want to frighten her. "Okay, since you won't look at me anyway. Close your eyes, I want to give you something if you think you can trust me."

Inhaling deeply, then letting it out slowly, she closed her eyes, softly. Quietly he took the ring off the edge of the desk, taking her hand he put the ring back on her finger. Her heartbeat rose, her brow furrowed.

Coming near, whispering in her ear. "This was a gift of love from me to you. Don't ever take it off again, my darling. You are twice blessed, in love. I have and will continue to love you 'as long as I shall live, forsaking all others…'". A tear slid down her cheek. Keep your eyes closed. Tilting her chin-up gently, a little further, he placed a kiss on her sweet mouth.

She instantly wrapped her arms about his neck giving into love. The tears coursed down her cheeks as she kissed him back, she felt his tears mingle with her own. When they parted, he brought her to himself holding her close.

"Oh Marie, I love you so. If your feelings for me have changed, will you promise to be mine forever? But only if you truly love me." Breathing huskily, "Tell me you love me, too." He pulled her away from himself so he could look into her eyes. In turn she searched his gaze seeing love, compassion and a fierce devotion within their depths, she smiled.

"Yes, I Love you. I will promise to be yours one day very soon, 'til death do us part, my love."

Unable to resist he pulled her close. He could certainly get used to this. God was indeed good. She sighed contentedly, held in his fierce embrace. For the joy that rose inside her, she sighed her request, "One more kiss?" Relishing in the fact that love had found her... Once Again.

Printed in the United States
by Baker & Taylor Publisher Services